ANGEL OF VENGEANCE

Anna Fehrbach is an MI6 operative in the heart of the Nazi establishment who has just found out about the Final Solution, but convincing her British employers proves next to impossible ... Meanwhile, she must organize the assassination of Hitler's probable successor – who also happens to be Anna's lover. But will Anna's nerve of steel hold out as those around her fall to pieces?

ANGEL OF VENGEANCE

Christopher Nicole

Severn House Large Print
London & New York

This first large print edition published 2009
in Great Britain and the USA by
SEVERN HOUSE PUBLISHERS LTD of
9-15 High Street, Sutton, Surrey, SM1 1DF.
First world regular print edition published 2007 by
Severn House Publishers Ltd., London and New York.

British Library Cataloguing in Publication Data

Nicole, Christopher.
  Angel of vengeance. -- (The secret service series)
  1. Fehrbach, Anna (Fictitious character)--Fiction.
  2. World War, 1939-1945--Secret service--Germany--
  Fiction. 3. Suspense fiction. 4. Large type books.
  I. Title II. Series
  823.9'14-dc22

  ISBN-13: 978-0-7278-7818-2

Printed and bound in Great Britain by
MPG Books Ltd, Bodmin, Cornwall.

This is a novel. Except where they can be historically identified, the characters are invented and are not intended to depict real persons, living or dead.

Vengeance, deep brooding o'er the slain,
Had locked the source of softer woe;
And burning pride and high disdain
Forbade the rising tear to flow.

Sir Walter Scott

PROLOGUE

Sitting beside Anna Fehrbach on her naya, looking down into the Jalon Valley six hundred feet below us, always had my pulse racing. I suspect it would have had the same effect on most men. The view was of course breathtaking, but irrelevant. What tingled the blood was the awareness, the very thought, that one was sharing a certain mental intimacy with a woman who had been the most beautiful – as well as the most deadly – female of her time. That had been long ago, but it was still an ever-present fact of life, even after sixty years. And Anna Fehrbach had moved through those years, to some an utterly sinister figure, to others – a privileged few – a dream they would never forget. Did I dare count myself amongst those few?

I had tracked her for some thirty years, whenever I had been able to spare the time from earning a living, ever since I had first come across her name when researching a novel set during the Second World War. No one had seemed quite certain as to who or what she had been, or indeed, what had become of her. But every reference had mentioned her beauty and her cold-

7

blooded ruthlessness. And every reference to this woman, who had been at the heart of some of the most dramatic events of the Hitler War, and afterwards who had rubbed shoulders – and more than that if the stories were to be believed – with the great and the grotesque, the heroic and the hellish, had made her the more fascinating. The fact that, when she had decided that her career was over, she had disappeared almost without a trace, had turned her into my life's obsession.

And so I had traced her. I remembered our first meeting, here on this very naya, when I had felt as if I were stepping into a cage with a lioness, not knowing if I might be spending my last moments on earth. I knew that she was well into her eighties, but after only a few seconds in her company I had been left in no doubt that the reports of her beauty as a young woman had not been exaggerated, just as to look into her deep blue eyes had convinced me that, while perhaps she would no longer be able to destroy me with her bare hands – I am a large man – she would have no hesitation in using the pistol she kept concealed on her person at all times, should she consider it necessary.

But she had been charming. My appearance had of course been fortuitous. Having turned her back upon assassination and espionage so many years ago, Anna Fehrbach, so-called Countess von Widerstand (which loosely translates as Countess of Resistance), had had to devote a great deal of time to disappearing. Too

8

many of the people she had been required to seduce and then destroy had relatives or comrades who had also survived, and who would dearly have liked to lay hands on her. She had accomplished her Houdini act successfully, until my appearance. But by the time this happened, she had grown weary of anonymity, of being forgotten where once she had been feared, and she had realized that her enemies could no longer harm her, as she would soon be dead in any event. She wanted to go out in a blaze of glory – one of the only two human weaknesses she had ever truly revealed – and I, as a writer, was a means to that end. It was a tantalizing thought that, had I come upon her even forty years earlier, she might have seduced me as well. But then, she would surely have disposed of me afterwards, as she had always disposed of any man or woman who came too close to the true Anna Fehrbach, Countess von Widerstand, the Honourable Mrs Ballantine Bordman.

So instead of being her lover, I had become her confidant. This was perhaps even more compelling, as she was allowing me to look into the soul of the most remarkable woman I had ever met, and perhaps had ever existed. And was I also her friend? I dearly wanted to feel that I was, and bathed in her smile as she handed me a glass of champagne from the bottle waiting in its ice bucket on the table beside her, placed there by her ever-attentive Spanish maid, Incarna, a woman who almost equally fascinated me, not because she was the least attractive

9

when compared with her mistress, but because I had to wonder just how much she knew about that mistress.

'It is good to see you again,' Anna said, speaking English with the still discernible brogue she had inherited from her Irish mother. Her voice was low and husky; I could not imagine it ever rising in anger or fear or pain, although from what she already had told me I knew it must have done so, for each reason, often enough in the past. This aspect of her was no less fascinating than everything else about her. She was a tall woman, only an inch under six feet in height, and remained slender. I had never seen her legs, as nowadays she always wore trousers, but they were obviously long, and from the bare ankles and feet thrust into her sandals I could not doubt that they were as perfectly formed as the rest of her, while the gentle swell of her shirt was sufficient to remind one of the formidable sexual weapons she had once possessed, and used to such dramatic effect. And yet all was secondary to her face, exposed as her once waist-length golden hair was now quite white and short. But the flawless bone structure, slightly aquiline in shape, remained unchanged, even if the skin was perhaps drawing a little tight. Her jewellery, which she had not changed since our first meeting, fitted perfectly into the aura she created. Her earrings were tiny gold bars dangling from gold clips; the gold crucifix resting on her bodice was a reminder of her Roman Catholic youth, the huge

10

ruby solitaire on the first finger of her left hand an indication of her wealth, and the man's gold Rolex on her left wrist a warning not necessarily to expect any feminine weaknesses: she had told me that the secret of her success, her survival, had been the ability to think, and act, more quickly than the average person. This jewellery was the other discernible weakness in her character. It had never actually been legally hers, but had been given to her by her Nazi masters, more than sixty years ago, to enhance the image they wanted her to project – that of a fabulously wealthy aristocrat. I think she took great pleasure in the knowledge that the Nazis had disappeared, while she was still around – and still had the jewellery!

Now she smiled. 'Have you formed a judgement about me yet?'

I drank champagne. 'I do not know enough about you to arrive at a judgement.'

She made an entrancing moue. 'I thought I had told you everything you wished to know.'

'You have told me of the beginning. But you were just twenty-one when you left Moscow and returned to Germany,' I reminded her. 'And the previous three years had been a little crowded.'

'That is one way of putting it.'

'Well, let's see. Your entire family was arrested in Vienna in March 1938 because your father was an anti-Nazi newspaper editor. You all should have gone to a concentration camp, but the arresting officer realized that he had got hold of something special in you, not only

11

because of your looks but because you had an IQ of 173, were head girl of your convent, and a top athlete.'

'His name was Hallbrun,' Anna reminisced. 'And he recognized nothing, save that I was a beautiful seventeen-year-old virgin, waiting to be deflowered. He offered me to his boss, Glauber, as a mistress. It was Glauber who saw the potential and sent me to the SS training school.'

'And it was Glauber who told you that if you worked for the Reich your parents and sister would be kept in safe but not harsh custody, but if you did not...'

'They would be sent to a concentration camp, yes.'

'What were your feelings about that?'

'I hated him. I hated the entire Reich.'

'But you worked for them, with brilliant success.'

'Christopher, I was eighteen years old when I graduated from that SS school. I did not see that I had a choice.'

'I understand. And so Glauber passed you on to the SD, the Sicherheitsdienst, and to Heydrich.'

'Yes.' She spoke as quietly as ever, but with enormous passion.

'And on their instructions you seduced and then married the Honourable Ballantine Bordman, son of Lord Bordman, and a diplomat at the Foreign Office, and became the darling of London society. It was during this period that you became a double agent. But that happened

12

in Berlin, didn't it?'

'Yes,' Anna said, her voice brittle. 'It wasn't something I had planned. Oh, I hated the Nazis and everything they stood for, especially for what they had done to me and my family, but I knew there was nothing I could do about it – nothing I could think of, anyway. But when I returned to Berlin in the spring of 1939 for a visit, I was accused of breaking the rules by carrying secret documents in my handbag instead of sending them through the designated channel, so Heydrich decided I should be disciplined.' She paused to drink some champagne, her fingers so tight on the glass I expected the stem to snap; I had heard enough about the strength of those fingers. 'Do you know what they did to me?'

She had told me, at one of our earlier meetings, but I could tell she wanted to recall that dreadful day, so I said nothing.

'They stripped me naked,' she said, every word a drop of vitriol from her lips, 'and strapped me over a bar while they caned me, as if I were a delinquent schoolgirl.' Her lip curled. 'I suppose I was, to them. Then they strapped me to a table and put electrodes into my anus and my vagina and turned on the current. Have you ever had anything like that happen to you?'

'Ah ... no.'

'I felt that I was being split in two. And yet, you know, the humiliation was worse than the pain. And they were just trying to discipline me, not destroy me.'

13

'And you were...'

'I was coming up to my nineteenth birthday.'

'Many a girl of eighteen would have been destroyed by such an experience.'

Anna Fehrbach put down her glass to gaze at me, and I felt a sudden chill as I recalled that on her record, even at eighteen she had outclassed most girls her age. 'So you determined to destroy them.'

'How simple you make it sound, in retrospect. No, Christopher, as I have said, in March 1939 I was not yet nineteen years old. I was a physical wreck after that session in the SD torture chamber. I spent three days in bed. Then I went out for a walk, and encountered Clive Bartley.'

'Who you already knew.'

'Yes. The previous year he had been Ballantine's minder in Berlin, when Ballantine had been there setting up the visit of Neville Chamberlain that resulted in the Munich Agreement. That was my first real assignment, to seduce Ballantine and find out just what the British were about. That was the way the Nazi mind worked; they could not believe a prime minister would go to see Hitler merely to agree to every German demand. They thought he might be coming with an ultimatum. Not one of them, not even I, realized just how good I was at my job. I seduced Bally so successfully that in addition to reassuring me that Chamberlain had no intention of going to war with anyone over anything, he fell in love with me and asked me to marry him. Of course he did not know that I was

14

a middle-class Irish-Austrian schoolgirl called Annaliese Fehrbach. He accepted entirely the form in which I was presented to him by the Nazis: Anna, Countess von Widerstand, heiress to a fortune.'

'What was your reaction?'

'I thought it was a joke. But Heydrich jumped at it. He could immediately see the possible rewards. But I was horrified. I mean, Bally was twice my age and not the least bit physically attractive. But I had to do what they wished.'

'And Clive Bartley?'

'He was even more horrified, from the opposite point of view. He was an MI6 agent, trained to be suspicious, and he later told me that he was certain that I was Gestapo from the moment he met me, at an SS ball; he had no idea that I actually worked for the SD. He even tried to stop the marriage, but Bally was determined. So when I took up residence in London he kept me under surveillance.'

'But could never pin anything on you until that day in Berlin.'

'Not even then. He was in Berlin on another matter, and he assumed I was still in London. Our meeting was a complete accident. And you must remember that I was still in a very mixed-up state. I was angry and humiliated. I wanted to hit back at them, and I didn't know how. And then suddenly, there it was. They had taught me how to seduce men, manipulate them to order. Why should I not seduce a man to my requirements, and even manipulate him? That I knew

15

he was an MI6 agent just made the idea more attractive.'

'So you invited him to bed. But it didn't work out the way you had intended.' As always, when discussing her many sexual adventures, I found myself imagining the young, vibrant, beautiful Anna of the long golden hair and the all-consuming body, naked in bed with a man, and wondered if I was turning green.

'I don't know how it might have worked out,' Anna said thoughtfully. 'We were interrupted, in bed, by Elsa Mayers.'

'Your minder.'

'My SD controller. She was Heydrich's creature, and I knew she would report what she had seen to Heydrich. In fact, she told me she was going to do that. You see, she also knew that Clive was a British Secret Service agent.'

'So you killed her, with a single blow to the neck.'

'Well,' Anna said modestly. 'They had taught me how to do that, too.'

'What was Clive's reaction to all this?'

'He was ... what is the word they use nowadays? Gob-smacked. I don't think he had ever known a woman who could kill with a single blow.'

'So, after some more ... discussion, you agreed to work for MI6, while still working for the SD. You surely knew that was going to be incredibly dangerous.'

'Perhaps I did not realize just how dangerous. But I never regretted the decision.'

'How did you explain Frau Mayers' death to Heydrich?'

'As soon as Clive had left, I telephoned the SD headquarters and told them what had happened, without mentioning him, of course. I reminded them that Mayers was a lesbian, as they well knew, and told them that when I had rejected her advances she had attempted to rape me, and I had hit her too hard. In self-defence. Heydrich accepted my story.'

'And for over a year you fed them whatever information MI6 told you to. But they got to you in the end.'

'No, they didn't. Not the SD in Berlin, or I wouldn't be sitting here now. The Gestapo spy ring in London, which had been receiving information from me for transmission back to Germany, began to suspect me, and tried to take me out. Fortunately, they did not report their suspicions to Berlin, but decided to act on their own. They sent three agents to arrest me.'

'But they didn't succeed.'

'I shot them all,' Anna said.

My turn to drink some champagne. She spoke in such a calm, matter-of-fact tone. And she had been just twenty years old!

'But it was clearly becoming too dangerous,' Anna continued. 'On every front. Ballantine had insisted I become a British citizen, and the Special Branch were also becoming interested; Britain and Germany had then been at war for six months, and were I to be arrested as a spy, I would have had to confess all, break with

17

Germany, and remain in England. But I couldn't do that.'

'Because Heydrich still held your family hostage.'

'Yes. So MI6 rigged up an elaborate scam, got me out of England, and broke the story of how the glamorous Honourable Mrs Ballantine Bordman had turned out to be a Nazi spy who had unfortunately managed to flee the country before she could be arrested. Heydrich was delighted with the publicity. And with my escape.'

'So much so that he made you his mistress.'

Anna's mouth twisted. 'I was his possession. He regarded me as his creation.'

'And Bordman?'

'Oh, he promptly sued for divorce.'

'Did you love him? Had you ever loved him?'

Anna had been looking out over the valley. Now she turned her head to look at me. 'One does not share a man's bed for a year without sharing other things as well. But love? No. Besides, I had known from the beginning that I was betraying him. I believe he had a nervous breakdown when he discovered what he was told was the truth. I mean, that I had always been a German spy. I am sorry about that. I can only say that when I was acting as his wife, I gave him everything he wanted, sexually. He enjoyed that.'

'And so you returned to Germany, and the SD, only now you were working for MI6.'

'I had been created in Hell,' she said thought-

fully. 'And I returned to Hell. But even Hell can be bearable, as long as there is hope. Clive, MI6, gave me that hope.'

'But they could not save you from being sent to Moscow, and the Lubianka.'

She made a moue. 'That should not have happened. The Lubianka, I mean. I was betrayed to the Soviets. But if it had not been for Clive I would have been there still. Or in a gulag somewhere in Siberia, being raped and beaten every day.'

'I thought it was Joseph Andrews who got you out.'

'Joe was inspired by Clive, and acting as his agent. But Joe...' A strangely dreamy look drifted across her face. 'He was quite a guy.'

'And so it was back to Berlin, and Heydrich. What exactly were your feelings for Heydrich at this point?'

'Of all the men I have ever known, I hated him the most.'

'You must have been pleased when he was killed.'

'Yes,' Anna said. 'His death pleased me.'

I frowned. 'You weren't involved in that, were you?'

Anna Fehrbach smiled.

One

The Final Solution

The young woman ran round and round the gymnasium. Tall, with long, slender legs, she took even strides, her waist-length golden hair floating behind her, although, as she had been running for some time, it was now becoming heavy with sweat. As were her singlet and shorts, which, along with a pair of gym shoes, were all she wore. Now the clothes clung to her like a second skin, much to the appreciation of the instructor, as he watched the movement beneath the thin material, the breasts rising and falling with increasing regularity, the buttocks seeming to revolve against each other. No less fascinating to him was her face, its slightly aquiline yet perfectly carved features, the lips parting and then closing again in time to each breath, and above all, the utter innocence of her expression, the soft blue of her eyes.

Stefan was a young man, only recently appointed personal trainer to the SD's most highly rated agent. This was in fact the first time he had been left in sole control, as it were. But he did not think he would find Anna Fehrbach any the less exciting if he had been here for several months. The thought that at this moment she was his to command ... but was she ever anyone's to command? It was impossible to watch all of that magnificent femininity, that calm and so relaxed face, and believe any of the stories that were told of her. And yet ... She was running towards him now, and in a moment would be passing, for the twentieth time, the table on which sat the gun. He drew a deep breath. 'Now,' he said.

Anna Fehrbach checked her stride without a moment's hesitation, whipped the Luger from the table, turned, sighted, and emptied the entire magazine at the target – a full-size cardboard portrait of a man – on the far side of the room, all in no more than fifteen seconds. She laid down the pistol and would have gone on running, had he not said, 'Enough.' She halted, still breathing deeply, her hair now settling on her back, the muscles in her thighs rippling.

Stefan stepped past her and walked the twenty metres to the target, stroking his chin as he inspected it. Every one of the nine shots had hit: six on the torso and three on the head. He turned and walked back to her. She had gathered her hair in both hands to hold it away from her neck.

'Nine shots, nine hits,' he commented. 'Where did you aim?'

Anna looked surprised at the question. 'Where I hit. Three times to the head, six times to the body. The head was first. Had this been for real, the other eight shots would have been unnecessary.'

Stefan picked up the gun to remove the empty magazine; standing this close to her, inhaling the compelling mixture of perfume and fresh sweat, her nipples clearly visible through the wet singlet, he had to do something with his hands to stop himself from touching her. 'That is the most remarkable shooting I have ever seen. After just having run a quarter of a mile, and without pausing to get your breath back.'

'Thank you ... Stefan, is it?'

To her, he thought, he was still just an anonymous trainer. 'Stefan,' he agreed. 'So, do you ever miss? Have you ever missed?'

'If I were in the habit of missing, I would not be here now. Are we finished?'

'For today.'

Anna nodded, and went towards the showers. Stefan followed, having trouble with his own breathing, as he wondered how far he could go, how far she would let him go.

'So, tell me your secret.'

She had reached the swing door. Now she paused, and half turned her head. 'Concentration, Stefan.' She pushed the door and went through.

Another deep breath and he followed. 'And you have had to shoot at living men, from time to time?' He knew she had, but he wanted to find out all he could about her, what made her tick, what made her so deadly – apart from her mind-paralyzing sexuality.

23

And she had still not objected to his presence. Instead she was stooping to take off her trainers, her hair falling past her face. Again he kept his hands at his sides with an effort; the temptation to touch the smooth flesh in front of him was overwhelming.

Anna straightened, lifted the singlet over her head and threw it on the one chair. Stefan caught his breath, less because of the perfectly sculptured breasts, the gold chain that allowed the small gold crucifix to lie in the centre of the valley between them, than at the realization that she was actually going to strip in front of him. But his anticipated delight was tempered by the equal realization that she was undressing with no thought of seduction or even coquetry, but simply in order to have her shower; that his presence was of not the slightest importance to her.

'It goes with the job,' she agreed, and dropped her shorts on the floor.

Stefan had to swallow before he could speak. 'I have been told that you have killed. Seven times.'

Seven times, Anna thought. Neither he, nor anyone in Germany, could know of the other seven, because they had been either at the behest of MI6, or for her own survival. But still, to have fourteen deaths on her conscience should have been a nerve-shattering situation for a twenty-one-year-old woman. But she did not have a conscience. She could not afford one. She was fighting a war, as much as any infantryman in the front line, for the protection of her family, and any enemy standing in front of her had to be destroyed. Nothing else mattered until the war was over. That she happened to be better at her job than anyone else was her good fortune. 'Not all were with a gun,' she remarked as she stepped into the stall.

Stefan watched her turn on the taps and test the water. 'Because you are as good with your hands as with a pistol,' he suggested.

'I have been well trained.'

The water was steaming. 'A cold shower would be better for you than all that heat,' he remarked.

Satisfied with the temperature, Anna stepped beneath the jet, soaking her hair. 'I do not like cold showers.'

'Because you had to suffer them in your convent?'

Anna stepped from beneath the jet, her hair wet and sticking to her shoulders. She left the water playing on her back while she soaped, slowly and luxuriously. 'Because I was a prisoner of the NKVD for several days.'

'And they made you take cold baths?'

Anna replaced the soap in its tray and turned back into the shower. 'They used cold water as an interrogating technique. Do you know about this?'

Stefan licked his lips. 'No.'

'They use a hose,' Anna said dreamily, allowing the hot water again to pound on her head. 'They reduce the stream to a pencil-thin spray, and then they put it into you.' She half turned her head. 'You understand what I am saying?'

Stefan swallowed again. 'It must have been...' He hesitated, unsure how to continue.

Now she turned to face him, the water flooding past her shoulders, down her back, across her breasts and stomach. 'Sexually stimulating? It could be that, if they wished it. It could also be very painful, if they wished it. More often they wished to cause pain,' she added thoughtfully.

'What are your feelings towards the men who did that to you?'

'They were women. One woman in particular.'

'Ah. Do you hate her?'

'Not now,' Anna said. 'I never hate the dead.'

'You know she is dead?'

'Certainly I know this. I killed her.'

'You killed her? In the Lubianka Prison?'

Anna smiled as she turned her attention to her hair, using the bottle of shampoo that rested on the shelf behind the shower. 'Actually, I hit her on the neck. Forgive me. Yes, it was in the prison.'

'And you still escaped. I thought it was impossible to escape from the Lubianka.'

'I had friends,' Anna said dreamily. One in particular, she thought.

Her eyes closed as she massaged her scalp. Stefan continued to study her, and now he bent forward. 'That mark...'

'It is a bullet wound.'

'You have been shot?'

'That is how one gets a bullet wound, yes.'

'But...'

Anna opened her eyes and tossed water from her hair. 'It did not kill me, as I am sure you can see ... That feels better.'

The thought that she had been both tortured and shot, and yet was standing here in front of him ... He now threw caution to the wind. 'Anna, may I shower with you?'

'Of course.' Her eyes opened, and she stepped from the stall. 'I am finished anyway.'

'Oh. Ah...'

For the first time she looked at him as if actually seeing him. 'I think you would like to have sex with me, Stefan.'

'Should I not? I think you are the most beautiful woman I have ever seen.'

Anna picked up her towel. 'You say the sweetest things. I shall enjoy working with you.'

'But...?'

She massaged herself, her hair now a damp golden stain down her back. 'I do not think it would be a good idea for us to have sex.'

'Because you do not like men? They say...' Another hesitation.

'That I am a lesbian?' Suddenly her voice was hard. 'They say so many things about me. But the only truth is that I am Anna Fehrbach. I work for the SD, for General Heydrich. I do what he tells me to, without question.' At least, as far as he knows, she thought. 'As he has not instructed me to have sex with you ... I am sure you

27

understand.'

Stefan licked his lips. 'Are you never tempted to break the rules?'

'That is not a very good idea, where General Heydrich is concerned.' She dropped the towel, picked up a clean one from the pile on the chair, and wrapped her wet hair in it. Then she made to step past him, but he caught her arm.

'Anna, I would risk anything to have sex with you.'

She looked down at his hand. 'Please release me, Stefan. I have said it is not possible. I do not wish to have to hurt you.'

'You, hurt me? I am a karate expert. I *train* people how to hurt.'

Anna gazed at him. 'That is exactly it. You train. I *do*.'

He hesitated. As always, she looked quite calm, unemotional; her breathing was perfectly normal, and her voice was again soft. But the soft eyes had become glacial.

The door at the far end of the gymnasium opened. 'Countess!'

Stefan released her and stepped away. Anna left the showers and picked up her cami-knickers. 'I am here.'

The young officer gazed at her as longingly as Stefan had done. 'You are wanted, Countess.'

Anna stepped into the garment, made sure her breasts were comfortable, and adjusted the shoulder straps. 'I will be there, as soon as I have dried my hair and changed my clothes.' She put on her shirt.

'Now, Countess. I am to take you now.'

Still as calm as ever, Anna pulled on her slacks, thrust her feet into the waiting sandals. 'Are you arresting me, Herr Captain?'

'Of course I am not, Countess. But you are required at the Wilhelmstrasse, now.'

At last he had caught her interest. 'The Wilhelmstrasse? I work from Gestapo Headquarters.'

'Today it is the Wilhelmstrasse, Countess. The Fuehrer is waiting to see you.'

Anna stared at him, and Stefan realized that she actually could be surprised, disconcerted, and perhaps even frightened at times. 'The Fuehrer?' she asked. 'I am to see the Fuehrer?'

'He is waiting.'

'I cannot possibly see the Fuehrer like this. I need to dress properly, dry my hair, make up my face, put on some jewellery...'

'The Fuehrer is waiting, Countess.'

'Would you refuse the Fuehrer, Countess?' Stefan asked slyly.

Anna glanced at him, then picked up her shoulder bag.

'I have a car outside,' the captain said, holding the door for her.

Anna stepped past him, walked along the corridor, passing the other gymnasiums, where people were training, men and women, but these were in groups; there was only one Anna Fehrbach. Remembering that had always given her confidence in the past. But at this moment she had no idea where she was going, what she might encounter, how she should react.

Outside the building, while she put on her dark glasses to repel the bright August sunshine, the uniformed chauffeur held the car door open for her, and she sank on to the cushions; the captain sat beside her. She had never seen him before, but he wore the black uniform of the SS, which was understandable; the SS provided Hitler's personal bodyguard. But he was entirely respectful: even the SS knew their place as regards the SD.

'Would you have any idea what this is about?' Anna asked as they drove through the fairly empty streets. It was the middle of a warm summer morning, and most of Berlin was at work. It was difficult to comprehend that the German armies were engaged in a titanic struggle only a few hundred miles away, but in this August of 1941, as those armies gained an almost daily succession of great victories, the war was receding at an ever increasing rate, with certain victory over the hated Communists already in sight. Apart from the casualty lists, which were never extreme, and the few craters or damaged buildings left by the sporadic RAF raids, the war had not yet interfered with the lives of ordinary Germans, save that there had been sufficient triumphs to keep them in a state of euphoria. Poland had been overrun in under a month, France and the Low Countries in hardly more than a month. True, Great Britain had not yet been conquered, but according to the Nazi

Government she had been eliminated as a power capable of interfering in the affairs of Europe, and could be dealt with at leisure after the destruction of Soviet Russia.

The German people had never known anything like it, whether in the memories of those who had experienced the Kaiser's Germany and the catastrophe that had followed, or those who had to seek their history from books. Be-fore the coming of Adolf Hitler, the national hero had been Frederick the Great, but even he had lived, and fought, on a knife edge, with almost as many defeats as spectacular victories. Hitler's Wehrmacht had never lost a battle.

Living in the midst of such a society, employed by its inner core, it was very difficult not to believe it. But if it were true, Anna knew that her future was inconceivable, and that her family, who she protected by apparently loyally serving the Reich, did not have a future at all. So she had to believe the reverse of the coin as projected by her English employers, so certain of ultimate victory, even if unable to name either a date or a means by which such a victory could be achieved. So ... she now turned her head to look at the officer.

He was looking at her. No man who had the least interest in women could resist the temptation to look at Anna Fehrbach, Countess von Widerstand, whenever possible. 'I'm afraid I am not in the Fuehrer's confidence, Countess. I can only tell you that I was summoned to his office, told where you could be found at this hour, and instructed to bring you to him.'

Anna considered this. 'When you were summoned, was there anyone else in the office with him? With the Fuehrer?'

'Why, yes. Reichsfuehrer Himmler and General Heydrich were with him.'

Her master and his master. With their master. That was surely reassuring. Had she somehow been betrayed, had Antoinette's Boutique – her Berlin contact for MI6 – been infiltrated, she did not doubt that Heydrich would have dealt with it personally, as two years previously he had dealt personally with her perceived breach of discipline when she had been caught carrying secret documents in her handbag instead of sending them through the prescribed route out of London.

She could still remember, she would never forget, the way he had stroked her flesh as he had inserted the electrode into her, the almost loving way he had switched on the current. Just a touch, he had explained, as her body had arced away from its bonds in agony. He did not wish to destroy her, only to remind her that she was his creation, and thus his servant, bound always to obey without question.

She supposed the most remarkable aspect of that horrendous experience was the manner in which, once she had been released to curl herself into a tight ball of misery, he, and the people who had assisted him, immediately reverted to being her friends. Their imaginations could take them no further. She had broken their rules, and

32

she had been punished, not severely in their eyes, as if she had been a child, and was not supposed to resent her chastisement. Not long afterwards, Heydrich had even taken her to his bed.

That entirely summed up the Nazi philosophy. In their eyes, subordinates, conquered peoples, were not allowed personalities of their own. They existed for the benefit of their masters, were given regular treats as long as they behaved and obeyed, were savagely punished if they transgressed, but once the punishment was over were expected to revert to unquestioning servitude. That they might dream of revenge for what had been done to them was unthinkable. Subservient, they were supposed to possess neither the intelligence nor the courage ever to consider mutiny.

This limited, if very effective, philosophy had so blinded their judgement that they could not accept there might be exceptions to the rule. People like Colonel Glauber, who controlled the SD training programme, and Hannah Gehrig, who had implemented it, had selected the schoolgirl Anna Fehrbach for inclusion in their ranks because of her looks, her exceptional intelligence and her easily demonstrated powers of decision and speed of thought, which enabled her to determine what needed to be done, and then to do it, before even a highly trained antagonist could act, handicapped as he or she invariably was by a subconscious reluctance to hurt or destroy so much beauty. But having selected her, and trained her, they had forgotten why she had been chosen in the first place, had supposed she would henceforth be theirs, obedient and unquestioning, even after being punished.

That she could ever be a threat, an enemy determined enough and talented enough to bring them down, had apparently never crossed their minds. Actually, she knew that it had never crossed her mind either, until that so fortuitous encounter with Clive Bartley – which had happened only three days after her punishment, when her body and her mind were still a molten mass of pain and anger. Clive had known nothing of her, had concluded that she was either a Gestapo agent or a German fortune huntress who had managed to marry into the British aristocracy and who therefore had to be regarded with suspicion by any conscientious member of the Secret Service. But he had been able to discern that, for whatever reason, the glamorous Honourable Mrs Ballantine Bordman was in a highly distressed state. He had set out to seduce her, she suspected, with utter cold-bloodedness. She was still not certain, after more than two years, whether after he had been to her bed and learned the truth about her he regarded her more as a woman he could potentially love, or simply as the most ruthless and deadly – and therefore immensely valuable – secret agent he had ever encountered.

She could not feel that way towards him. For the first time since her arrest by the Gestapo in

March 1938, Clive had brought a ray of hope into her life. She did not know if she loved him. She did not know if she was capable of love any more. She was keeping her parents and her sister alive by faithfully working for the Nazis – as far as they knew. But as that was all they could be allowed to know, Johann and Jane Fehrbach had totally rejected her as a traitor and a whore. As for men, she had been trained only to seduce and then destroy. As the seduction involved the ability to make her victims feel she loved them, she had no idea if she would recognize the real thing if she ever experienced it. But Clive had made her feel that she was more than just a robot trained to kill; that she, with him and his superiors, had a vital part to play in restoring the world to better times. That was all she had to live for, until those times arrived.

'Are you nervous, Countess?' the Captain enquired, bringing her back to the present as the car pulled into the courtyard.

'Why should I be nervous?' Anna asked as the door was opened.

She was, in fact, less anxious than preoccupied, with a mixture of apprehension and curiosity. Although she had committed several horrendous crimes in the name of this man, and undoubtedly at his bidding, she had never actually met Hitler, had only ever seen him from a distance. This was the first time she had even entered the Chancellery. And to do so now in such a state of dishabille ... She had taken off the towel in the car, but her hair was still wet, clinging to her neck and down the back of her shirt, and she wore no make-up and only the shabbiest of clothes. If she had no doubt of her beauty, she also believed in enhancing it whenever possible, and had never before allowed herself to appear before her employers as anything less than perfectly turned out – with the exception, of course, of Heydrich, who had explored her naked body often enough.

She half expected to be turned away by one of the smartly dressed and immaculately groomed young female secretaries who peered at her as she entered the building, taking off her sunglasses and blinking in the sudden gloom. Instead one woman, older than the rest, her severely handsome face exposed as her hair was drawn back in a tight bun, came forward. 'Countess von Widerstand? I am Frau Engert. Will you come with me, please?'

Anna fell into place at her side as they approached the wide staircase leading up to the first-floor gallery. 'I am sorry about my dress. I was given no time to change.'

'I was told you would look delightful in sack-cloth, Countess. I was not misinformed.'

This was promising. They reached the steps and started up them; a guard at the foot stood to attention, and Anna reflected that he could not possibly know who she was, and therefore he had to be acknowledging her companion's rank. But Frau Engert was very simply dressed as a secretary, in black skirt and white blouse, black tie and black stockings, and black court shoes. There was no visible evidence of any rank. 'You are...?' she ventured.

'I am Herr Hitler's private secretary. One of them.'

'I see. So would you know why he has sent for me so urgently?'

'The Fuehrer does most things urgently, Countess. This morning he wishes to meet you.'

Anna wasn't quite sure what to make of that, but they had reached the gallery and were entering a large, high-ceilinged lobby. Here there were several desks, seated at which were more secretaries who regarded Anna with interest. At the rear of the room was another pair of enormous doors, stretching very nearly to the ceiling, in front of which were two armed SS guards. They stood to attention, and then one of them opened the doors.

'Frau Engert, my Fuehrer.'

Frau Engert gave a brief nod of the head, and gestured Anna into the room. They stood together as the doors closed behind them, and saluted. 'Heil Hitler!'

Anna blinked in the sudden bright light streaming in through the huge windows behind the desk. It was a relief to see that Reinhard Heydrich, her master in all things, was still there. Tall and blond, his yellow hair brushed back from his forehead, only his thin gash of a mouth and the coldness of his blue eyes robbed his face of handsomeness. She was not so pleased at the presence of Heinrich Himmler, overall commander of the Secret Services, and therefore her ultimate commander as well. She had only met him twice before, and found him disconcerting because his eyes, no less cold, were half obscured behind rimless glasses, and his face, large and bland, with its small, curiously irrelevant pale moustache, was utterly expressionless. She could not imagine what he would be like when angry, or in the throes of passion. If such a man could ever feel passion. But he, she knew, was the ultimate arbiter of her fate, at least until the Allies won the war ... supposing that was ever going to happen.

But neither of these men, so ruthlessly powerful in their professional capacities, mattered the least when in the presence of the ultimate arbiter of *their* fates, and the fates of everyone in Germany, not to say Europe. Anna was not surprised by Hitler's appearance – she had seen enough photographs of him to expect the dark, un-Aryan hair, one lock drooping over his forehead, an obviously deliberate style, the carefully trimmed black moustache. His clothes were as nondescript as she had expected, certainly when compared to the pristine black uniforms of his two henchmen; he wore a simple brown tunic over black pants, his only decoration the Iron Cross First Class at his neck, legitimately earned, she knew, as a despatch rider in the Great War.

What did surprise and disconcert her was his complexion – which was mottled red and white, suggesting that he was not in the best of health

– and his height. At five feet eleven inches in her bare feet, Anna was taller than most men. One of the reasons she had first been attracted to Clive Bartley was that he was six feet two. But Hitler was several inches shorter than that. She wondered if this would upset him, but he was smiling as he came forward, both hands outstretched.

'Countess! I have heard so much about you.'

Anna hesitated, uncertain whether she was about to be embraced, but as this did not happen, she extended her own hands, and had her fingers grasped and squeezed. 'You flatter me, my Fuehrer. I must apologize for my appearance. I was working out in the gymnasium and was told to come at once.'

'A beautiful woman is a beautiful woman is a beautiful woman, Countess. It is not necessary to gild the lily. And working out! Anyone can see that you are superbly fit ... Yes, yes, Engert.'

The secretary had apparently left the room after escorting Anna into it, but had now returned with a silver tray on which were a glass of water and two rather large capsules. 'It is nine thirty, my Fuehrer.'

'Already?' But he swallowed the pills. 'They fill me full of this rubbish,' he explained. 'There is a pill for this, a pill for that, and a pill for something else. Come, sit down.' He led Anna to a chair in front of his desk, and then, still holding her hand, sat beside her, another chair having been hastily placed there by Heydrich. From the click of the doors behind her she

39

gathered that Frau Engert had again withdrawn. 'You are an Austrian.'

'I have an Austrian father, my Fuehrer,' Anna said carefully.

'And an Irish mother.'

Another surprise: he had not referred to any notes. 'Yes, my Fuehrer.'

'Who managed to escape the British clutches after the Easter uprising of April 1916.'

'Ah...' Anna had to make an immense effort to stop herself glancing at Heydrich, who was standing on her other side. He certainly knew the truth, that her mother had had no part – and as far as Anna knew, no interest – in the Irish Independence Movement, had indeed worked and gained her reputation as an investigative journalist with a London newspaper and had amazed both her employers and her friends when, on being sent to Vienna in 1919 to cover the many horrendous tales of starvation and indeed cannibalism reputed to be taking place in that erstwhile capital of empire, so devastatingly isolated from food and succour in those traumatic days following the end of the Great War, had stayed there to marry a relatively obscure Austrian editor. But if her boss had chosen to tell his boss something different... 'She does not like to talk about those days,' she said, with absolute truthfulness.

'Oh, quite. I can understand that. And you were born in Vienna, which makes us fellow countrymen. I lived for a while in Linz, and I intend to retire there when my task here is finished. It is a lovely place.'

'But you also lived in Vienna,' Anna ventured.

A shadow passed across Hitler's face. 'It was necessary to earn a living. But it was not a happy time. Vienna is the most beautiful city in the world. But not all of the people are what one might hope, or expect. Still...' His expression brightened. 'Those days are history. I am told that you are one of the most faithful servants of the Reich. That there is nothing you would not do for the Fatherland.' He gave her fingers a gentle squeeze. 'That means for me, you know.'

Oh, my God! Anna thought. Sleeping with Heydrich was an ongoing purgatory, but at least she was used to it by now. Sleeping with this man was unthinkable.

'Even if you are not always successful,' Hitler remarked gently.

Anna stiffened. The interview had been going just too well, whatever the undercurrents.

'Tell me about Marshal Stalin. He is still alive, is he not?'

'I was betrayed before I could carry out my mission, my Fuehrer.'

Hitler nodded. 'Those scum have been dealt with. But tell me, why were you betrayed? By your own people. My people!'

Anna turned her head to gaze at him. 'Both men wished to have sex with me, my Fuehrer. I did not wish to have sex with them. So they avenged themselves by handing me over to the NKVD.'

'You did not like these men? Or is it that you

41

do not like any men?'

Anna felt that she was picking her way through a minefield; there was no way this man could be snubbed as easily as she had snubbed Stefan. 'I did not like those men, my Fuehrer.' Again she was sticking to the absolute truth.

'Yet did you not once save the life of Herr Meissenbach by killing two would-be assassins with two shots?'

His knowledge of her past was encyclopaedic and alarming. 'It was actually four shots. That was in the line of duty, my Fuehrer; it was my business to protect Herr Meissenbach. He had not yet revealed any ... wish to know me better.' Now that was a lie, but she did not see how even Hitler could know that.

He smiled. 'Although perhaps the event created that wish. But that too is history. It is the future that matters. I have in mind to entrust you with a most important mission.' Anna held her breath, but he again surprised her by asking, 'What is your feeling towards the Jews?'

The sudden change of direction was disconcerting. But reading *Mein Kampf* had been part of her training, and she had a photographic memory even greater than his appeared to be. 'The Jews are the enemies of the Reich, my Fuehrer.'

'Quite. But I would like to know your personal opinion of them.'

'I do not know any Jews, my Fuehrer. I am a Roman Catholic.'

'Of course.' To her consternation, he released

her hand to hook his finger in the chain of her crucifix and gently pull it out from beneath her shirt. 'This is very beautiful. It matches its owner, and would appear to live a most fortunate life.' He peered at her. 'Do you ever take it off?'

Even sitting down, Anna felt that her knees were turning to water. Those eyes had a magnetic quality she had never experienced before. 'Not as a rule, my Fuehrer.'

'What a lucky charm.' Carefully he dropped the crucifix back inside her shirt. 'Do you know, I am also a Roman Catholic? When I have the time. But I would like you to think about the problem. Because it is a problem. The Jews are like weeds in a beautiful garden. Unchecked, they will strangle all the flowers. But merely cutting them back is not a solution. They simply sprout again, more profusely than before. And unlike weeds, they do not just exist in our garden. They are everywhere. Tell her, Himmler.'

The Gestapo chief spoke for the first time. 'It seems there are more Jews in Russia than anywhere else. We have had to detail special squads – we call them Einsatzgruppen – to shoot these people. But it is an exhausting business. And morale suffers, you know. These men are highly trained members of the SS. They would happily die for the Fatherland, for their Fuehrer. But even they find the business of having to line up a hundred or more Jews – men, women, and children – almost every day, make them strip naked, and then dig a vast pit and force them to stand on the edge of it, and then shoot them so that they fall into the pit ... it's a demoralizing business. I have had men breaking down under the stress.'

Anna wondered what stress the victims felt, just before being shot. She felt slightly sick, especially at the thought that, from his detailed description of what happened, Himmler had obviously personally attended at least one of these executions, and probably been titillated by it.

'Why are they made to strip?' Hitler asked, interested.

'Well, my Fuehrer, their clothes are often extremely useful.'

Hitler did not look entirely convinced, while Anna was trying to work out why she was involved in such a conversation.

'And of course,' Himmler went on, now in full complaining flow, 'it is such a tedious business. There is no end in sight. Do you realize, my Fuehrer, that it is estimated there may be as many as five million Jews in Russia? Even if we shoot a hundred a day, we are still talking of, well...' He scratched his ear.

'Just short of a hundred and thirty-seven years,' Anna said absently.

The three men all turned to look at her.

'I'm sorry,' she said. 'It just slipped out.'

'But that is marvellous,' Hitler said. 'Absolutely marvellous. Do you realize what you have here, Heydrich?'

'I do, my Fuehrer. However, Anna's genius

44

merely highlights the problem. There are also several million Jews here in Germany, and probably an equal number in the rest of Europe. On that basis, if the Reich really is going to last a thousand years, most of them will be used up before the problem is finally solved.'

Hitler patted Anna's hand, then got up, and sat behind his desk. 'I do not find that amusing.'

'But it is true, sir. One cannot argue against mathematics. However...' He paused.

'Yes.'

'It is possible to alter the figures.'

'I do not understand. What are you proposing to do? Take a zero off the end and proclaim that there are really only several hundred thousand instead of several million?'

'No, sir. The only figure that can be altered is the number of Jews that can be disposed of every day. If, instead of a hundred, we got rid of a thousand a day, that would bring the required time down to thirteen years. Is that not correct, Anna?'

Anna stared at him. These people are talking about human lives, she thought. As if they were unnecessary sheets of paper. She heard herself say, 'As far as Russia goes, Herr General.'

'And,' Heydrich went on, 'if the figure is raised to ten thousand a day, we are talking of little more than a year and a half.'

'A year and a half,' Hitler mused. 'That would be wonderful. And say another year and a half for the rest. The Jewish question solved, in under four years.'

'With respect, my Fuehrer,' Himmler said, 'that proposition is absurd. I have just explained that maintaining, much less recruiting, my Einsatzgruppen squads is proving increasingly difficult. Now you are asking me to expand them a hundred-fold? We happen to be fighting a war. I simply do not have the men.'

Hitler looked at Heydrich, and then at Anna, as if supposing she might have the answer to that question as well. But for one of the very few times in her life Anna's brain was paralyzed.

'With respect to you, Herr Reichsfuehrer,' Heydrich said. 'You are approaching the business from the wrong end. You are treating it as a military problem, whereas it is really a civil problem, and as such, should be dealt with by the police.'

'You are expecting the police to go around arresting Jews and shooting them? Not even the Gestapo are trained for anything like that. You would have a morale problem that would make mine irrelevant.'

'I am not suggesting that the police shoot anybody,' Heydrich said patiently. 'But the Gestapo are surely capable of arresting people. Have them arrest every Jew they can find, and incarcerate them.'

'The outcry would be enormous.'

'Not if it is done properly. You simply announce that all Jews are to be resettled, somewhere in the east. There is no need to be specific.'

'And where in the east are you proposing to

46

send them? We are still at war in Russia. Even after the victory, there will be a great deal of cleaning up to be done.'

Anna could tell that Heydrich was only suppressing a sigh with difficulty; this man was his boss. He looked at Hitler.

'I do not think General Heydrich really means that we should resettle the Jews, Heinrich,' the Fuehrer said quietly. 'But to house several million people in concentration camps that are already full ... even to build sufficient new camps to house them all, the expense...'

'With respect, my Fuehrer, we only need one or two additional camps.'

'To house five million people?'

'Not to house them, my Fuehrer – except on a temporary basis – but rather to process them. The turnover can be fairly rapid.'

Hitler gazed at him for several seconds, then looked at Himmler. To Anna's relief, none of the men looked at her. She could not believe what she was hearing, what Heydrich was proposing. She had shared a bed with this man more often than she cared to remember, and would have to do so again, perhaps this very day.

Himmler snorted. 'I have just explained that I am having trouble maintaining the morale of the Einsatzgruppen, carrying out a hundred or so executions a day. Now you wish to increase that number, perhaps a hundredfold? Even if they are locked up in a camp, the men will not do it.'

'I agree,' Heydrich said, again smoothly. 'I am not proposing that we use the SS for this task,

47

save for operating and maintaining the camps, as they already do. Nor am I proposing the use of firing squads; we surely have better use for our bullets, and besides, as you say, sir, it would be too slow. But it is possible to dispose of several hundred people at a time by the use of gas. If the subjects are herded into a large sealed chamber, and gas introduced into that chamber, they will be disposed of in just a few minutes. Then the bodies can be removed, and another lot sent in.'

'You think they will go?' Himmler asked. 'There would be a riot.'

'Not if they are properly handled. Consider, Herr Reichsfuehrer. They have been assembled, and have been taken to what they will be told is a holding camp before they proceed to their resettlement area, their new homes. They are then told that before they can depart, they must be bathed with a special de-lousing soap. They will accept this; most of them are riddled with vermin anyway. These people are essentially passive. As long as there is hope of an improvement in their situation, they will obey orders. Once they are inside the "bath house" and the doors are sealed, it does not matter if they then realize what is about to happen.'

'And you expect my SS to handle all of this?' Himmler demanded.

'The SS will oversee it. I acknowledge that they will have to be specially selected for the task, and there would have to be extra pay and privileges. The actual handling of the bodies would be done by concentration camp inmates, who would also receive special privileges. There will be no difficulty in finding volunteers.'

Himmler looked at Hitler, who was stroking his chin. 'How can you be sure this gas will kill an entire group of more than a hundred people at a time?' the Fuehrer asked. 'I have experienced gas poisoning, you know, in the Great War. I was very ill, and spent some time in hospital. But I did not die. Nor did many of my comrades.'

'Forgive me, my Fuehrer, but science has advanced a good way since 1918. I have been in talks with various chemical firms, and they tell me they have developed a pellet, nothing larger than that, which, dropped through a ventilating shaft, will dispel enough gas to kill everyone in a sealed chamber. Very quickly, too. They will not suffer for more than a few seconds.'

How humane, Anna thought, feeling sick.

'I must say,' Hitler commented, 'that if such a plan would truly work ... it would have to be kept top secret, of course.'

'Of course.'

Hitler looked at Anna, who suddenly felt very cold.

'Anna is absolutely trustworthy, my Fuehrer,' Heydrich declared.

'I did not doubt it for a moment.'

'But it will, of course, leak out,' Himmler said. 'Certainly when construction of these special camps commences.'

'The important thing is that the German people should not know of it,' Hitler said. 'As for world opinion, by the time they know what is happening we shall be masters of all Europe. The Japanese will certainly not object, and Africa is irrelevant.'

'And the United States?'

'Are you not now about to gauge US opinion?' The three men all looked at Anna, who again felt a sudden chill, which only increased as Hitler smiled at her. 'That is going to be your responsibility, my dear. Does that please you?'

Anna was still finding it difficult to think coherently, but she managed a faint, 'Yes, my Fuehrer.'

'Excellent. Well, Reinhard, you do seem to have come up with a solution to our problem. Do you not agree, Heinrich?'

'You understand that General Heydrich will not be here to oversee this programme, my Fuehrer? Or have you changed your mind about sending him to Prague?'

'No, no. He has a job to do there which I suspect only he can do efficiently. You will supervise this programme, Heinrich. You will hold talks with these chemical experts about this wonder pellet, and you will commission architects to design and build the new camps. Ah...' He frowned and looked at Heydrich. 'Where exactly would they be located? I do not think it would be a good idea to have them here in Germany for the reasons I have stated.'

'I agree, sir. But there is a lot of open country

available in Poland, and it will be easier to seal off these areas from the general population than here in Germany.'

'Of course. That is good thinking. Well, gentlemen, Anna, I congratulate you. It seems to me that we have achieved...' He looked at Heydrich.

'I would say, my Fuehrer, that we have achieved a Final Solution to the Jewish problem.'

Two

The Abwehr

Sitting between the two men in the back of the car as it drove away from the Wilhelmstrasse, Anna felt as if she were about to suffocate.

'You have scored a victory,' Himmler remarked. 'I hope for your sake, my dear Reinhard, that it works.'

'It will work,' Heydrich said, 'if it is carried out with the proper efficiency. That is now your province, Herr Reichsfuehrer.'

'Yes,' Himmler said thoughtfully. 'Do you think it will work, Anna?'

I prefer not to think of it at all, Anna thought. *It is the most horrendous plan I have ever heard.* She knew there had been unbelievable massacres before at various periods in history, whether for military or political reasons, but for destroying an entire people just because they were there one had to go back to the Assyrians. So she had to think about it, and she had to tell the world what was going to happen, supposing the world was capable of doing anything to prevent it. But the risk that would involve, when

52

she had virtually been sworn to secrecy ... She was grateful for her glasses, which effectively concealed her eyes, and said quietly, 'It is an overwhelming concept, Herr Reichsfuehrer. May I ask why I was included in this meeting?'

'You weren't intentionally. The Fuehrer just wanted to meet you, to find out if everything we had claimed about you was true. So your presence was accidental, although he did wish to ascertain your opinion of the Jews, your attitude towards them, in view of the mission you are to undertake. And you did very well. The Fuehrer was very taken with you. He may well wish to ... how shall I put it? See more of you.'

Anna drew a sharp breath and Himmler smiled. 'Now, that is an overwhelming thought, is it not?'

'This mission, Herr Reichsfuehrer...'

'We will discuss it later. Over dinner, perhaps.'

Anna looked at Heydrich, who was also smiling. 'The price of fame, as well as beauty, Anna. But you see, as you may have gathered, I will not be here for a while.'

'You are going to Prague.'

'A place I am sure you remember well.'

'I was there for less than twenty-four hours.'

'But in that brief space of time you accomplished one of your greatest triumphs.'

Or suffered one of my greatest misfortunes, Anna thought. 'I did my duty, Herr General,' she said primly. 'But ... there is trouble in Bohemia?'

Himmler snorted. 'The Czechs are the most impossible people on earth. They must be made to understand their place in the Reich; that they belong to the Reich, not the Reich to them. And von Thoma – you remember von Thoma, Countess?'

'We never met. As I said, my visit was very brief.'

'She just arrived, killed two enemy agents, incapacitated a third, and was recalled.' Heydrich's voice was proud. 'I did not wish her to become exposed to any publicity.'

Enemy agents, Anna thought. She had often wondered what she would have done had she known those unfortunate men had been British agents. At that moment, her job had been to protect Meissenbach, and they had intended to kill him. But what a catastrophe would have been avoided had she just let them get on with it.

'Extraordinary,' Himmler commented. 'But then, you are an extraordinary woman, Countess. I look forward to working more closely with you.'

Anna turned her head to look at Heydrich again. He continued to smile. 'As Reichsfuehrer Himmler has indicated, it has been decided that General von Thoma is not capable of ruling Bohemia-Moravia, and therefore I am going to replace him.'

'You're going to be governor-general of Czechoslovakia?'

'Do keep up to date, Anna. Czechoslovakia no

54

longer exists. I have been appointed Reich-Protector of Bohemia-Moravia. Do not look so alarmed. The appointment is only until I have taught these people how to be good citizens of the Reich. I estimate it will take not longer than a year. Then I will be back in Berlin. Until then...' He looked at Himmler.

He gave another of his cold, emotionless smiles. 'You will be working directly under my command, Anna. As I have said, I am looking forward to this. As are you, I am sure.' He squeezed her hand. 'I will come to see you, this evening, and we will discuss your next assignment.'

Anna followed Heydrich into his office, attracting surprised glances; no one in Gestapo Headquarters had ever seen the Countess von Widerstand anything less than immaculately groomed and dressed. But she ignored them all, closing the doors behind herself without waiting for any of the secretaries to interfere. Heydrich, taking off his cap and belts, turned in apparent surprise, as if he had not realized she was behind him. 'Anna?'

Anna took off her glasses, restored them to the pocket of her shirt. 'Can this be real, Herr General?'

Heydrich sat behind his desk. 'I am not sure to what you are referring.'

I'm referring to anything I have heard today, she thought. But the bigger subject was just too big for discussion, certainly with the man who

had thought it up. 'I mean that you are aban-
doning me to this ... this...'

He held up a finger. 'Please, Anna. Reichsfuehrer Himmler is supreme commander of the
German Secret Services. That means he is the
supreme commander of everyone in the Secret
Services. And that includes you, whether you
like it or not.'

'Will he wish to have sex with me?'

'I would be very surprised if he does not.
Mind you, I have no idea what his tastes are. But
you are quite capable of taking care of any
tastes, are you not?'

Anna placed her hands on the desk and leaned
forward. 'Reinhard, I am a human being. I have
feelings, believe it or not.'

'Do you know, I have often doubted that. Oh,
you are a consummate actress. But I have
observed you, when apparently in the throes of
an orgasm, clearly thinking of something else.
Or some*one* else.'

Anna straightened; he was getting rather close
to the truth. 'I have never faked an orgasm in my
life.' Which was not a lie.

'I am sure of it. That is one of your greatest
assets. That you can become totally absorbed in
your sex, while at the same time determining
what should happen next. Perhaps even something like killing your partner.'

'So I stay alive.'

'Because you are valuable to us. Continue being valuable to us, and you and yours may enjoy
a long and profitable life.'

Anna's nostrils dilated. The threat contained in the words 'and yours', which he had so casually slipped in, was the nightmare that dominated her life.

He was a believer in crossing t's and dotting i's. 'Tell me, when did you last see your parents?'

'When you permitted me to visit them, in July of last year.'

'But that is more than a year ago. That is very neglectful of you. I will give you an authorization now.'

'I do not wish to visit my parents at this time, Herr General.'

Heydrich raised his eyebrows.

'They have learned, from their guards, that I am working for the Reich, and thus regard me as a traitor, both to Austria and to their beliefs.'

'That is a pity. But have they not also learned that they are alive and well just because you have embraced our principles?'

'I do not know. It is better that they should not. I think they would find that unacceptable.'

'It is remarkable how some people refuse to accept reality. Fortunately you, Anna, have never suffered from tunnel vision. Nor must you now. Your value does not depend merely on your unusual skills; it equally lies in your beauty, your sexuality, which makes any normal heterosexual man want to get his hands on you. Reichsfuehrer Himmler is, as far as I know, a normal heterosexual man, and he is, as of now, the most important man in your life. I say this with some sadness. But as I have told you, I would hope to complete this Prague business within a year, at which time I shall return, and hope to reclaim you. Now go away and prepare to entertain the Reichsfuehrer tonight. I am sure you will find him ... different.'

As she waited on the pavement for her taxi – Heydrich's determination to preserve her anonymity meant that he would not allow her the use of an official car, which suited her purpose well enough – Anna wondered who she loathed more, Heydrich or Himmler. But while she knew Heydrich very well, she did not know Himmler at all. It was the cold-fish demeanour of the Gestapo Chief that was so off-putting. And tonight she would have to give him everything he wanted, with the loving enthusiasm he would want as well. She wondered if Heydrich had ever discussed her sexual skills with his boss.

But there were more important things in life than sex. The death of millions! The car door was opened for her, and she sank on to the cushions. 'I wish to go to Antoinette's Boutique,' she told the driver.

He grunted, and the car moved away from the kerb. But he was watching her in his rear-view mirror, and while he clearly liked what he saw, she knew he was wondering if such an untidy and shabbily dressed young woman could afford the fare – and what he should ask for if she could not. Equally, he would be wondering if she could possibly afford to shop at such an expensive emporium.

'I will not be long,' she said as the taxi stopped outside the lavish exterior. 'Wait for me.' She gave him a note. 'There will be another of those when you have taken me home.' Again he did not comment.

Anna entered the show room. 'Countess! Countess?' The woman, pertly attractive with curling dark hair, peered at her. Like everyone else, she was unused to seeing one of the Boutique's most valued customers in anything other than the height of chic. And for her suddenly to appear after so long an absence... 'Are you all right?'

Anna took off her glasses. 'Good morning, Edda. Is Signor Bartoli free?'

'He is with a client, Countess. Perhaps I can help.'

'I wish to see Signor Bartoli. Will you tell him this?'

'Ah ... of course. Will you not sit down?'

Anna nodded, but she preferred to stand, moving restlessly from showcase to showcase. There were several other customers in the store, and they cast curious glances at so much beauty encased in shapeless slacks and a crumpled shirt, and with her still-damp hair loose and somewhat untidy. Anna ignored them, and a moment later Edda Hedermann returned. 'If you will come in, Countess.'

Anna followed her, not into the fitting room where she usually saw her Berlin boss, but into

Bartoli's office.

'Signor Bartoli will be with you in a moment.'

She closed the door, and Anna sat down and crossed her knees. The enormity of what she had been told that morning was only slowly overshadowing her personal problems. It was in fact so great, so horrifying, that its exact implications were difficult to calculate. She knew she should go home and think about it, but going home meant preparing herself for Himmler's visit, and she wanted to get this problem off her chest before contemplating in detail such a mind-blowing prospect. And before allowing the personal risk to which she would be exposing herself get the better of her devotion to duty.

She got up, sat behind Bartoli's desk, pulled a block of his notepaper towards her, and wrote rapidly. Then she read what she had written, and blew a raspberry. She took the gold lighter from her shoulder bag, flicked it into flame, and carefully burned the paper. She did not herself smoke, but carried the lighter as a fashion accessory.

The door opened and Bartoli came in. 'What are you doing here?'

'Waiting for you.'

'You are supposed to make an appointment.'

'This is urgent. Would you like to sit down?'

Bartoli was a short, rotund man with a waxed moustache. As overwhelmed as any man when he had first discovered that the agent he had been appointed to monitor, and hopefully control, was quite the most exciting woman he had ever seen, his enthusiasm had dwindled as his attempts to get close to her had all been firmly rejected. 'It does happen to be my desk.'

Anna got up and moved back to her chair. Bartoli sat behind the desk and shot his cuffs. 'Where have you been, anyway? I have not seen you for a year.'

'My dear Bartoli, I have spent most of the last year in Moscow, as you well know.'

'The entire German Embassy staff was returned from Moscow on the twenty-third of June, the day after the invasion began. It is now the sixteenth of August.'

'I did not return with the Embassy staff. There were difficulties. And when I did get back, I felt the need to rest up for a few weeks.'

Bartoli frowned. 'You are not saying that the Soviets got on to you?'

'That is one way of putting it.'

His eyes gleamed. 'And they roughed you up?'

'That is also one way of putting it.'

'What did they do to you?' His tone was eager.

'If you hang around long enough, I will write my memoirs and you can read them and jerk yourself off.'

He flushed. 'One day you are going to come tumbling down.'

'Then I will put that in my memoirs too. Now listen, I have some information which I wish transmitted to London, urgently.'

'Very well. What is it?'

'The Reich Government intends to execute every Jew under its control on the continent of Europe. That is every country with the exception of Spain, Sweden and Switzerland. And Great Britain, of course.'

Bartoli stared at her. 'Are they mad? Or are you mad?'

Anna shrugged. 'You could be right on both counts. But it is going to happen.'

'You are talking about ten million people!'

'If none of them can escape, you are probably right there too.'

'How do you know this?'

'An hour ago I was at a meeting at the Reich Chancellery, with the Fuehrer, Reichsfuehrer Himmler, and General Heydrich, when the decision was taken. It cannot be implemented for some time, perhaps a year, as all the necessary facilities have to be built, but I can tell you that they are already killing Jews at the rate of more than a hundred a day in Russia.'

Bartoli's mouth had sagged open. Now he snapped it shut. 'And what part are you to play in this operation?'

'I have no part in it.'

'But you were there. Why?'

'I was summoned to a meeting with the Fuehrer, and the subject came up.'

'How fortuitous. And supposing I agree to send this rather absurd information to London, what do you expect them to do about it?'

'Luigi, I am not asking for your *agreement* to send this information to London. I am giving you vital information which *must* be sent to London, immediately.'

Bartoli glared at her. His problem was that he did not know how much clout she possessed. But he had to suspect it was considerable. 'I have asked: what do you expect London to do with it? Supposing they even believe you.'

'It must be handled carefully, as at this moment only four people know of it. But the secret may reasonably be leaked once construction of the required facilities commences. I think I will be able to discover when this happens and let them know. If they then reveal to the world that they know what the Nazis are planning, it will on the one hand warn the Jews of Europe what is hanging over them, and perhaps enable some of them to get out, and it may even restrain or perhaps entirely negate the policy. Although they pretend not to be, the Nazis are as susceptible as any government to international criticism, especially from America. Persecuting the Jews to a state when all who can have fled the country, leaving most of their wealth behind, is one thing. And that incurred enough neutral criticism, again principally in the United States. Murdering ten million people is another thing altogether. You get that information to London, Luigi, and tell them to wait for a further communication from me.'

She left the office and returned to the showroom, smiling at Edda, who was looking more po-faced than ever. Anna supposed that from the regularity of her visits the woman suspected she was Luigi's mistress, although ... She frowned. This was her first visit to the Boutique in a year.

She put on her glasses, went out into the warm August sunshine, and the taxi's engine started. But this was not the same taxi that had dropped her here.

'Who are you?' she inquired through the front window. 'Where is my driver?'

'He had to go off. That was longer than a few minutes, Fraulein,' the driver pointed out. 'He saw me passing, and asked me to take his place.'

Alarm bells began to ring in Anna's brain. But she got into the back of the car. 'I'm sorry I kept you, and him, waiting. One never knows how long it will take, with clothes.'

'That is an expensive shop,' he commented. 'Do you buy all of your clothes there?'

'I do not think that is any business of yours,' Anna said. 'Pull in over there.'

The taxi drew up at the kerb. 'Nice building.'

'I think so. Your fare?' Anna opened the door.

'It is here.' The driver half turned and presented a card that indicated he was a member of the Abwehr.

Anna felt the tension creeping through her body. She was well aware of the jealousy that existed between the Abwehr, which was the Military Intelligence Service, and the Gestapo. Equally, she knew that both organizations were inferior to the SS, much less the SD. But this man could not possibly know that she belonged to the SD. More importantly, why had he chosen to pick her up, masquerading as a taxi driver?

'I am impressed,' she said. 'But I do not understand what you want of me. In case you do not know it, I am the Countess von Widerstand.'

'So-called,' he sneered. 'Is there anyone in your apartment?'

'My maid.'

'We will go up there together, and you will dismiss your maid, and then we will ... talk.'

Anna regarded him for several moments. She did not doubt that he was a genuine Abwehr agent, but she did know that Abwehr agents, like those of the Gestapo, as a rule operated in pairs when on duty, and so it seemed this man was not necessarily on official business. She also deduced that, like so many men, he clearly regarded himself as necessarily superior to any woman, certainly one who was young and so obviously innocent of the ways of the world, even if he might suspect her of dealing in subversive activities. Equally, like so many policemen in Nazi Germany, he regarded himself as above the law, at least when bullying and perhaps enjoying an attractive victim.

But she needed to find out just how much he did suspect, or might even know, about both the Boutique and herself. So she allowed herself a hasty and obviously nervous lick of her lips. 'If that is what you wish.'

He followed her into the lobby and she greeted the concierge, who looked apprehensive. Like most people in Germany he could recognize a policeman when he saw one, and Anna was one of his favourite tenants. But as she merely smiled at him he made no comment; she knew that, as this building was owned by the SD, and all of its residents worked for that organization, he was required to note and report all non-resident comings and goings.

She led the man into the elevator, took off her glasses, placed them in her pocket, and faced him. 'Will you not tell me your name?'

'My name was on my warrant card.'

'I'm sorry, I did not notice.'

He held out the card again.

Anna studied it. 'Pieter Schlutz. Mine is Anna.'

'Anna what?'

'Anna, Countess von Widerstand.'

'You do not wish to make me angry, Anna.'

'Oh. Are you going to beat me up?'

'That would be very enjoyable, I am sure. Although there are other things I would prefer to do to you first. Or maybe after would be better.'

Anna shuddered. 'I do not like being hurt, Herr Schlutz. Please do not attempt to hurt me.' Which was all the warning he was going to get.

'Then do not make me angry. Then I will only hurt you a little.' He stepped against her, squeezed her hips, and then unfastened her slacks to pull them past her thighs to uncover her underwear, immediately sliding his hands under the hem of the cami-knickers to find the bare flesh beneath, thus rendering himself momentarily helpless. At this close range it was impossible to generate any real power, but in addition to her

66

skills at martial arts Anna was consummately trained at both judo and karate. It was judo, the art of using the opponent's movements to defeat him, that she needed here. His face and body had moved down her stomach as he sought her pubes, so she simply placed both hands on his head and pushed with all her strength. His knees struck the floor of the car, and as she was still pushing, he lost his balance and fell over; the cami-knickers ripped as his fingers tightened in search of balance. Anna stepped away from him and pulled up her pants. He pushed himself into a sitting position, lips drawn back in a snarl.

'Bitch! I will...'

Anna's toes, travelling in a perfectly timed kick, crashed into his jaw and he fell backwards to hit the wall with a thump. She fastened her pants, then stood above him to make sure he was out, at least for the moment, before kneeling to hunt through his clothes. There was a Luger pistol, which she tucked into the waistband of her slacks, and then she found what she really wanted: a pair of handcuffs. She removed these, rolled him over, dragged his arms behind his back, and secured his wrists.

The elevator car had by now arrived at the sixth floor, and stopped. Anna grasped Schlutz's shoulders and, using all her strength – he was a heavy man – dragged him into the doorway so that the doors could not close. Then she stepped over him, crossed the lobby, and opened her apartment door. 'Birgit!' she called.

'I am here, Countess.' Birgit hurried up the

corridor from the kitchen, drying her hands on her apron. A dark-haired young woman – although she was some years older than Anna herself – she had a short and slender body and pretty features, at this moment, as always when confronted by her mistress, contorted with anxiety. Anna knew that the maid had no real idea what she did for a living, other than that she worked for the Government, but as she had been in Anna's employ for well over a year now, and had been with her in Moscow, she did know that people had a habit of being found dead when in Anna's vicinity. As for the Russian debacle, Birgit, as a member of the Embassy staff, had been repatriated the day after the German invasion had started, when Anna had already been in the hands of the NKVD. No doubt Birgit had supposed she would never see her mistress again, however much she had pretended to be overwhelmed with joy and relief when she had suddenly turned up, a week later, apparently on top of the world.

Anna smiled at her. 'I need your help.'

'Countess?'

'Here.' Anna led her across the lobby and indicated Schlutz's body.

Birgit clasped both hands to her neck. 'Is he dead?'

'Not yet. I want him in the apartment. Come along.'

The alarm was buzzing as someone else was trying to use the elevator. The two women grasped a shoulder each and dragged Schlutz clear of the doors, which promptly closed. By now Schlutz had opened his eyes and was taking in his surroundings. Then he opened his mouth.

'Please do not make a noise,' Anna requested. 'Or I will hit you again, harder. In fact, it would be better if you did not speak at all, until I invite you to do so.'

Schlutz closed his mouth again, but continued to stare at her in a most vituperative manner.

'He is very angry,' Birgit suggested.

'Wouldn't you be, if you had just been kicked in the teeth? I think he can probably stand up.'

Between them they got Schlutz to his knees and then his feet, although he was clearly not functioning properly, and had to be held up. By now Birgit had noticed the pistol in Anna's waistband.

'He threatened you with a gun?'

'Not exactly. I just felt that we could have a more civilized conversation if I had it. The handcuffs are his as well. He's a policeman. Well, in a manner of speaking.'

'Oh, my God!'

'Just relax.' They got Schlutz across the lobby and into the sitting room. 'On the settee,' Anna said.

They sat him down, facing them. His chin was almost blue, and he was gasping for air. Seeing him sitting there brought back such memories. Gottfried Friedemann had sat there, with his arms round her, seconds before she had obeyed Heydrich's command and put the Walther automatic pistol to the back of his head and squeezed

69

the trigger. But then, Clive Bartley had sat there as well, with his arms round her, seconds before her life had taken on an entirely new dimension. Good and grotesque, happy and horrible, all sides of the same coin.

She adored this apartment, with its soft carpets, its panelled walls, its luxurious furnishings ... Her parents had been comfortably off, but there had been no money for extreme luxury in the Vienna house. Even so, when she had been taken away and placed in a Gestapo cell, and even more when she had been taken from the cell to go to the SS training school, she had supposed that comfort, much less luxury, had vanished from her life forever. But instead she had wound up here, in more luxury than she had ever suspected to exist outside of a palace.

None of it was hers, of course; a fact of which the man seated in front of her did not seem to be aware. She lived here because Heydrich – or was it actually Himmler? – required the Countess von Widerstand to live in a style to match her name and manufactured background. Here she could entertain, here she could seduce, and here she could execute, with an SD disposal unit only a phone call away – something else this unfortunate lout did not seem to know.

So here it was that she had sold her soul to the devil. Because she had had no choice. But it was also here that she had taken the fist step towards reclaiming that soul. Unfortunately, the devil still had to be serviced.

'What are we going to do?' Birgit asked.

There was no way Birgit could be allowed to overhear any of the answers she intended to extract from this man. 'You,' Anna said, 'are going to go out and enjoy yourself. I do not wish you to come back before six. But while you are out buy some nice food, and when you do come back, prepare a very good dinner. I believe we may be entertaining tonight.'

'But you, Countess. Will you be safe here with him?'

'I think we are going to get along just fine,' Anna assured her. 'Now, off you go. There is money on the dressing table.' Birgit hurried from the room, and Anna went to the sideboard and poured two glasses of schnapps. Then she sat beside Schlutz. 'I think you could do with this.'

She held the glass to his lips, and he drank eagerly enough. 'Do you know what they are going to do to you, Fraulein? What I am going to do with you, when I get free?'

Anna leaned away from him and sipped her own drink. 'You are counting chickens, Herr Schlutz, although perhaps I should start calling you Pieter, as we are liable to become very intimate. What should be concerning you is what I am going to do to you, now, if it becomes necessary.'

Birgit emerged, wearing her hat. 'I will go now, Countess.'

'Six o'clock,' Anna reminded her. 'Not a moment before.' She waited for the front door to close, then went to the sideboard and refilled the

71

glasses. 'So you see, Pieter, we have six hours to get to know each other. But we will stop just now for lunch.'

'Stop what?' he asked, for the first time apprehensive.

'Whatever we happen to be doing at the time.' Anna gave him another drink, then sat in a chair opposite him, leaning back and crossing her knees. 'Now, let us start at the beginning. You work for Military Intelligence. Admiral Canaris, is it? And you have for some reason determined that there is something suspicious about me, or my name, or whatever. Was this your own deduction, or that of Admiral Canaris?'

'I was directed to investigate you, yes.'

'And what have you found out?'

'I know that you are an Austrian adventuress who operates under a spurious title, but who managed to marry into the English aristocracy until she was discovered and thrown out.'

'Because I was an adventuress?'

'There was some talk of you actually being a spy, but I do not believe that.'

'You should be more trusting. You have still not told me what you have found out to make you want to interrogate me. I mean to say, if I am not a spy, what crime am I supposed to have committed?'

'I will tell you that when you are at our headquarters.'

'But we are not going to your headquarters.'

'Do you seriously think you can keep me here? For how long?'

72

'How does the idea of eternity take you?'

He stared at her. 'You? A chit of a girl? You would not dare harm an agent of the Abwehr. You would not know how.'

'Well, maybe I can pick it up as we go along. I asked you a question. Answer it.'

Her voice had suddenly taken on a sharp edge, and his head jerked. But he did not lack courage. 'Fuck off.'

'I have an idea that you came here with that in mind,' Anna said. 'And as you have reminded me, I am a simple young girl who only knows how to submit to men. So, you see, your wish is my command.' She stood in front of him. 'As at the moment I am doing you a favour, it would be very unwise of you to attempt to kick me. I am in a better position to hurt you than you are to hurt me, would you not agree?'

She unbuttoned his jacket, then released his belt and pulled his pants right off. Then she did the same to his drawers, while his breathing slowly increased in intensity. 'Hm,' she commented. 'I've seen better. But he is improving all the time. Now you have to wait a few moments.' She went into her bedroom, leaving the door open so that she could keep an eye on him while she opened her bureau drawers to find what she wanted.

He actually never moved, remained contemplating himself, obviously wondering if he dared believe the pleasure that seemed about to be his. She selected two pairs of handcuffs and a scarf, then returned to the drawing room. 'We don't want these getting in the way,' she suggested, and pulled his left ankle towards the settee leg to secure it with one of the cuffs. Then she pulled the right leg to the other side. This meant stretching him to the limit, but he made no effort to resist her; the very business of being spread so wide while naked from the waist down was intensifying his erection.

'There,' Anna said, standing up. 'Now, we don't want you screaming, either in ecstasy or in agony; this is a respectable building.' She moved behind the settee, draped the scarf round his mouth, drew it tight, and secured it on the nape of his neck. Now at last he attempted to protest, but it was too late.

'All set, I think.' Anna went to where her shoulder bag rested on a chair, and took out her lighter. 'I don't smoke myself,' she assured him. 'I think it is a disgusting habit. But so many of my guests do. From your breath I would say that you certainly do. You should give it up. But then, you're not a very strong character, are you? Your professional life has been spent ill-treating your victims; you have never been a victim yourself. But one should always experience both sides of every situation, don't you think? I have been tortured, you know. The experience either wrecks you forever, or it makes you twice as strong, mentally, as you were before. It did not wreck me. Of course, I was not physically damaged, except for a brief while. But once I start to burn you, you will be physically damaged, permanently. Because, as we are

74

not going to be interrupted until six o'clock this evening, I am quite prepared to go on burning you throughout that time. With a break for lunch, of course. Now, Pieter, you have admitted that you were sent to investigate me. I wish you to tell me how this happened, and how you knew to pick me up outside Antoinette's Boutique. I have a feeling that the two things are connected. If you are prepared to answer before I flick this lighter, nod your head.'

Schlutz stared at her.

'Your decision. Would you believe, Pieter, that I have never done this sort of thing before? Although there are quite a few men I have felt like doing it to. Well, one has to start somewhere, and yours is certainly big enough.'

She stood between his legs and flicked the lighter; it emitted a huge flame. Schlutz's chest rose and fell with great rapidity, and his head was moving too, up and down. Anna closed the lighter and laid it on the coffee table.

'That was a very wise decision. Please remember that if you attempt to make a noise I will hurt you very badly.' She moved behind him and untied the scarf. 'So talk to me.'

'A drink,' he gasped. 'I need a drink.'

'Why not?' She refilled the schnapps glass and held it to his lips.

He drained it. 'You are a devil from hell!'

'I think some people do believe that. But this is the hell, you know. Nazi Germany.'

'Masquerading as an innocent young girl...'

'I do not masquerade as a young girl. I am

75

only just twenty-one. That men choose to regard me from their own limited sexual point of view is their problem, not mine. But you have not told me anything that I wish to know. Unless you do so, now, I am going to replace the gag, and then I will burn you whether you nod or not. Do you know, I am getting quite excited about it.' She picked up the gag.

'Frau Hedermann,' he gasped.

Anna frowned. This could be more serious than she had supposed. 'Frau Hedermann works for the Abwehr?' How could Bartoli have been so careless?

'No. She is a friend of mine. And she is suspicious of Bartoli.'

'How am I involved? He is my dressmaker, nothing more.'

'She thinks there could be more. She noted this last summer, when you paid several visits to see him. It was supposed to be for a dress fitting, but she says the dress was a ridiculous thing, and that you never did take delivery of it. Bartoli burned it.'

Now that was careless of me, Anna thought; she had merely told Bartoli to get rid of the dress. That he would be so stupid as to burn it in front of his staff had never occurred to her; he was supposed to be her Controller.

'This all happened a year ago,' she pointed out. 'When did she tell you about it?'

'Well, when we got ... friendly. It was last autumn. But by then you had gone away.'

'Did she know where?'

'No. But I told her to contact me when you reappeared. If you ever did.'

Anna gave him an affectionate squeeze as a reward. 'And today was your lucky day. Or not, as the case may be. You say you told her to contact you when I returned from wherever I had been. Was this on orders from your superiors? From Admiral Canaris?'

'I had no orders. There was nothing concrete to present to my superiors.'

'So you were lying just now when you said you had been told to investigate me. You are acting entirely on your own. I am glad about that. Why were you so interested?'

'Well...' He flushed. 'I asked Frau Hedermann for a description of you, and she told me you were the loveliest woman she had ever seen.'

'So you got the idea that when I turned up again, you could flash your badge and bully me into having sex with you. You really are a despicable creature, Schlutz. But also a very stupid one. So I eventually returned from wherever I had been, and Frau Hedermann remembered that you were ... interested, and telephoned you. She is every bit as despicable as you. And you hurried down to the Boutique, and I suppose you flashed your badge at my taxi-driver and told him to clear off.'

'Well...'

'Now just tell me one more thing. You are quite sure that no one in the Abwehr knows anything about this. It is entirely between you and Edda Hedermann. Who, I assume, is your

77

mistress, and in order to retain your favours is prepared to pimp for you?'

'Well ... there were Edda's suspicions that you and Bartoli were engaged in possible subversive activities.'

'Of course,' Anna agreed. 'Suspicions which, if I do not agree to have sex with you, can easily be passed to your superiors, which could make life very difficult for me.'

'It need not happen. Anna, stop this silly game, release me and have sex with me, and I will agree not to take the matter any further.'

'I think that is a very reasonable proposition,' Anna said.

'Well, then, let me go.'

'But I don't think it would be safe for me to agree to it. I cannot bring myself entirely to trust you. But I will make you very happy. Oh, dear, your little man appears to be going to sleep.' She knelt between his legs and began to play with him.

'Anna,' he gasped. 'Oh, Anna. Take him into your mouth, Anna.'

'I do not wish to do that.'

'You...'

'I would not like you to think that I have anything against fellatio,' Anna explained. 'But I do need the physical evidence that you were trying to rape me when I ... defended myself ... There we go. Wasn't that fun?'

He was panting, his chest heaving. But his brain was starting to work again. 'You ... What are you saying?'

'Give me a moment.' Anna went into the bathroom and washed her hands.

'Anna!' he called. 'Come back. I have said I will drop the investigation against you.'

Anna returned. 'Oh, I am sure you will never do that, Pieter.' She walked round the back of the settee. 'I would like you to know that your company, although most distasteful, has also been quite stimulating. It has taken my experiences to new heights. Although I suppose it is actually depths.' She was now standing behind him. 'But I will wish you good fortune in whatever future you may be going to.'

She drew a deep breath and swung her right arm from behind her shoulder, getting all of her 120 pounds into the movement, holding her hand rigid, and crashed it into the side of Schlutz's neck, just above where it joined his shoulder.

Three

Going West

Schlutz slumped without a sound, his head sagging sideways on to his shoulder. Anna waited for a few moments, then rested two fingers on his neck. There was no pulse.

She released his ankles, then rolled him over and freed his wrists. Another roll and he tumbled on to the floor, on his back. She knelt beside him and picked up his discarded pants, replaced his handcuffs on his belt, then restored his Luger to its holster; in each case wiping the article clean of her prints. Then she let the pants lie beside the body, dropping the drawers on top of them. Her own handcuffs she restored to the drawer in her bedroom.

Then she washed the glasses they had used, and stood above him for a moment, finger on her chin while she considered. She was working, as she had been from the moment she had realized that he was too dangerous to be allowed to live, her mind entirely concentrated on what needed to be done. Normally in these circumstances she would telephone Heydrich, and he would send a disposal unit to remove the body. But he would want to know what had happened, and how it had happened. The way the body was lying, its appearance, and the semen would certainly back up her story that he had been endeavouring to rape her and she had defended herself. But there was one considerable drawback to that scenario, at least as regards Heydrich. When in March 1939 she had been forced to kill Elsa Mayers to prevent the betrayal of her liaison with Clive Bartley, she had used that self-same story. Clive had long since departed, on her instructions, and she had told Heydrich that Elsa had tried to rape her, and that she had defended herself, violently. As he had known all about Elsa's proclivities, he had accepted that tale without question. But would he accept an almost exact repetition, two years later, even if the sex was different? She had a high regard both for his intelligence and his suspicious nature.

In any event, Heydrich had virtually washed his hands of her, at least for the time being. She needed to go to the top, to the person who was just working himself up to come to her.

She picked up the telephone, gave the number. 'The Reichsfuehrer does not take telephone calls,' the woman announced.

'Will you just tell him that it is Anna, that something very serious has happened, that I need his help, urgently, but that I cannot come to him.'

'Really, Fraulein,' the woman said. 'Do you

expect the Reichsfuehrer to be interested in your domestic problems?'

'Yes, I do, and I recommend that you do as I say or it may be unfortunate for you.'

There was a brief hesitation. Then the woman said, 'I will need your full name and status.'

'Anna will do.'

Another hesitation, then the woman obviously laid down the phone and went off. Anna sat absolutely still, staring at the dead man. Number fifteen! Soon enough, she knew, she would be overtaken by an enormous surge of guilt and remorse, of self-horror at what she had done, a sense of disbelief that she, Annaliese Fehrbach, who not four years ago had been a convent schoolgirl, considered by the nuns as almost the perfect pupil, brilliant and inventive, and yet always obedient and polite, could possibly be sitting here contemplating the body of the fifteenth adversary she had killed with ruthless efficiency. One day, when it was all over, she would go to confession, something she had not been able to do for all of those three and a half years. She wondered what her penance would be; half a dozen Hail Marys would hardly fill the bill.

But at this moment, Annaliese Fehrbach did not exist. She was the Countess von Widerstand, applying herself to the task of survival and eventual success with all the enormous concentration and determination she had at her command, which would allow nothing and no one to stand in her way, to threaten her existence, and, by projection, that of her family.

'Anna? What has happened?'

'Oh, Herr Reichsfuehrer! I have a problem.'

'A problem? What problem?'

'There is a dead man here.'

'What? Where?'

'In my apartment.'

'A dead man? In your apartment? How did he get there?'

'He was alive when he came here. He forced his way in and tried to rape me. So I defended myself. I must have hit him too hard...'

'My God! Listen, do nothing. Touch nothing. Just wait. I will take care of it.'

'Oh, thank God! I knew you would not fail me, Heinrich. Oh, I do apologize, Herr Reichsfuehrer. That was unforgivable.'

'Not at all. I would like you to call me Heinrich, at least in private. We are working together, are we not? I will be there in fifteen minutes.'

Anna replaced the phone and took another look around the room. Then she grasped the front of her shirt and tore it open; the buttons burst and scattered. She released her belt and slid down the slacks. Her cami-knickers were already torn where Schlutz had grasped them in the lift, but she tore them some more, to expose her crotch entirely. She pulled the pants back up, fastened them, then seized them and jerked them open; again buttons flew. Then she refastened the belt. A last look round the room, then she sat down to wait. This was one of the occasions when she wished she did smoke.

***

'My dear girl! My dear, dear girl.' Himmler looked as if he would embrace her, but thought better of it. The room was full of men; even the concierge had come up to discover what had happened to his favourite resident. So Himmler contented himself with grasping her shoulders while holding her at arms' length, peering at her torn clothing. 'Are you all right?'

'Now that you are here, Herr Reichsfuehrer.'

'I meant are you hurt in any way?'

'I do not think so. Perhaps you could examine me...'

He blinked at her in embarrassment, and she realized that with a man as sexually timid as this she would have to be careful. But his attention was distracted by the doctor, who had come to stand beside them. 'Well?'

'It would seem to be exactly as the Countess has said, Herr Reichsfuehrer. The man must have spent himself immediately before death. Well, you can see...'

'Of course I can see,' Himmler snapped. 'It is disgusting.'

'My people are cleaning it up now. There are just a couple of things...'

'Yes?'

'He appears to have been struck, violently, on the chin, at some time before death.' His gaze drifted to Anna.

'Yes,' Anna said, 'when he threw me down and started to take off my clothes, I kicked him.'

'I would say, going by the bruise, that you

must have laid him out.'

'I thought I had. But when I tried to get up, he caught hold of me and threw me down again.'

'But he did not actually penetrate you?'

'No, he was so worked up that, as you say, he came before he could complete. That gave me the opportunity to get my arms free, so I hit him.'

'You hit him with your hand, on the neck?'

'Yes.'

'Do you know that his neck is broken?'

'I'm sorry, Herr Doctor, I was trying to defend myself.'

The doctor scratched his head.

'What a horrifying experience for a young woman,' Himmler commented, leaving Anna to wonder if he had ever actually read her file in any detail. 'Well?' This to the SS captain who had accompanied him with four of his men.

'We found this, Herr Reichsfuehrer.'

Himmler took the rectangle of cardboard. 'Abwehr?' He looked at Anna.

'Yes. That is how he got in. He was pretending to be a taxi-driver ... I suppose the taxi is still outside...' She looked meaningfully at the concierge, who was clearly listening; there could be no holes in her story.

The concierge nodded. 'It is still there, Countess.'

'Well, when we got here, he showed me his badge and said he wished to speak with me. I did not wish a scene on the street, so I invited him up. I felt I should find out what he wanted.'

The captain looked at the concierge, who again nodded. 'That is exactly how it appeared to me, Herr Captain. The Countess did not look alarmed, so I saw no reason to interfere.'

'I had no reason to be alarmed,' Anna pointed out, 'until we got inside, when he assaulted me.'

'And he gave no idea what he wanted?'

'He wanted me, Herr Captain.'

'Yes, but...'

'You had better get on to Canaris,' Himmler said. 'Find out what he's after, interfering with one of our people.'

'With respect, Herr Reichsfuehrer,' Anna said. 'I do not think Admiral Canaris, or his office, had anything to do with what happened. This man, this Schlutz, told me so, when I asked what he wanted. Nothing, he said. Save a piece of your ass.'

'My God!' Himmler said. 'The scum these people employ. For God's sake, get this place cleaned up, Schuster. And remove that carrion. Doctor!'

'Ah ... Countess...' The doctor licked his lips.

'I think the bedroom would be best,' Anna decided. 'You'll excuse us.' Her remark included the entire room, but she knew Himmler was following as she led the doctor into her bedroom. 'What would you like me to do?'

'If you would undress...'

Anna began to remove her torn clothes.

'You do not mind if I stay?' Himmler asked.

'I am your servant, sir,' Anna said primly, and took off her cami-knickers.

Himmler stood against the wall, breathing deeply. The doctor was more professional, but he was clearly enjoying what he was required to do, the more so as he could find no reason for doing it. 'There are a couple of small bruises,' he said at last, reluctantly. 'Nothing the least serious. Would you like me to give you some ointment?'

'I am sure I have sufficient ointment in my medicine cabinet, thank you.'

'But this...' He bent forward.

Oh, Hannah Gehrig, Anna thought. If I hadn't had to break your neck to save Belinda Hoskin's life, I should have broken it to save your bullet from being such a nuisance. 'It was a bullet wound, Herr Doctor. It is perfectly healed now.'

'The Countess's English husband shot her,' Himmler said. So he had read her file after all, and, like Heydrich, accepted her account of the incident.

'Good heavens! Well, then...' The doctor looked longingly at her pubes.

'I have told you, Herr Doctor, that he did not succeed in penetrating me. In fact he did not get near penetrating me. So there is nothing for you to find inside me.'

'Ah. Yes, of course. Well...'

'Oh, get out, Doctor,' Himmler said. 'You are irritating the Countess.'

'Yes, sir. Well, good day, Countess.'

He closed the door behind himself, and Himmler and Anna looked at each other. 'May I put something on?' Anna asked.

'My dear girl! But, after such an ordeal, would you not like to lie down?'

'I am all right, really.' Anna put on a dressing gown, thrust her toes into slippers. 'What I would really like is a drink. May I pour you one?'

'That would be very nice.'

She led him into the drawing-room, where the SD men were removing the last traces of what had happened, and poured two glasses of schnapps. It seemed several light years since she had done this for Schlutz, but now she had an even stronger sense that she was feeling her way. If she had absolutely no desire at that moment to have sex or even get too close to anyone, her future existence depended on this man even more than it had ever done on Heydrich.

They touched glasses, and she sat on the settee. He waited a few minutes until the last of his policemen had left the apartment, casting longing glances at Anna's legs as they did so, and then sat beside her. 'This does not bother you? I mean, in view of what happened here just now.'

'I have to accept what happened.'

'Oh, quite. Absolutely. Your approach to life, your calmness, is astonishing in one so young. I think the man who could arouse your passion would be very fortunate.'

That was unanswerable. He had just suggested that he found her reaction to Schlutz and her near rape, as he believed it to be, close to

88

unnatural, so suggesting that he might be that man at this moment might be highly risky. But to indicate that she did not wish his company in bed might be equally risky. 'I am sure that man exists, Herr Reichsfuehrer,' she said. 'Would you like something to eat?'

He raised his eyebrows.

'I know you are coming here tonight,' she said. 'And in fact I have very little to offer you now. My maid is out buying what we are going to eat. But as you are here now, and it is past lunchtime...'

'And you are hungry. For food.'

'Yes. I am hungry. For food. There is some cold meat in the icebox. I can make us up a sandwich.'

'I think that would be very pleasant. May I watch you?'

'Of course.' She led him into the kitchen, began slicing bread.

He followed, stood in the doorway. 'Have you ever been to America? I mean, the United States.'

'No, Herr Reichsfuehrer, I have not. But I understand that you wish me to go. To do what, exactly?'

'What you do best.'

'Ow!' Anna exclaimed at the sudden sharp pain.

'Oh, my dear, you have cut yourself.'

'It is just a nick. You took me by surprise.'

'I am so sorry. Let me look at it.' He took her hand, raised it to his mouth, and sucked her finger. Anna was totally taken aback. Various men had sucked almost every inch of her body, but never her finger ... And this man was about to start murdering people on a scale unimagined even by Genghis Khan. But then, he was already shooting them at the rate of more than a hundred a day.

He took his mouth away; the bleeding had certainly stopped. 'Is the idea distasteful to you?'

'You are sending me to kill someone?'

'To kill ... Oh, good heavens, no! You are to gather information. Points of view. Opinions. Possibilities. I thought you understood that that was the reason the Fuehrer wished to meet you, to see for himself if everything we had told him about you was true. As for the assignment, you are perfectly qualified. You are fluent in English, are you not? In fact, I am told that you speak English with an Irish accent. The Irish are very popular in America, at least on the east coast, which is where you will be going.'

Anna buttered bread. 'I believe so. But...'

'And you have a friend there already, have you not? Ah ... Joseph Andrews. An important diplomat, I believe.'

Anna, spreading slices of ham, turned her head sharply.

'Is he not the man who got you out of the Lubianka?'

'Yes,' Anna said. 'He is.' She added lettuce leaves and mustard, put the sandwiches together, slowly and carefully. 'Would you like

90

some wine?'

'That would be very nice. He was your lover?'

Anna placed the plates on the dining table, opened the icebox and took out a bottle of hock. Joe had never laid a finger on her. He had saved her life because his friend Clive had asked him to, but he had known of their relationship and was too much of a gentleman even to consider muscling in. But to protect herself, she had told Heydrich that he had been the man she had been meeting clandestinely in the Hotel Berlin in Moscow. Heydrich had not approved, but he had been prepared to accept that she was a woman of strong passions, and Joe had been a neutral American.

At this moment, however, the important point was that Heydrich might well have noted the impropriety on her file... 'Yes, Herr Reichsfuehrer, he was my lover.'

'And he proved his love by getting you out of the Lubianka, at some risk to himself, I understand.' Himmler seated himself at the table, making no effort to help her with the corkscrew. 'Have you been in contact with him since?'

Anna placed the bottle and two glasses on the table and sat down opposite him. 'He wanted me to go to the States with him, but of course I could not do that. My duty is here, to the Reich. So we agreed to part. We have not corresponded since.'

Himmler masticated, somewhat noisily. 'But if you were to turn up in his life again...?'

'I have no idea what his reaction might be. Are you suggesting...?'

'Yes,' Himmler said, and drank some wine. 'You will go to America to join the Embassy staff in Washington, and you will contact Andrews, discreetly, of course – you should allow him to make the first move towards resuming your relationship, as I am sure he will – and make it plain to him that you are available. And then, from your privileged position at his side, you will commence your operation. It is roughly the same assignment as you carried out so successfully in Russia over the last year.'

So successfully, Anna thought, and sipped her wine. But she could feel relieved that she was not being instructed to murder anyone. At least for the moment.

'As I am sure you know,' Himmler went on, 'our relations with the United States are ... difficult. They pretend neutrality, yet they are providing all the aid they can to Great Britain and now, it seems, Soviet Russia, a nation to which they have always shown considerable hostility in the past. This man Roosevelt is particularly difficult. Had the Americans not broken their own rules and re-elected him for a third term last November, I do not believe we would still have a problem. But there it is. Our business is reality, not theory, and while the fact that they are providing aid to the Western Powers – we can hardly still call them democracies as one of them is a Communist dictatorship – is a nuisance, that in itself will hardly affect the eventual outcome of the war. I mean, it is obvious that Russia is defeated, and will collapse entirely before this coming winter, after which Great Britain can be dealt with at our leisure. The Americans obviously realize this. Yet they are still pouring weapons and munitions into England and Russia. They must have a plan, Anna. We need to know what that plan is. We need to know whether Roosevelt is doing this on his own or at the behest of the Jewish lobby, whether he has the backing of the country as a whole, and whether he has already made up his mind to go to war, at some stage. And, most important of all, when will that stage be reached? Of course, we need to know if our plan to rid Europe of the Jews, should it become known in America, will affect any of those decisions, in view of the huge Jewish lobby over there. You are the woman to get us that information.'

'You flatter me, Herr Reichsfuehrer.'

'No one could flatter you, Anna.' He wiped his lips, finished his wine, and stood up.

Oh, my God! she thought. *Here it comes.*

He moved round the table to stand behind her, ran his fingers through her hair. Now she would have to wash it again, to get rid of the butter.

His hands moved from her hair down to her shoulders, pulling the dressing gown apart to expose her breasts, slipping down to give them a quick, but at least a gentle, caress. More butter! Then he moved away. 'Show me your legs.'

Anna turned in her seat and opened the

dressing gown entirely. In for a penny, in for a pound.

To her surprise, he did not touch her again, just gazed at her for several seconds. At last he said, 'I do not believe there is a man in the world who could resist your body, your charm, your charisma, Anna. Not even that poor cripple in the White House.'

She remained sitting, making no effort to cover herself up; her heart had actually slowed now the moment had come. But to her surprise, he turned away and picked up his cap. 'In the circumstances, I do not think it will be necessary for me to come here for dinner tonight. You will receive your passages, your travelling funds, and all other requirements, tomorrow. You will travel by an American ship out of Naples, and our submarines will be warned under no circumstances to attack the vessel. I will wish you good fortune, and of course, success.'

'My maid...'

'Oh, yes, your maid. Someone will telephone you to get her name and particulars for her documentation. Very good, Anna. I will look forward to getting to know you better when you return.'

Anna stood up and closed the dressing gown. She was having a little trouble with her breathing, and inhaled deeply. 'Herr Reichsfuehrer, there is something you should know.'

Himmler had gone to the door. He now turned back, frowning. 'Tell me.'

'Two things, actually. The first is that Joseph Andrews is not an important diplomat. He is a

94

Government Agent.'

'He seems to have carried some clout with the Soviets.'

'He had a personal acquaintance with Lavrenty Beria, and was able to persuade the commissar that it would be in his interests to let me go.'

'I would say that proves he is a man of some influence. He will certainly know the right people for you to meet in Washington.'

'Perhaps. But the second caveat is the more important. Andrews knows that I am a German assassin.'

Himmler came back into the room. 'How does he know this?'

'Beria told him. Andrews only knew that I had been arrested. He did not know why. So he went to Beria, as boss of the NKVD, to find out and intercede for my release. Beria told him that I had been sent to Moscow specifically to assassinate Marshal Stalin. He had the proof, supplied by the traitor Meissenbach.'

'And yet he let you go, because Andrews asked him to?'

'He did not let me go. He committed me to Andrews' custody. Andrews told him that I was wanted in the States for attempting the murder of President Roosevelt.'

Himmler frowned. 'That can't be true. We never ordered that.'

Anna suppressed a sigh; this dimwit virtually ruled Europe! 'Of course it was not true, Herr Reichsfuehrer. Andrews made it up. It was the day after our troops invaded Russia. The country was in a panic. Those in power knew immediately that they were in deep trouble unless they could get outside help, and there was only one source from which that help could come. But they did not then know that America was going to help them. Andrews told Beria that the best way to obtain American support would be to convince Washington that the Soviet Government wanted to cooperate in every possible way, and a quick early way to prove that would be to allow him to take me back for trial and almost certain execution.'

'He is a devious man, this American of yours.'

'Yes, sir. But the point is that he knows exactly what I am.'

'No, no, Anna. The point is that, knowing what you are, he still rescued you. And then turned you loose to return to Germany. That is not love. That is adoration. I think you will do very well in America.'

The door closed, leaving Anna staring at it. However much she had detested the thought of having to share her body with such a man, she had been mentally braced for it. And in the end he had hardly touched her, while repeatedly assuring her that there was no man who could keep his hands off her if the opportunity arose. Perhaps he was one of those men who did not believe in sleeping with the help. Or, equally likely, his essentially timid sexual personality could not accept the idea of sleeping with a woman who had just killed a man.

And he was convinced that he could deduce the reason behind everyone's actions, based on his peculiar mental make-up of cold-blooded ferocity and wild romanticism, and, she was concluding, rather limited powers of perception. It apparently had not occurred to him that there could be a far more prosaic reason for Joe having helped her: simply that he had been asked to do so. Of course, Himmler could not know, or even be allowed to suspect, that Joe's reason was because Clive had called on him, and in order to do that he had had to convince him that she was actually a British double agent. Even if he had been sworn to secrecy, and she was sure that he was trustworthy, it had still been an enormous risk for Clive to take. Would it stand up to her suddenly turning up in Washington, when Joe would have no doubt that she was there to work?

But whatever happened, once again she was being sent out of Germany, to a neutral country, where all things might be possible. Which meant, in the short term, that there was a great deal to be done.

Anna had a bath, washed the butter from her hair, then dressed and put the hair up under a cloche. She had had enough of taxis for one day, so she walked; it was only a few blocks and this enabled her to make sure she was not being tailed.

'Countess?' Frau Hedermann was clearly astonished to see her again, perhaps because this was the first time Anna had visited the Boutique twice in one day.

'Is Signor Bartoli in his office?'

'Oh, yes. But...' Frau Hedermann looked left and right, as if wondering whether or not to summon help. But while there were three assistants present, there were also several customers.

Anna ignored her, crossed the room, and opened the office door.

'What the shit...?' Bartoli stared at her, and the young woman seated on his lap hastily rose and pulled down her skirt, which had been gathered round her waist.

'Exactly,' Anna said.

Bartoli squared his shoulders. 'You had better leave, Erika.'

'Yes, Signor Bartoli,' the girl gasped. 'Yes.' She sidled round Anna and through the door, which Anna closed and locked behind her.

Bartoli was doing something under his desk, which she assumed meant he was putting his own clothes back together. 'You have no right to come barging in here without even knocking.'

'I have every right, in the circumstances.' Anna advanced to stand before the desk. 'Has my message gone?'

'Of course it has not. I do not send messages from here. It will go tonight.'

'Good. You will have to add something to it.'

'You seem to forget that I am your Controller.'

'And you seem entirely unaware of what is going on around you.' Anna sat down. 'When I left here this morning I was arrested.'

98

'What? My God!' He looked past her as if expecting to see a Gestapo agent appear in the doorway. 'What happened to you?'

'I hate to disappoint you, Luigi, but nothing happened to me.'

'But, if you were arrested...'

'Fortunately for us, the man who arrested me suffered from the same problem as you.'

'He ... what?'

'So I disposed of him.'

'You ... My God!'

'Which is something you should bear in mind. However, he did have a reason for arresting me, apart from a desire to get his hand under my skirt.'

'But ... got rid of him ... the police...'

'Something else you seem to have forgotten is that here in Berlin I *am* the police. Concentrate. Agent Schlutz had been informed that there is something underhand going on in this boutique, specifically involving you and me. The tip-off came from one of your people.'

'One of my people? That is impossible.'

'In fact, it was your top woman, Edda Hedermann.'

'Edda? I cannot believe that.'

'I suggest you ask her, as soon as possible, but I would also suggest you do it when you and she are alone and no one else is within earshot. Ask her to remain here this evening after closing time to discuss something with you.'

'But ... Edda ... If she has betrayed us to the Gestapo...'

'She has not betrayed you to the Gestapo yet. She betrayed me to Agent Schlutz, who was Abwehr, and who happens to be her lover.'

'Edda? A lover?'

'Did you suppose she had eyes only for you?'

'This man Schlutz...'

'Calm down. I do not believe, from what he told me before he departed—'

'You said you disposed of him.'

'I mean I broke his neck, Luigi.'

Bartoli swallowed.

'As I was saying, I am sure that he had not yet filed a report. Edda suggested I was worth investigating, and he looked me over, and decided that I was indeed worth investigating, but not necessarily for subversive activity. Now, as I have said, I have sorted that out and he will not trouble us again. However, we have no means of knowing what Edda's reaction will be when she discovers he is dead. If she is in any way suspicious of you, and me, she may well decide to take the matter further.'

Bartoli pulled a handkerchief from his pocket to wipe his brow. 'You are saying...'

'Yes, Luigi. That is what I am saying.'

'My God, my God, my God! How will you do it?'

'I am not going to do it. It is your responsibility.'

'*Mine?* You are the expert.'

'There are two reasons why I cannot be involved. It will have to be an accident, and it will have to be done right away. Now, I have just killed a man and explained it to the satisfaction of my SD employers. I feel that for me to have to explain another fatal accident within twenty-four hours, or even forty-eight, might get them wondering if I am safe to be allowed out.'

Bartoli put away his handkerchief; he was obviously wondering the same thing.

'The other reason is that I am leaving the country within forty-eight hours, and I have a lot to do.'

'You are leaving Germany? Again? You have been back less than two months.'

'I seem to be popular.'

'Where are you going?'

'I am going to America.'

'You are getting out?'

'Chance would be a fine thing. Of course I am not getting out. I am going as an agent of the Reich.'

'To kill somebody?'

'No. To get information.' But the warning beacons that always flickered in Anna's brain were suddenly very bright. Himmler had insisted that her mission was solely to gain information as to American intentions. But she had been sent to England in 1938, also to get information. It was only after she had been there for nearly two years, and established herself on the London social scene, that she had suddenly been informed she was required to assassinate Winston Churchill. It had taken the combined efforts of the Special Branch and MI6 to get her out of that mess. And last year she had been sent to

101

Moscow, again to 'get information', only to be informed, just two months ago, when once again she was established in the Russian social scene, that the Reich required her to kill Marshal Stalin, the day before the German invasion. That she had survived was thanks to Joe Andrews, to whom she was now being sent, to 'gain information'. Who was going to rescue her from that terminal situation, when it arose?

Bartoli was gazing at her. She smiled. 'Naturally, I wish London to know of it. So, write down the additional message, and make sure they both go off tonight. And then attend to Edda.'

Bartoli's nerves seemed to have settled down. He copied down what Anna had to say, and then raised his head. 'Is it blood you have in your arteries? Or iced water?'

Anna stood up. 'You may believe, Luigi, that my blood is a good deal hotter than yours. Especially right now. Ciao.'

'Despatch from Basle,' Amy Barstow said brightly. 'Out of Berlin. It is very interesting.'

She laid the original paper and the decoded translation on Clive Bartley's desk and waited, nose twitching. It was impossible to work closely with someone in such a tension-filled and occasionally lethal – if usually for other people – business as secret intelligence, and not become at least mentally intimate. With her sharp features and slightly overweight figure, Amy knew the intimacy would never become anything more than imagined, but that made her even more interested in her boss's undoubtedly chaotic emotional life. She knew he had what might be termed a close relationship with a high-powered London fashion editor. But she also knew that every time a despatch arrived from Berlin he became quite agitated. And she also knew the name, or names, of the lady involved. She personally had never met Anna Fehrbach, the Countess von Widerstand, the Honourable Mrs Ballantine Bordman, but she had seen photographs of her. The trouble with photographs, especially when they were in black and white and on the page of a newspaper, was that while they could portray extreme beauty, and in the case of Anna Fehrbach most definitely did so, they could convey nothing of the personality, the charisma, the charm, which the woman apparently exuded and could have almost all men grovelling at her feet. Nor could they indicate anything of the deadly purpose she could apparently reveal. To meet this reincarnation of the Gorgon one day was one of Amy's great ambitions, providing they were on the same side.

But for the time being she had to see her through the eyes of her boss, whose reaction was entirely as expected. Clive Bartley snatched the paper, scanned it, and leaned back with a sigh. 'She's all right.'

Amy snorted. It bothered her to see Clive so emotionally at the mercy of a woman's well-being. It did not fit the man. Clive Bartley was six feet two inches tall, with thinning dark hair and a big chin, which went with his generally craggy features. He was powerfully built, had a spectacular record in the field when it had been necessary, and had a few fatalities to his own credit, again when it had been necessary. Amy considered that to allow any single agent, however attractive, to get this far under the skin was positively obscene, if not dangerous. 'One would like to think so, sir,' she remarked. 'It does sound a little far-fetched.'

Clive was studying the transcript again. 'But not unbelievable.'

'You mean you are going to accept it?'

'I am certainly going to take it upstairs.'

'And,' she said, acidly, 'as to the second half of the message, does this mean you will be going to New York in the near future?'

Clive grinned. 'Do you know, Amy, I think that may be a very good idea.'

'Good morning, Billy,' Clive said brightly. 'Despatch from Berlin via the Basle office.'

Billy Baxter raised his head to peer across the desk. 'Don't tell me your inamorata has surfaced?'

In the strongest contrast to Clive, Billy Baxter was a small man, and far from looking like a retired athlete, rather suggested a still hard-working academic, his clothes shabby, the patterned sweater he always wore under his jacket, even at the height of summer, embedded with strands of tobacco from his invariably absent-minded filling of his pipe. Clive had worked for him long enough to know that the façade was a deliberate sham; Billy Baxter possessed one of the most acute and ruthless brains he had ever encountered, and this bothered him, in the present instance, because he also knew that Billy had never been able to bring himself quite to trust his most glamorous double agent. So he said now, somewhat stiffly, 'It is from Anna, yes. Frankly, I had not expected to hear from her again so soon. She had to recover from her Russian ordeal. But this is dynamite.'

Baxter had been studying the transcript. 'Yes,' he said. 'She was in the hands of the NKVD for a while, wasn't she?'

'Yes,' Clive said grimly.

'And they used their water torture on her.'

'Yes,' Clive said, even more grimly.

'It would appear that some of it, quite a lot of it, must have got on to her brain and is still there.'

'Just what do you mean by that?'

'Oh, come now, Clive. This has to be absolute balderdash. There is no civilized government in history would conceive of such a plan.'

'With respect, sir, aren't you making a fundamental error in supposing that the Nazi regime is a civilized government?'

'Have you any evidence that it is not?'

'Well...'

'Oh, I know they wage war with utter ruthlessness. But that is why they are winning. Did

105

not an American national hero – and, incidentally, a president – say that moderation in war is madness? When we get around to adopting that philosophy we also will start to win. But to declare war on your own people simply because they practise a different religion, I mean, that is sheer barbarity.'

'We did it, on the Roman Catholics, not four hundred years ago.'

'We required them to keep a low profile and out of politics. Those who actually got burned at the stake had stuck their chins out.'

'That is a matter of degree.'

Baxter peered at him. 'I know you would like to believe this latest hysterical outburst, but...'

'Billy, with the humblest possible respect, you are a male chauvinist pig of the worst kind. I have known Anna now for three years, and I have seen her in some of the tightest imaginable corners, and I have never found the slightest trace of hysteria in her make-up. You remember last year when we were just about to get her out of England and the Gestapo sent three thugs to arrest her? She was unarmed and alone when they got to her flat. When I arrived fifteen minutes later they were all dead and she was drinking a glass of sherry.'

'I remember that very well,' Baxter agreed. 'I also remember that only a couple of months later she was in Prague and shot dead two of our agents who she thought were about to assassinate her current lover.'

'I beg your pardon. She did not know they

106

were our people, and she was protecting Meissenbach, who at that time was her boss.'

'All right, all right. I apologize. She is not hysterical. But she is also a young woman I would not like to get too close to when she is in a bad mood. And what we have managed to agree on is that she reacts very quickly and very positively to anything she doesn't like. She may have overheard some conversation in which the concept of this "final solution" was thrown out – rather like Prince Hal when, at least according to Shakespeare, he was asked what would be the first thing he would do when he became King Henry V, replied, "hang all the lawyers". No one took him seriously and, needless to say, he didn't.'

'So you don't propose to take this any further.'

'Not without a whole lot more proof than the opinion of a twenty-one-year-old girl, however valuable you may think she is. For God's sake, Clive. We are trying to unite the world against Hitler. What do you suppose the reaction of presently confirmed neutrals would be if we started flying this kite? England must indeed be desperate if she is reduced to propaganda as low as this. I'd be laughed out of my job.'

'So you need proof. The first thing we should do is talk to Anna and find out where she got this information from.'

'Just how do you propose to do that?'

'Well, she's on her way to New York...'

'Shit! I'd forgotten that. I suppose we had better warn Washington that a very lethal bomb is about to explode in their midst.'

'I don't think that is the least bit funny. However, the point is that this is a heaven-sent opportunity for us to contact her...'

He checked as Baxter leaned back in his chair. 'Your effrontery takes my breath away. Us? You mean you! Is that all you can think about, getting your hand into her knickers?'

'She doesn't wear any. But I am the only one of us she trusts and will confide in.'

'Listen. Go home and have sex with Belinda and straighten yourself out.'

'Billy, you are letting your prejudices get in the way of your duty.'

Baxter sat up again and reached for his pipe; this was at least a sign that his brain was working overtime. 'So you would like to be present at her execution, is that it?'

'Say again?'

'Doesn't that fellow Andrews know she's a German spy? A German assassin?'

'He also knows she works for us.'

Baxter filled his bowl, slowly and messily. 'And you think he'll have kept that to himself?'

'He gave me his word, and I believe he'll keep that word.'

'Until pushed. Which will happen when he discovers that Anna is in Washington on some secret mission for the Reich that invariably means someone is for the high jump!'

'Listen, America and Germany are not at war, and if Anna is going to Washington as a member of the Embassy staff, she will have diplomatic immunity. If the State Department decides it does not like what she is doing, all it can do is put her on the next boat back to Europe.'

Baxter struck a match and puffed smoke. 'Then she might even get torpedoed, and all our troubles will be over.'

'I'll overlook that,' Clive said. 'But all that nonsense you have just spouted makes it all the more important for me to get over there, to act as referee and to keep her out of trouble. Surely even you can see that.'

'I can see a great many things.' Baxter took his pipe from his mouth to point it. 'You will complete your current assignment. Don't bother to shake your head. Jerry is not going to send Anna to Washington and then call her back the next day. And if she gets into trouble and is thrown out, it is probably better that you should not be there. If she can survive for a couple of months, we can feel reasonably sure that she is behaving herself. And when you are free, I will allow you one month. A week to get there, a week to get back, and a fortnight in the States. And if you get torpedoed, you're fired.'

Clive opened the door of his flat and inhaled. 'That smells good.'

Belinda Hoskin emerged from the little kitchen. 'Are you referring to the food or my perfume?'

'Both.' He crossed the room and swept her up off the floor. This was necessary if he was going to kiss her, as she was only five feet two inches

109

tall, and slender with it. Pretty enough, with clipped features and crisp black hair which she wore cut just below her ears, her principal asset was her intense personality, although this could be exhausting.

But Clive knew that her main attraction, to him, was the total contrast she presented to Anna Fehrbach, which he knew made him several kinds of cad. His defence was that Belinda had been his on-and-off partner for several years; they had come together before either of them had had the faintest idea that anyone named Anna Fehrbach even existed. He had then found Belinda both compelling and attractive, so much so that he had asked her to marry him. She had declined.

As she clearly liked both his looks and his bed manners, she had had to come up with an explanation for her refusal, and this, or rather these, had been straightforward enough. She had then been thirty years old, and having just achieved the position of Fashion Editor of a leading London weekly, had not felt like giving it up to be a housewife. As this had not been an essential concomitant of his proposal, she had had to come up with a back-up, so her second reason had been his job, which he had felt obliged to reveal to her, without of course going into any detail.

But she could gather, certainly at that time when he had been less senior than now, that it entailed a great deal of field work, more often than not out of England, and that it also involved, from time to time, a certain amount of physical danger. She had told him that she did not feel like becoming a widow just then. But the message had been clear: ask me again when I've enjoyed my position for a few years and you are senior enough to stay at home.

Now she slid down him. 'It's only bangers, I'm afraid. It's goddamned difficult to get anything else. I would have thought that now the Blitz is over things would improve.'

He followed her into the kitchen. 'Is the Blitz over? Nobody tells me anything.'

Belinda blew a raspberry. 'There hasn't been a raid for a week.'

'I think that's probably because Jerry is a trifle occupied somewhere else, as you may have heard. Anyway, the situation in the shops doesn't depend on the Luftwaffe. It's a matter of the U-boats, and they certainly haven't gone away.'

'Well, I wish they would.' She stood above the hob, turning sliced onions with her spatula. 'Now tell me what's on your mind.'

'Is there something on my mind, except for sausages and a drink and a bit of nookie?'

'Darling, I can always tell when there's something on your mind. But you can pour us a drink.'

The real reason she had refused to marry him, Clive knew, was that she was a control freak. She ran her office with an iron fist, albeit usually in a velvet glove, and she intended to operate her domestic life in the same way, which was

111

not a practical proposition when your husband has a job about which you can know nothing and can never discuss, and which is liable to remove him from your orbit for weeks or even months at a time. And so they had been overtaken by events. By one overwhelming event in particular, even if she was not yet fully aware of it.

Clive could remember as if it were yesterday the first time he had seen Anna Fehrbach, Countess von Widerstand. It had been October 1938, and he had been in Berlin as minder to the Honourable Ballantine Bordman, sent to finalize the details for the visit of Prime Minister Chamberlain the following month, which had turned out so disastrously. This could not actually be laid at Bordman's door: it was now known that what would happen at that meeting had long been determined by the Nazis. His job was merely to rubber-stamp the agenda.

But as it had been recognized that Ballantine Bordman was both not very bright and regarded himself as God's gift to the female sex – he had only got the assignment because he was the son of Lord Bordman – it had quietly been determined that instead of a simple detective, he should be accompanied by a senior MI6 agent, just to make sure he didn't get into trouble. And that had been a complete failure, although Clive would argue to himself that the odds had been too great for even him to overcome. From that moment at the SS ball, to which they had been invited and which Bordman had insisted they attend, they had been lost.

They had been standing together on the edge of the dance floor, watching the array of brilliant uniforms and bare shoulders and flashing jewellery in front of them, when the Countess von Widerstand had entered the ballroom on the arm of an SS officer, rendering all the other previously beautiful women tawdry. Clive now knew that Anna had been born on 21 May 1920, and so in October 1938 had been just eighteen and a half years old. He had recognized at first sight that here was a girl of exceptional beauty, charm and charisma, even if he had not then known anything of her exceptional brainpower – or her lethal training. But neither had he doubted for a moment that she was there simply as a guest. She could not be.

What had followed had been both predictable, at least with hindsight, and too fast for his reactions. That Ballantine should require an introduction had seemed reasonable enough. That he should spend the rest of the night dancing with her had been over the top, but not immediately dangerous, even if the fact that no other man had dared approach her during that time must have been suspicious. That Ballantine should have been invited to a party at her apartment the next day had been disconcerting but not yet critical. That he had not returned that night had started alarm bells jangling. But when he had returned, the next morning, to announce that he was going to marry the girl, Clive had felt closer to a heart attack than at any time in his life.

It had transpired that Ballantine had spent the

night in her bed, and too late had discovered, or been convinced, that she was a virgin, and had felt compelled to do the honourable thing and ask her to marry him. But he had been desperate to do so in any event; having got his hands on that body and his mouth on those lips he had had no intention of letting them go again. As Clive was now in a similar situation, he could understand that determination.

What had never appeared to cross Ballantine's mind was why a young girl, beautiful and apparently very rich, should wish to tie herself to a man who was more than twice her age, definitely overweight and not particularly attractive in any event, and completely lacking in any charisma of his own. It had certainly occurred to Clive, but there had been nothing he could do about it. Even if he had had no doubt that she was a Gestapo plant, he had still not been able to deduce the reason. He now knew, because Anna had told him, that for all their apparent confidence the Nazis had been afraid that Chamberlain might not after all have been coming to accept their demands for the dismemberment of Czechoslovakia, but instead was coming to threaten war after all.

Ballantine had been able to reassure his glamorous bed mate that war was not on Chamberlain's agenda, no matter what concessions he might have to make. Then he had discovered blood on the sheet, which had decided things for him, from the point of view of an English gentleman, even if he hadn't believed that heaven had fallen into his lap.

Anna had told Clive that her SD masters had known it had fallen into theirs, however horrified she had been at the prospect of becoming an English housewife, even if she would be wealthy and socially in demand. He had been helpless, swept away on a tide of events he had not been able to combat. Even his attempts to convince Baxter that she had to be a spy had fallen on deaf ears. 'Proof,' Billy had said, as usual. 'This woman is top drawer now. I have to have cast-iron proof before the boss will let me put her under surveillance, much less have her openly investigated. You just don't like the woman.'

That might even have been true, in October 1938. It could even have still been true in March 1939, but he doubted it. Otherwise he wouldn't have been standing outside her apartment building in Berlin, looking up, wondering if she still maintained it now that she had an English home, and she had walked out of the swing doors and virtually bumped into him. But that had not been the Honourable Mrs Ballantine Bordman. Even less had it been the Countess von Widerstand. It had been a frightened, distressed and utterly vulnerable little girl, who had been all the more beautiful and desirable for that. But she was a little girl who had also been very angry.

Clive often thought that by stretching her naked across that bar to torture and humiliate her – or disciplining her, as they saw it – the

Nazi hierarchy might have signed their own death warrants. He knew of no one, not even Winston Churchill, who was more dedicated to bringing them down, and certainly no one who was better placed to do it – if only his superiors would trust her enough to give her full rein.

He had known none of this when he had accompanied her upstairs 'for a cup of coffee' that fateful morning. He had been fully aware that to seduce this girl, who he had still been certain was a Nazi agent, might be for the good of the state. But he had also been fully aware that to seduce this girl, the wife of a man with whom he was quite friendly, at an obviously low ebb in her life, would be an absolutely caddish thing to do. But as with everyone else who came into contact with Anna, even those who knew her well, he had not really understood the personality he supposed he could dominate, the deadly force and ice-cold determination that lay behind that beautiful mask.

So before he had known what had hit him, she had seduced *him* with consummate skill. And when, half an hour later, he had been lying beside her on her bed, utterly sated, both mentally and physically, believing she was too, and the door had opened, he had watched her leave the bed in a long avalanche of naked glory, and destroy an intruder with a single blow to the neck.

That had been a moment he would never forget to his dying day, even as he realized that if such beauty, such charm, such skill, and such instant, lethal, uncompromising powers of destruction, could be harnessed and controlled, he would possess one of the most potent forces in existence. It had taken time. Anna herself had been willing, even eager, to work towards the destruction of her tormentors. As she had explained, it was necessary for her to keep on working for them to safeguard her family, and this had actually been a bonus, although it was one he had hated to use. Baxter had been less enthusiastic. He had gone along with the idea when Anna had proved how valuable she could be, but he still regarded her as a ticking time bomb that would one day have to explode. As for actually controlling her, for all her apparent subservience, at least when in his company, Clive knew in his heart that despite their intimacy Anna did indeed have an agenda of her own, one that was known only to her.

But the thought that in another month or so he would be able to hold her in his arms once again ... He poured the two glasses of scotch.

'So keep your beastly secret,' Belinda said, forking sausages on to plates. 'Listen, do you know that next month is my mother's seventieth birthday?'

'Good lord! Is she all right?'

'Of course she's all right. But I think we should go and see her. Spend a couple of days with her. You can manage that, can't you?'

'Ah ... where exactly would we be going?'

'Perth.'

The drink he was sipping went down the

117

wrong way and he did some choking, watched without sympathy.

'I am not talking about Australia, idiot,' she said when he had got his breath back. 'Scotland.'

'And when exactly does this event take place?'

'Her birthday is twenty-ninth September. That's a Monday. We could go up on the Sunday, and come back on the Tuesday.'

'Ah ... I'm afraid I will be away over the end of September.'

Belinda placed the plates on the table with great care. 'You told me, when you came back from Moscow two months ago, that you would not be travelling again.'

'I know I did. But the fact is—'

'And the time you went away before that,' Belinda said in a somewhat sinister monotone, 'you wound up in hospital for several months.'

'My darling, that wasn't my fault. I wasn't flying the plane. I was merely a passenger. I suppose I'm lucky to have survived the crash.'

Belinda drank some whisky. 'So where are you going this time?'

'Now, you know I can't tell you that.'

'It's to do with that woman, isn't it?'

'Ah...' One of the great unsolved mysteries of Clive's life was what had transpired between the two women on the one occasion they had met. But neither would ever tell him. He knew the facts. Anna had been with him in this flat when Belinda had entered unexpectedly. That scenario

118

had been dreadfully reminiscent of what had happened to Elsa Mayers in Berlin, and for one terrible moment he had feared it might happen again in London. But Anna had understood from a glance at his face that this was an embarrassment, not a danger, and in any event, Belinda had left again without a word.

An hour later, she had been outside Anna's Mayfair flat. Clive knew, because she had told him, that she had identified the woman as the Honourable Mrs Ballantine Bordman from photos she had seen in the glossies, and had simply gone to her home and waited for her rival to return. Anna had let her in, and the two women had been engaged in conversation when catastrophe had struck.

Clive would dearly love to discover what they were actually saying. But whatever it was, Hannah Gehrig, Anna's 'maid', who was actually her SD controller in England, returning unexpectedly, had found it sufficiently conspiratorial to require executive action. She had drawn her pistol, and Anna had disposed of her with another of her phenomenal personal attacks, only this time – Hannah Gehrig being a more positive character that Elsa Mayers – she had stopped a bullet that had put her into hospital for several weeks.

That Anna had so nearly died while saving Belinda's life had of course earned her eternal gratitude, and as the circumstances and the necessity to hush the whole thing up had involved bringing Belinda into the picture, at least partially, even the fact that Anna had been found in a compromising position with Clive could be explained as perhaps a necessary exchange of secret information. But Belinda now knew that Clive was Anna's MI6 controller, and she also knew that the pair had made contact on more than one occasion over the past two years. Gratitude had not been that eternal.

His hesitation had given him away. Belinda finished her drink, pushed back her chair, and stood up, ignoring the plate of sausages. 'In that case,' she said, 'I had better bugger off. Actually, on second thoughts, *you* can bugger off.'

She slammed the door behind her.

Four

Lovers

Joseph Andrews looked up from his desk as the office door opened. 'Mr Fisher is here, Mr Andrews,' Margaret said.

'Oh. Right. Show him in.'

Andrews stood up. He was a tall, underweight man – he kept his figure under careful control – with thinning hair and a long, somewhat lugubrious face, although his smile could be charming. He was smiling now. 'Larry! How's the Bureau standing up?'

'Without you, hardly at all.' Lawrence Fisher, short and tubby, shook hands and sank into the chair before the desk. 'What's it like, working for Wild Bill?'

'One could say exciting. Although we haven't really got off the ground yet. The department was only founded a couple of weeks ago.'

'Yeah. And Hoover is already wondering how the hell he allowed you to be seconded.'

'Two reasons, I guess. Donovan is a hard man to refuse, and our business is mainly Europe. That's why he wanted me. It's a part of the

121

world I happen to know.'

'Doing what, exactly? I mean, Office of Strategic Studies. What the hell is that?'

'That is whatever you wish to make of it.'

'But what are you going to do?'

'Now, that, you will have to ask Wild Bill. I think he's in the building. Shall I get Margaret to see if he's free?'

'Screw that. Listen, as you say, you know Europe. So maybe you can help us. That's actually why I'm here.'

'Any time.'

'Well, we were wondering if the name Countess von Widerstand might mean anything to you?'

Andrews had been leaning back in his chair, comfortably relaxed. Now he slowly sat up. 'Say again?'

'Yeah, I know it's a goddamned mouthful. And I'm told it don't mean a shitting thing, either. Something like "Countess of Resistance". But the fact is, this chick is one hell of a classy broad. And she really is a chick. According to her passport, she's only twenty-one, but ... Say, you all right?'

'I am waiting,' Andrews said, speaking very slowly, 'for you to tell me what this is about.' *Christ*, he thought. *If something has happened to Anna...*

'We don't know what it's about,' Fisher confessed, 'or if it's about anything. It's just that this dame landed in New York last week, on passage from Naples, Italy, on her way to join the German Embassy here in Washington. No big deal about that, except that she's a knock out, which ain't illegal. But, you know how it is, the entry was passed on to us as a matter of course, foreign nationals and all that stuff, and Harry Brice – you remember Harry?'

'I remember Harry,' Andrews said, with an effort keeping himself from grasping his friend by the lapels and shaking him. 'Are you saying that Anna ... the Countess von Widerstand, is here in America, right this moment?'

'I reckon she's just about five blocks away, right this moment. The point is that Harry Brice says he knows this bit, and it ain't good news. Harry was in the UK a couple of years ago, remember? And he remembers a scandal about this dame – she was apparently calling herself the Honourable Mrs Bordman then – who turned out to be a German spy and fled the country just before being rounded up by the Special Branch or whatever. It caused quite a rumpus because no one knows how she did it – I mean, got away with it – and the intelligence boys aren't saying. Well, as it was clearly their fuck-up to let her slip through their fingers, you can't blame them. But you were in England around then, weren't you? You remember anything about it?'

'Is it that important?' Andrews asked while he tried to think.

'Well, do we really need any slinky Nazi femme fatale wandering around over here? J. Edgar ain't seen this yet, but I reckon he's gonna

123

do his nut when he does.'

'Perhaps you shouldn't show it to him.'

'Are you kidding? It's my ass on the line.'

'Well, then, when you do, ask him to lay off, at least for a while.'

'You'll have to explain that, old buddy. You saying you do know the dame?'

'Yes. I knew of her, in London, and I actually met her, when I was in Moscow.'

'And you took a shine to her.'

'Who wouldn't?'

'Even if she's a Kraut spy?'

'You need to reserve judgement until you meet her. The important point is, why is she here?'

'Yeah. That's exactly the question J. Edgar is gonna ask. And he's gonna want answers, too.'

'I can give you those answers.'

Fisher raised his eyebrows. 'You been holding out on us?'

'I said I took a shine to her. What matters is that she took a shine to me. I was ... able to do her a favour.'

Was he telling the truth, or just airing an impossible dream? He remembered having dinner with Anna on the banks of the Moscow River or walking with her in Gorky Park ... But those memories were overlaid with others, of that naked, crumpled but compelling figure standing against the wall of her Lubianka cell, and even more, of the flaming angel of vengeance she had suddenly become when Chalyapov had tried to overrule Beria's orders and prevent her leaving the prison. Two sides of the same coin perhaps. But where one side had been the purest vulnerable femininity, the other had been more deadly purpose than he had ever seen in any other human being, male or female. He had no doubt that she had been grateful to him for saving her from an unthinkable fate. But could he seriously doubt that if he got in her way she would blow him away like, according to Clive Bartley, she had blown away more than a dozen other people, men and women, as and when she had considered it necessary?

But the thought of seeing her again, of perhaps even being allowed to touch that velvet flesh ... He flushed as he realized that Fisher was staring at him. 'What I am saying is that I reckon I may be able to get through to her, find out what you want to know, whereas if you try to muscle in she might just clam right up.'

Fisher grinned. 'It might be fun to have her in one of our interrogation rooms and see what she's made of.'

'I don't think that would be a good idea,' Andrews said, and hastily added, 'I mean, if she has been posted here as a member of the German Embassy staff, she has diplomatic immunity.'

'Yeah,' Fisher agreed, regretfully. 'But I don't think the old boy will go for letting you have first crack of the whip. He's still brooding on the way you upped and left the Bureau.' He held up his hand as Andrews would have spoken. 'OK, OK. I know you had no choice in that matter. Whatever Donovan wants for this new super-department of his, Donovan gets, and he wanted you. But it rankles with J. Edgar. He'll get over it. But right now, cooperation is the last word in his dictionary. The lady is our territory, and she's gonna stay that way. Until we have everything we want or can get. Then maybe we'll let you have a go.' He got up. 'I'll give her your regards.'

Andrews remained staring at the closed door for several seconds. He had given Clive Bartley his word that he would never reveal to a soul that Anna was a double agent. But keeping her out of the clutches of the FBI had to override that word, whether she was here for the Germans, or actually for MI6. And either way, he had to find out why she was here. What Fisher, and therefore Hoover, did not know was that Anna was less a spy than an assassin.

He pressed his intercom and Margaret came in. 'Mr Donovan in the building?'

'I believe so, sir. I'll just check.'

'If he is in, I want to have a meeting, now. Tell his secretary it is a matter of the utmost urgency.'

Margaret raised her eyebrows, but hurried off, and fifteen minutes later Andrews was seated in a leather armchair before the large walnut desk.

'Your girl said it was urgent,' Donovan remarked. 'Our first problem? I hadn't expected it to come up quite so soon.'

Bill Donovan was a big man with deceptively peaceful features and a quiet manner. But he had earned his soubriquet of Wild by his ability suddenly to produce bouts of almost demonic energy and purpose – not unlike Anna herself, Andrews supposed. Just as he also supposed it was that quality that had made President Roosevelt select him to form and head this newest and most secret of departments.

'Neither had I, sir,' Andrews agreed. 'May I assume that anything I say to you will never be repeated to a living soul?'

Donovan regarded him for several seconds. 'That is a damned odd thing to say to me, Joe.'

'I apologize, sir. But this is a matter of the utmost urgency, and also of life and death.'

Donovan stroked his chin. 'I had got the idea it was a domestic matter. Personal.'

'It is, and it isn't.'

'Yeah? Well, you'd better put it on the line. This conversation is becoming a little convoluted for so early in the day.'

Andrews took a deep breath, and began to speak. Donovan listened in silence, hardly moving. When Andrews had finished, he said, 'You're a guy with a formidable background, Joe. Far more formidable than I ever suspected. Let me just get this straight in my mind. This young woman is not actually a countess, or even a German. She is a half-Austrian, half-Irish knockout named Anna Fehrbach who happens to be a genius as well as a glamour girl as well as a professional murderess. Sounds great. So she works for the SD, killing people whenever told to do so. But she does this with the blessing

127

of MI6, for whom she also works. It seems to me that our prime requirement is to establish beyond a shadow of a doubt just which of those is the one that matters.'

'MI6.'

'Because she says so?'

'I was given this information by a senior member of that organization. She works for the Brits. She works for the SD simply in order to keep her family alive. That is also confirmed by MI6.'

'Well, I guess we have to hope that she, and they, are worth all of these dead bodies she seems to leave lying about. Now, we need to know what she is doing here. Is she spying, or killing? And who is she doing it for, the Brits or the Krauts?'

'That is what I propose to find out, sir. But she has to be handled carefully.'

'I'll bet.'

'What I mean is, I can't accomplish anything if the FBI are breathing down her neck and mine.'

'So you would like me to warn Hoover off.'

'Do you have the clout to do that?'

'The President tells me that I have the clout to do anything I want, providing I don't interfere with his prerogatives. That sort of power kind of leaves a man breathless. But it has to be used with the utmost responsibility. You're sure it wouldn't be best just to round the young lady up and put her on a boat back to Europe? That would sure be most convenient, and prevent any

128

sore toes.'

'With respect, sir, I feel that would be desperately counter-productive, for two reasons. The first is that if we start picking up German Embassy employees, certainly those with diplomatic status, and bouncing them back across the Atlantic, they're liable to do the same to our people in Berlin. The second is that now she is here in our back yard, this is our opportunity to find out a lot more about her, her employers, and their plans. And maybe even to turn her a little further.'

'And the third reason,' Donovan said, 'is that this is your opportunity to renew your acquaintance and perhaps get up close and personal.'

'Well...' Andrews flushed.

Donovan grinned. 'I'm not blaming you, Joe. Maybe I'm a little envious. I'd like to meet the young lady, if the opportunity presents itself. OK, you got it. I'll clear away all possible weeds. But, Joe, God help you if anything goes wrong. I'm particularly thinking about the possibility that one of our top people suddenly has a heart attack. Good luck.'

Joe knew that Donovan was absolutely correct in his initial reaction that the safest course would be to have Anna immediately deported, but his heart was singing like a rampant canary at the thought that she had just been delivered exclusively to him. Supposing he could handle it. Handle her! But as he had been given carte blanche...

'Margaret,' he said. 'Have we got anyone worthwhile in the German Embassy?'

'Several, I would say.'

'I'm not talking about the FBI. I mean us, the OSS, exclusively.'

'Well, no, sir. I mean, we're still operating on a skeleton staff. Mr Donovan is very sticky about who he takes on. He wants only the best.' She paused to regard her boss with arched eyebrows; Joe had been one of Donovan's first choices.

'I want you to find someone who might be prepared to work for us, exclusively. We'd make it worth his while.'

'Well, strictly off the top of my head, there's Hans Luckner. He's a junior filing clerk, but he's been very helpful to the Bureau in the past, and he's always short.'

'Good enough. Get hold of him and tell him I want a rundown on the movements of the Countess von Widerstand, who has just joined the Embassy from Germany. It is urgent.' He looked up and found Margaret gazing at him. 'It is also confidential.'

'Yes, sir.' Margaret left the room, and Joe leaned back in his chair.

She was there, only a few blocks away. Would anything come of it this time? Could anything come of it? That of course would depend on what she was here to do. But if she really was working for the Brits ... The last time, Clive Bartley had been very much in evidence, and their relationship had been too obviously intimate for him to consider intruding. But had it really been an emotional relationship? Or merely a matter of keeping in with the boss?

And suppose she was here for the Nasties, with something very nasty in mind? Well, he reckoned he could cross that bridge when he came to it. But as he had told Donovan, it had to be handled very carefully, and he had to find out everything he could about her before reminding her of Moscow, just in case. Patience, boy, patience.

Bridget Losey could tell her boss was in a bad mood. Lawrence Fisher stamped into the outer office and threw his hat at the stand. It missed. 'Get me an interview with the Chief,' he snapped.

'Yes, sir. Ah...'

'What?'

'Mr Kronsky is waiting to see you.'

'What in the name of God ... Where is he?'

'I gave him a seat in the lobby. It was his idea to wait.'

'Well, I guess I'll have to see him. Put the Chief on hold.' He arranged his features into a smile, opened the door to the lobby. 'Comrade! What can I do for you?'

The Russian was a heavy-set man with a permanently sad expression. 'It is an urgent matter.'

'Isn't it always? Come in.' He ushered his visitor into his office, closed the door. 'Have a seat and tell me your troubles.'

The Russian looked more pained than usual,

but over the past few months he had become accustomed to the peculiar American sense of humour. 'We need your assistance, your co-operation, in a small matter.'

'I was under the impression that you were getting our assistance, and our cooperation, in every possible matter.'

'It is very reassuring to hear you say so, Mr Fisher. It has recently come to our attention that you are harbouring in this country one of the world's most dangerous criminals.'

'Tell me about it. Which one did you have in mind?'

'A woman who masquerades as the Countess von Widerstand.'

Fisher, who had been moving gently to and fro in his swivel chair, came to a halt and sat up. 'Say again?'

'The title is of course entirely spurious. It does not exist. Her real name is Anna Fehrbach. She is an Austrian by birth, and she is an agent for the Nazi Government of Germany.'

Fisher regarded him for some seconds before speaking. 'And as such I can see that you would regard her as an enemy. But as you know, the United States is not at war with Nazi Germany. Therefore, providing their travel documents are in order, there is nothing to prevent a German citizen from visiting us. That is of course pre-suming that you are right and that she is in the country. May I ask, what is your interest in the young lady?'

'My dear Mr Fisher, you know she is here.

132

You have just revealed that knowledge by describing her, accurately, as a young woman. As for our interest, we wish to ... interview her regarding her attempt on the life of Premier Stalin, not three months ago.'

'Attempt on the life ... You guys have got to be mixing this countess up with some other female. According to her passport, she is only just twenty-one years old.'

'You do seem to know a lot about her,' Kronsky remarked. 'And she may be just twenty-one years old, but she is a highly skilled assassin. That is what she does for the Nazis. She works for the Sicherheitsdienst. You know of this?'

'I know of the SD,' Fisher muttered. 'But I still can't believe it. She's ... well...'

'A very handsome young woman. The use of her beauty is her stock-in-trade. But she can kill, and does, with knife, gun or her bare hands.'

'You have got to be kidding. How do you know all this?'

'She spent most of the past year in Russia. During that time we know, because there are witnesses, that she killed two senior Soviet officials, in the course of her escape from the Lubianka Prison, and she is strongly suspected of two more suspicious deaths in Moscow. So—'

'Wait, wait, wait, wait, wait!' Fisher said. 'You're losing me. You are saying this dame escaped from the Lubianka? No one escapes from the Lubianka.'

'We were tricked. Fehrbach was being held

there awaiting trial for her attempt on the life of Premier Stalin, which fortunately she was prevented from carrying out. However, an American diplomat, a Mr Joseph Andrews—'

'Holy Jesus Christ!' Fisher said.

'Absolutely. This Andrews tricked Commissar Beria into releasing her into his custody, to be brought to the United States, where she would be tried for the attempted murder of President Roosevelt.'

Fisher stared at him.

'The order of release was actually rescinded before Andrews could remove Fehrbach from the prison, so she killed the two people who tried to re-arrest her, one of whom was a senior commissar, and she and Andrews left the country before our people could catch up with them. You must realize that this took place on twenty-third June, the day after the Nazi invasion began, and there was a considerable amount of chaos.'

'Yeah,' Fisher conceded. But his mind was already roaming elsewhere.

'Well, it was supposed at the time that Andrews was following an agenda of his own. But we did have his assurance that she was being returned here for trial. Instead of which, here she is – what do you say? – as bold as brass. And entering this country from Germany, which would indicate that Andrews never brought her back here in the first place, and probably never intended to do so. We wish her arrested, and tried and convicted for her crime here, or failing that, handed over to us for trial in Russia.'

'And conviction, of course,' Fisher suggested.

'Oh, she is certainly guilty.'

'Well, Comrade, I will certainly look into the matter.'

'Look into it? Mr Fisher, this woman is certainly here to commit some crime or other.'

'As you say. Unfortunately, you see, we don't go in for preventive detention, and she has not as yet committed any crime in the United States. She is also here as a member of the German Embassy staff. That is to say, she has diplomatic immunity. Now, if we can find out, and prove, that she once tried to assassinate President Roosevelt, or participated in any un-American activities, we can demand her expulsion, but that will be done by the Germans themselves, and she will necessarily be returned to Germany.'

'Germany is the enemy of all mankind.'

'I'm inclined to agree with you. But right this minute, she is not legally our enemy.'

'You are refusing to assist us in bringing a known international terrorist to justice.'

'I am going to assist you in every way I can. However, in this country, we don't make up the laws as we go along, we merely abide by them. I will have this lady thoroughly investigated, and then I will come back to you. Until that investigation is completed, Comrade, I most earnestly entreat you not to do anything stupid.'

Kronsky stared at him for several seconds, then got up and left the room.

'He doesn't look a happy bunny to me,' Bridget remarked as she came into the room. 'Don't tell me the Reds have managed to lose another army, or whatever.'

'Listen,' Fisher said. 'Get me that spot with the Chief. And this really is urgent.'

'The view is spectacular, don't you think?' Erich Stoltz spoke anxiously. He was an earnest young man who had never cut a great figure with women; his inferiority complex had prevented him from ever trying. That he had been instructed to squire the most glamorous young woman he had ever seen had left him completely out of his depth.

The Countess von Widerstand was not, on the surface, a difficult woman to escort. She was always pleasantly good-humoured, fell in with most of his suggestions, was both punctual and utterly graceful in her habits as well as always being perfectly dressed and groomed. But she was obviously far more important than her apparent position as a Chief Secretary at the Embassy indicated. For one thing, the very posting of Chief Secretary was a bit much for a girl of twenty-one. For another, the Ambassador treated her with an inordinate amount of respect. And for a third, she had been thrust straight into the whirl that was Washington society, attending a cocktail party or a dinner party virtually every night. In no more than a month she had become a social phenomenon, with no hostess feeling that her party was a success unless her guest list

136

included the Countess von Widerstand.

But today she was having a quiet lunch with him in this restaurant on the seventh floor of the hotel overlooking the Potomac. As always she was attracting glances, but that was entirely because of her looks, dressed demurely as she was in a pale blue summer dress hemmed just below her knees to reveal her superb calves, a high-necked but extremely well-filled bodice, her long, straight, silky golden hair floating down her back and restrained only by a single pale blue band on the nape of her neck. Her jewellery was enough to attract admiring glances, the small gold bars dangling from her ears, the delicate gold crucifix resting on her bodice, the gold Junghans watch on her wrist, and above all, the huge ruby solitaire on the forefinger of her left hand.

Today was also the first time Stoltz had observed a certain tension in her demeanour, a slight impatience. As if she were waiting for something to happen, and was irritated that it had not yet done so. Now she said, 'Yes, it is a lovely view. Do you suppose we could order?'

'Of course. I do apologize. The clams here are very good.'

'Then let us have the clams.'

He snapped his fingers and the maître d' hurried over. Stoltz ordered, then looked up in concern as he discovered another man standing beside them. But the man ignored him, preferring instead to address Anna.

'Countess! What a pleasant surprise.'

'And for me, Mr Andrews.'

'May I join you?'

'I would like that. In fact, Erich, would you be a dear and leave us alone?'

'Ah...' Stoltz was dumbfounded. 'You know this gentleman?'

'Well, that would appear to be obvious, wouldn't it?' Anna's tone remained softly sweet.

'And...' He looked from one to the other.

'Mr Andrews will both pay for the meal and see me home afterwards.' She looked at Joe.

'Surely.'

'Well...' Stoltz stood up. He had been told by the Ambassador that he should obey without question any instructions given him by the Countess. So he clicked his heels, and left.

Andrews sat down. 'That was a little rough on the lad.'

'He is such a Nazi. And you know, apart from their ideology, they are the most boring people on earth. We have ordered clams. Do you like clams?'

'I like anything, so long as I can eat them looking at you.'

'You say the sweetest things. But I have waited nearly a month for you to contact me. You did know I was here?'

'I did, yes.'

'Yet when we were finally at the same party the other night, while we looked at each other across the room, you made no move to approach me. I felt quite neglected.'

'Seeing you took me entirely by surprise. I

138

knew you were in the country, but I needed to do a little background work, and then some thinking. Are you saying that you are in Washington simply to see me?'

'Well, you did save my life. In some philosophies, when you save a life that life belongs to you.'

'Now that is a statement worth hearing. If only I could believe it.'

'You should try me some time.'

'That is just about my dearest wish.'

They gazed at each other, and then the meal arrived. The waiter raised his eyebrows at the replacement of one diner by another but he poured the wine and withdrew. 'There's a sadly puzzled lad,' Joe commented. 'Now, are you prepared to tell me why you're here? I mean the true reason.'

Anna pouted. 'I thought I already had. However, if it's that important to you, I am taking American opinion on our decision to invade Russia. My people regard the fact that you are pouring millions of dollars worth of lend-lease into that country as a hostile act.'

'Your people?'

'As far as you are concerned, that is how it has to be.'

'Unfortunately, it's not quite as simple as that.'

Anna put down her fork.

'If you will take out your compact and powder your nose, you will be able to see, seated three tables behind you, a gentleman – I use the word loosely – having lunch.'

Anna did as he suggested, dabbed her nose with the powder puff, closed the compact and restored it to her handbag. 'One of yours?'

'Again, loosely. FBI.'

'Explain.'

'You could say that he is keeping you under surveillance at the request of the Soviets. The Reds have discovered you are here, having arrived, on your own, via a ship from Europe. I'm not quite sure what their attitude is to your having disposed of Chalyapov and Colonel Tserchenka, but they were certainly under the impression that I was bringing you back here to face trial. That was the deal with Beria, remember?'

'And as I obviously am not in custody ... What exactly do they have in mind?'

'I hope we have warned them off doing anything. They applied to the FBI to have you arrested to await extradition.'

'And got nowhere. Good old FBI.'

'It's not that simple in that direction either. The Bureau took the correct line that as you are employed at the German Embassy you possess diplomatic immunity. But it has discovered, on its own, that you are a German spy. Now it has been informed that you are also a German assassin. If it cannot touch you, legally, it certainly wants you out of here. That is to say, it would like to have you expelled. That could be tricky if you were to find yourself on a neutral ship bound for Europe and discovered you were sharing a table with a couple of NKVD heavies.'

'How soon is this liable to happen?'

'It's not going to happen at all, as long as you behave yourself. I was able to put a block on any FBI activity, at least overt activity.'

'But you're FBI yourself, aren't you?'

'I used to be. Now I belong to a senior organization. You could call it our version of the SD, although I would hope that our hands are just a bit cleaner.'

'But I am being shadowed by an FBI agent.'

'They're hoping you'll give them a handle to pull that might enable them to go over my head. Whether they do or not is up to you. I'm sorry. I can stop them arresting you or demanding your expulsion, but I can't control how they handle their internal affairs.'

'And what are the Russians doing all this time?'

'I have no idea. They seem to have accepted our decision that you cannot be touched.'

'Surely you realize that the Russians never accept anything they have not instigated in the first place.'

'Agreed. But they know they can't touch you without a just cause or without risking a diplomatic incident, and right now they are too dependent on our support to fight their war to chance that.'

'You are terribly reassuring,' Anna said with a touch of sarcasm. 'It seems to me—'

'That you just have to ignore them and get on with your business. And, Anna, I hope your business does not include bumping off anyone you suspect to be a Red who happens to get too close. That would be absolutely fatal.'

Anna smiled. 'Yes, it would, wouldn't it?'

'Anna...'

She rested her hand on his. 'Just joking. I'll be good. Now I'd like to ask you the sixty-four-thousand-dollar question.'

'Which is?'

'I have been in this country a month, as you well know. Yet you have only now approached me.'

'Yes. I'm sorry. I explained—'

'That you were also waiting to see if I would put a foot wrong? If I might have come here to assassinate someone? I presume you have also been having me shadowed, rather more subtly than the FBI. So what has brought you out of the woodwork now?'

'You have every right to be angry. Perhaps ... perhaps I knew that if we were to get together...' He gazed into those ice-cold blue eyes, which could suddenly reveal so much warmth. He had seen the warmth when she had looked at Clive Bartley on that unforgettable day in Moscow, just as a few hours earlier he had seen the cold immediately before she had killed Commissar Chalyapov on her way out of the Lubianka. Now he felt he was looking at the warmth again. Or was he just being optimistic?

She had left her hand lying on his. Now her fingers gave his a gentle squeeze. 'But I belong to you, Joe. Remember? I am yours to command.'

'Ah, right. So maybe we could spend the afternoon together. Where would you like to go?'

'I would like to look at your apartment,' Anna said, getting up, and still holding his hand.

Joseph Andrews closed the lobby door, made sure the latch had clicked, waited for a moment to allow his heartbeat to even out. He was forty-four years old, and had had his share of women. He had even been married once, briefly. But that had been a long time ago, and since then he had regarded the opposite sex with a vague suspicion. Presumably he should regard this woman with more suspicion than most. Save that he felt he knew all of her secrets ... and she knew that he did.

Besides, in his heart, even if he had known she had come here to kill him, he would still want to be here, with her. From the moment he had seen that naked figure in the Lubianka cell, she had dominated his thoughts. On that occasion she had very rapidly found some clothes to wear, but then, when Chalyapov had attempted to stop her leaving, she had gone into action with that speed and accuracy, that unhesitating decision, that he found breathtaking. Clive Bartley had told him about the real Anna, as opposed to the languorous beauty of the evening gowns and the dinner parties, and he had not entirely believed him. Now he was finding it difficult to believe that this moment was real, as he watched her walk across the lounge to the picture window overlooking Washington, slowly stripping off her

143

gloves, her hair and her scent drifting behind her. He wondered just how many men, apart from Clive himself, had gazed at that view with such a mixture of apprehension and wild anticipation. And had they lived to remember it? But did that matter, when he was the man in possession, and with the knowledge that right now, at any rate, she needed him even more than he wanted her.

'What a lovely view,' she remarked. 'And high enough not to be overlooked.' She turned to face him, took off her dark glasses. 'I am not very good at seduction,' she said ingenuously. 'When I am required to take off my clothes, well, things just happen. Would you like me to take off my clothes?'

'Only if you would like something to happen.'

'I'm here, aren't I?' She stepped out of her shoes.

He had to think of something to say, something that would not reveal him to be, as at that moment he felt, a gauche teenager on his first date. 'I see you're still wearing your jewellery.' How gauche could you get?

'I never thanked you for returning it to me.' Anna lifted her dress over her head and laid it on a chair, shook out her hair.

Joe inhaled deeply. 'It was not a problem. It wasn't damaged, I hope?'

'Not at all. Not even the watch.' Anna took off the Junghans and laid it on the table, placed her ring and her earrings beside it, then slipped the straps of her cami-knickers from her shoulders.

144

Her movements, so innocently casual, entirely lacking in coquetry, were almost as compelling as the flesh she was uncovering. As she had said, so innocently, when she started to take off her clothes, things just happened.

But he had to regain some measure of control. 'Wait!'

She paused, eyebrows arched, breasts half exposed.

'There is only so much that a guy can absorb all at once,' he explained. 'I have never even kissed you.'

'I know that.' She waited, still holding the bodice of the cami-knickers in place, but she released it to put her arms round him as he came up to her. Her tongue was soft, utterly yielding to his, as her body seemed to glue itself to his. 'Is that better?' she asked when at last he moved his head.

At least there were pink spots in her cheeks. He stood back and watched the cami-knickers slide down to her hips, and then down her legs to the floor. *Those legs*, he thought. He had only ever seen them once before, on that day in the Lubianka. He felt the suspender belt and stockings were an unnecessary excrescence, as she apparently understood.

'Would you like me to take these off as well?'

'Do some men wish you to keep them on?'

Anna made an enchanting moue. 'Some men do not exist, at this moment.'

'I would like you to be naked.'

Anna released the belt and rolled down the

stockings, bending over to do so. Joe could resist no longer, rested his hands on her buttocks, then slid them round her thighs to hold her pubes. He half expected a violent reaction, but she merely said, as she discarded the second stocking, 'I was wondering when you would do that. Tell me, do you like to be on top?'

'Eh?'

'It's just that, if I am to be on top, this might damage your teeth.' The crucifix moved gently to and fro in time to her breasts as she gave a little shimmy.

'Ah ... can't we do it both ways?'

Anna lifted the crucifix over her head and again fluffed out her hair.

He lay on his side to look at her, as she lay on her side facing him. Her eyes were half shut, and her lips parted slightly. Her hair was scattered across her shoulders, some strands in front to lie on her gently heaving breasts, a few even wisping across her face, to be disturbed by her breathing. Somehow the destruction of her immaculate coiffure conveyed a sense of intimacy superior even to the feeling of lying between her legs, feeling the insides of her thighs moving against his hips.

He was absolutely sure she had climaxed, at least once, even if he knew that one could never be certain with a woman like Anna. But he was not going to be quite so gauche as to ask. Instead he said, 'Did you find that utterly prosaic?'

Her eyes opened, and she blew hair away from

her mouth. 'Can making love ever be prosaic? But if you want something more ... how soon will you be ready again?'

'I would say not too long, if you're going to stay there.'

'I have nowhere to go, at the moment.'

'And if you would like something different...?'

'When I am in bed with a man,' Anna said, 'I like anything he likes.'

'What I actually would like,' he said, 'is to lie here looking at you, and maybe touch you from time to time.'

'That sounds rather attractive,' she agreed. 'But...'

'Oh, yes,' he said. 'Nature will undoubtedly call.'

'But when it does, if we just progress from where you happen to be touching at that moment, it might be very pleasant.'

He touched her breast, stroking across the nipple and then down into the valley, very deep as the breasts were crushed together by the angle at which she was lying. He had not actually touched her before, after they had got to bed. They had both been ready, and if there had been no sense of haste, there had also been no desire for any elaborate foreplay. Now he allowed his finger to stroke down to her stomach and across her ribcage, and then raised his head. 'This mark...'

'I know,' Anna said. 'It is very embarrassing. Every time I take off my clothes I am asked about that scar.'

He touched it. 'It's not exactly a scar. More like a sort of stain. Is it painful?'

'Not at all, not now.'

'Am I allowed to ask?'

'I got in the way of a bullet'

'Oh, good lord! Anna...'

'My profession has its ups and downs, as you may have noticed. Don't worry about it. The bullet smashed a couple of ribs and then exited. It was two years ago and I am perfectly healed. And the lady who fired it is now dead.'

'You mean you shot her in turn?'

'No. I broke her neck. Now, Joe, if we are going to progress, from what might be called a standing start, you will have to try lower down.'

'Anna! I have fallen in love with you.'

Just for a moment a shadow passed over her face. 'You don't know me.'

'I know just about everything about you that anyone knows. Clive Bartley told me.' Now his eyes were watchful as he tried to read her expression.

But her own eyes had drooped shut again, and they did not open now. 'He must have great confidence in you,' she murmured.

'Confidence,' he said, and drew a deep breath. 'A confidence I have betrayed.'

'By having sex with me? You are too much of a gentleman, Joseph Andrews. Clive knows that no man can possess me – all of me all of the time – until this war is over. Not even him.'

'But it is still possible to betray him. And you.'

Anna frowned as her eyes opened. 'I do not understand. Are you saying...?'

Those eyes had not yet frozen. There were some things even Anna needed to consider before taking action. He wondered if she could kill him while lying naked beside him, or if it would be necessary for her to get off the bed. Whatever the answer to that, he had to hurry. 'Not in the sense you are assuming. I have said that I love you. I have no intention of letting any harm befall you. But ... you know that in order to enlist my help in getting you out of the Lubianka, Clive had to convince me that you were actually a British agent?'

'Yes.' Her voice was slow, and thoughtful.

'I swore I would never reveal that to anyone. But in order to save you from the FBI, and by projection, the Russians, I had in turn to convince my boss.'

'The man Donovan.'

'The man Donovan. But you can forget about him, Anna. He is beyond your reach. Not only is he entirely reliable, but I would no more dream of letting anything happen to him than I would dream of allowing anything to happen to you. He is operating the most secret government organization in this country. We keep our secrets.'

Anna swung her legs out of bed and went to the bathroom. Joe waited for her to return, but she did not get back in beside him, and instead stood above him.

'Would your protection, and that of Donovan,

continue if you discovered that I am actually here to commit some crime against your government?'

Joe caught her hand. 'For God's sake, Anna, tell me you're not serious.'

'At this moment, I have no assignment apart from discovering if there is any chance of America entering the war against Germany.'

'Then I can give you a categorical answer. There is no chance whatsoever of America entering the war.'

'How can you be so sure?'

'Because not a year ago Roosevelt was re-elected on a pledge that he would never send American troops to fight in a war in Europe.'

'No matter what might happen?'

'No matter what. Within the bounds of reason. I mean, if in a maniacal fit your Fuehrer were to send a Luftwaffe squadron to drop a load on New York, well, our people would demand that we go to war. But I don't think even he is that crazy. And in any event, there is no bomber in the world with the range to get across the Atlantic and back. So I think I can give you a guarantee that there will be no war. Does that make life easier for you?'

'If you will answer a hypothetical question.'

'If I can.'

'Suppose, just suppose, there were a plane capable of bombing New York or Washington ... You say your people would then clamour for war with the aggressor. Are they capable of fighting a war?'

'You mean because we're supposed to be interested only in making money and enjoying the luxuries that money can bring? You tell me first, is there such a plane in existence?'

'No. I said the question was hypothetical.'

'Will you swear to that?'

'Certainly. I will swear to God that, so far as I know, there is no aircraft in existence, or even one planned, with that capability.'

'And I will accept your assurance. As to how we would respond to such an attack, if it happened, I would have to say that our options would be limited, in the short term. We don't have much of an army, by your standards, and we don't have much of an air force either. Bringing those up to the required standard to fight a war with, say, a European power, would take time, months, maybe a year or so. But we do have the most powerful fleet in the world, and the ships would protect us while we mobilized. What any would-be aggressor needs to know is that this nation, while it likes money and its pleasures, has resources of men, money and raw materials unequalled by any other country. But more important than that, it has a passionate pride in itself and its inviolability. What your Nazi masters should always remember, Anna, is that if by some means they got involved in a war against us, they can forget any idea of gaining a few victories and then negotiating a profitable peace. If this country ever has to take up arms, it is not going to rest until the last vestige of Nazidom has been wiped off the face of the earth. I hope that is what you came here to find out.'

'It just about completes my mission.' She snapped her fingers. 'Just like that. But what about the Jews?'

'They largely control the media, and thus a lot of public opinion. But they don't control the Administration.'

'You know they are being persecuted in Germany, in every part of Europe that is Nazi-controlled?'

'I guess everybody knows that.'

'Does everyone know that they are being systematically murdered?'

He frowned.

'And that these murders are likely to become ... well ... wholesale?'

'Are you serious?'

'Even I do not joke about things like that, Joe.'

He held her hand, drew her down to sit beside him. 'Can you prove it?'

'I have no documentary proof. But I move in high Nazi circles. That is my job for MI6: to listen and report.'

'And what has been London's reaction to that report?'

'I don't know. I left Germany for here almost immediately after sending it.'

'So they're sitting on it. Well...'

'But they are already at war with Germany. I need to know if that knowledge, should it become known to your Administration, could lead to war with America.'

152

He stroked her flesh. This was the cold-blooded, working Anna. But still the most desirable woman in the world. 'Somehow I doubt it. There is enormous sympathy for the plight of European Jewry here in America. But there is even greater hostility to the idea of ever again getting involved in a European war. So, barring that actual attack I mentioned earlier, I would say the answer is no.'

'Then I may as well hop on the next boat back to Europe.'

He squeezed her against him. 'Don't do that.'

'Well, maybe I should have that opinion confirmed from other sources.' She frowned. 'You said something about two betrayals. Is the other as good?'

Joe sat up. 'It's the reason I stopped observing you from a distance, and moved in today. I reckoned it might be the only chance I was going to have.'

'Don't tell me you're being sent back to Europe?'

'It's on the cards, but not immediately. No, Europe is coming to us. Actually it has already done so. Clive Bartley landed in New York yesterday.'

Five

NKVD

Anna did not move, and as Joe had pulled her forward so that her head was resting on his shoulder, he could not see her face. He inhaled the scent of her hair, which was clouding his nostrils. 'I guess you're fully entitled to kick me in the teeth and walk out of here,' he whispered. 'But I'll still love you forever.'

Still she did not move. But she asked, in hardly more than a whisper, 'Do you know why he is here?'

'No. But I can make a pretty good guess. I assume you informed London of your visit?'

Now she did move, slowly pushing herself away from him. 'You think he came all this way just to see me?'

'Well, he sure travelled to Moscow earlier this year just to see you. New York and Washington are no further.' He grinned. 'Who knows, maybe he just wants to keep in touch.'

He wants to discuss the Final Solution, Anna thought. But also to keep in touch. Oh, yes.

'So, all I can say is that I just knew that I had

to get in first, or I wouldn't ever make it,' Joe admitted. 'I'm a louse. You're fully entitled to hate me.'

'Why should I hate you? That was fun. And you have paid me a great compliment.' Anna got up and picked up her suspender belt.

'But that's it between us?'

It should be, she thought, sitting down to put on her stockings. *I have repaid you for saving my life, and you have given me the information I was sent here to obtain.* But she reckoned he was about the straightest man she had ever met. Certainly he was straighter than Clive. And even if, despite that certainty, she valued Clive the more, she still couldn't do without him. 'I hope not,' she said aloud.

He swung his legs out of bed. 'You serious?'

Anna put on her cami-knickers, draped the crucifix chain round her neck. 'I need you.'

'Name it.'

She adjusted her slip. 'I am employed by the German Embassy. Questions will be asked as to why I got rid of Stoltz and went off with you this afternoon, but I can explain that; getting close to you is part of my job, and you have given me valuable information.'

'Glad to have been a help,' he said bitterly. 'I appreciate your frankness, but that is pretty devastating.'

'Silly man,' she said. 'That is what I have to convey to my employers. I cannot remember when last I told them the truth, about anything. But I cannot just take off for an afternoon with

155

Clive. He is an enemy of the Reich.'

'The penny is dropping. You know, you're asking quite a lot, much as I like the guy.'

'There is no other way. He is certain to contact you, at which time you will set it up and invite me to have lunch with you. All above board.'

'It'll still be risky. I'd bet my bottom dollar that your Nazi friends are keeping an eye on you. Should a known British agent show up at lunch, even if I'm present...'

Anna put on her dress, added her jewellery. 'He won't show up at lunch. He'll be here, where you will bring me after lunch, just as you have done today.'

He gazed at her. 'Do you wrap every man you meet around your little finger? That is, when you are not actually killing them?'

She sat beside him. 'Now you are angry with me.'

He kissed her mouth. 'Angry with you? No, Anna, I could never be angry with you, not even if I knew you were about to put a bullet in my brain. That's your great strength, I guess.'

'Then you will do it?'

'Sure. I need my head examined, but I'll do it.'

'I will make it up to you. If you would like me to.'

'I would like to take you away to a desert island where no one could ever come near us again.'

She got up to find her handbag and peered in the mirror to start applying make-up. 'You would be bored.'

'You mean you'd be bored. May I ask you a question?'

'Certainly.'

'Will you answer with absolute honesty?'

'Ask me the question.'

'Are you in love with Bartley?'

Anna carefully etched in her mouth. 'I owe him my life. Just as I owe you my life. I also owe him my sanity. Above all, I owe him any hope I may have of the future. But then, I probably owe you those things as well.'

'Are you saying that you're in love with both of us?'

Anna put away her lipstick and brushed her hair. 'I am saying that I must be the most fortunate woman in the world, to be loved by two such men.'

Joe went to his jacket, and took out a card. 'This is my private number. Call me if you need anything at all.'

'Thank you.' She put the card in her handbag, kissed him, and went to the door. 'Do invite me out to lunch again soon.'

Love, she thought as she rode down in the elevator. Men always talk of love, when what they really mean is sex. The sad thing was that she felt she could probably love either of them, even if they were crippled and confined to a wheelchair. But that was self-deception. The only man with whom she had ever enjoyed sex before today was Clive, and how much of that had been because of the hope he held for the

157

future, she could not be sure. But she had enjoyed today as well, and Joe was strictly the present, never the future.

Equally was there no use in denying that her heart was singing at the thought that in a very short space of time she would be with Clive again, however briefly. Of course she wanted the reassurance, the confidence, that he always brought with him, but she also wanted so much more than that.

She smiled at the concierge, put on her glasses, and pushed open the doors to the street. It was a magnificent early October afternoon. According to the people at the Embassy, the Wehrmacht were in the suburbs of Moscow, and expected to control it within a fortnight, although it was equally expected that the Soviets would fight with greater determination than usual for their holy city. It was more difficult than ever to deduce from where the eventual British victory was going to come, especially if the United States was definitely not interested, but she did not doubt that Clive would be able to reassure her on that point as well.

She stood on the edge of the pavement, spotted a yellow cab, and raised her hand. The cab had actually been stopped against the kerb only a few yards away, obviously having just dropped a fare. Now it obligingly pulled in again.

'The German Embassy,' Anna told the driver, and settled herself back on the cushions. She was enjoying a delicious sense of relaxation. Of course Stoltz would have reported the strange goings-on at lunch to his superiors, and the Ambassador would no doubt want a word, but he was a dear old soul and very obviously in total awe of her – and in any event, as she had told Joe, she had only been doing her job.

And the job was done. She could take the next boat to Europe, after having made sure Himmler knew exactly when and how she was travelling, so that the U-boats could be warned off. But there need be no hurry. That was the beauty of her situation. No one, least of all Himmler, would expect her to have completed her mission so rapidly and with such a successful result. Indeed, part of her own euphoria was that such a result had come about so suddenly, when she had just been growing impatient at her lack of progress. She could stay here, certainly for as long as Clive was able to, and even after he returned to England, Joe would remain ... She remembered that when he had first made advances to her, in Moscow, he had said that if she ever came to the States he would show her his home in Virginia.

She realized that she had almost been nodding off, and also that they seemed to have been driving for a very long time. She hadn't been in Washington very long, but she had gathered from her outings with Stoltz that it wasn't a very large city, and now they were ... She looked out of the window. They were in some sort of deserted suburb.

She leaned forward, tapped on the glass,

which was obligingly slid open. 'Excuse me,' she said. 'But I wish to go to the German Embassy, not a drive in the country.'

'We stop now,' he said, and stopped so suddenly she nearly bumped her forehead on the glass. She jerked her head backwards, and both the rear doors were opened, to admit a man to either side of her.

'No noise, now,' one of them said, and held a knife to her breast.

Anna inhaled, aware that she, of all people, had allowed herself to drift on to Cloud Nine. She certainly didn't like the look of either of the men. But in the confined space of the car, and with the knife blade pressed against her, there was nothing she could do, at least for the moment. So the best thing to do was nothing, save act; her greatest strength, when people tried to take advantage of her, was that they never knew of just what she was capable.

She panted. 'Please don't hurt me. Look, there's money in my handbag. Take it. Just don't hurt me.'

The man on her other side grinned at her. 'We wouldn't dream of hurting a pretty doll like you. All we want to do is take you for a little ride, see?'

'No, no,' Anna gasped. 'I won't give you any trouble. Just don't hurt me. Please.'

'Then you behave. But we'll just make sure.' From the side pocket of his jacket he produced a little box. This he laid on his lap, opened it, and took out a hypodermic needle.

Shit, she thought. Once again she had been taken by surprise. But still there was nothing she could do while the knife blade was resting on her breast. And a moment later the needle was being driven into her arm.

Anna awoke to a headache and a bitter taste in her mouth, and a peculiar feeling of half comfort and half pain. She realized that she was tied to a bed, spread-eagled, each wrist handcuffed to the outside bar of the iron bed head, and each ankle similarly to the bars at the foot. She was also naked. But this was not even a nuisance, however much her captors might suppose she would be so humiliated and embarrassed she would be the more ready to surrender to their demands. But every man, and every woman, beginning with Dr Cleiner at the SS training school, who had had her in their supposed power, however briefly, had begun by removing her clothes. The room was warm, and as far as she could tell they had not done anything to her yet.

Far more disturbing was the fact that they had taken her jewellery, and her watch, but when she turned her head, she saw them lying on the table on the far side of the room, and gave a little sigh of relief.

She heard movement, and turned her head the other way. A woman had been seated in a chair by the window. Now she got up and came to stand above her. She was a mature woman, in her mid-thirties, Anna estimated, and had a cold face. 'Have we met?' she asked.

161

The woman turned away and opened the door. 'Comrade Kronsky!' she called. 'She is awake.'

Shit! Anna thought again. She was in deeper trouble than she had supposed. Although had she been thinking clearly she would have guessed immediately who her kidnappers had to be. And she was absolutely helpless until they released her, and surely they had to do that eventually.

There were heavy feet on the stairs, and then Kronsky came in, accompanied by two men, one of them actually – and somewhat melodramatically – carrying a tommy gun. 'Countess,' Kronsky said, also standing above the bed. 'Do you know that you are every bit as beautiful as they say, and that your photographs suggest?'

'I don't think I know you,' Anna said.

'Boris Kronsky.'

'I assume you are Russian?'

'That is correct, Countess.'

'You are employed by the Russian Embassy?'

'Indeed. I am also employed by the NKVD, an organization with which I understand you are familiar.'

'May I have something to drink? My mouth tastes like a sewer.'

Kronsky snapped his fingers, and a moment later the woman was holding a glass to Anna's lips, raising her head to do so. But her wrists remained cuffed to the bed. The liquid was clear, but Anna knew it would be vodka, and so sipped rather than gulped. Her mouth burned, but some of the foul taste was gone. 'Would you not like to finish it?' Kronsky asked.

'No. Thank you.'

'Well, perhaps later. You are very calm.'

'I am very angry. I am a Chief Secretary at the German Embassy. Did you know that?'

'Of course.'

'Then you will know that you are on your way to prison. And if you rape me, you will be gone for a very long time.'

He sat beside her, held her jaw, and moved her head from side to side. 'What you do not realize is that I know everything about you. I know that you are not really a countess, but an Austrian assassin named Anna Fehrbach.'

His hand moved from her jaw to stroke her neck, caressing the flesh but squeezing just hard enough to give the impression of immense strength. For all her determination not to panic, Anna caught her breath.

'I also know that you were sent to Russia last winter, on a mission to assassinate Premier Stalin, but were prevented from carrying out your assignment by my colleagues.'

To Anna's relief his hand left her neck, but then slid lower. She realized it was going to be a very long evening.

'But you escaped them. No one seems to know quite how, because it was hushed up. But no doubt it will come out at your trial.'

'You hope to take me back to Russia for trial?'

His hand had reached her breasts, and he caressed her flesh before pulling her nipples, quite hard. Again she could not stop herself

163

catching her breath. 'I am told you enjoy this,' he remarked. 'Yes, Comrade, I am going to take you back to Russia for trial. I am told that Premier Stalin himself wishes to interview you before you are hanged. I am sure he will wish to be present then, too. To get out of the Lubianka you killed a friend of his, did you not? Commissar Chalyapov? As well as an NKVD officer, Ludmilla Tserchenka?'

His hand at last left her breasts and moved down to her stomach, where he gently massaged the soft flesh.

'You are going to have to pay for those crimes, before your execution. I believe you will beg for death before it comes.' He touched her scar. 'Did our people do this to you?'

'No. Do you think you can just kidnap me and ship me out of this country like a parcel?' Anna had not intended to reveal any weaknesses such as curiosity, but she knew where his hand was going next and needed to prepare herself for it.

She was not going to get the time. His hand moved between her legs, and his fingers began to probe. Now she forced herself to breathe evenly. 'Oh, yes,' he said. 'It will take a little time to arrange, but I will enjoy having you as my guest. I did ask the FBI simply to arrest you and hand you over to our custody, but they refused. They may be supporting us in fighting our war, but one has to feel that they do not really like us. So I am going to have to arrange transportation for you on a suitable ship, and as I say, that will take a little time. So I suggest that

164

you just lie back and enjoy it.'

Anna was now breathing very hard as, no matter how determined she was not to let him get to her, she could not prevent the sensation spreading throughout her groin and up into her stomach. To allow this bastard to bring her to orgasm ... If she could just get her hands free...

'Please,' she gasped. 'I need to use the toilet.'

'Of course.' At least he had to move his hand to snap his fingers. Anna took several deep breaths and worked her own fingers to restore all possible feeling, and then she saw the room fill with people. There were now two women and three men, as well as Kronsky, and one of the men was still carrying the tommy gun. She did not think they could possibly know all about her, but they were definitely afraid of her. 'The lady wishes to relieve herself,' Kronsky explained. He spoke Russian, but Anna had become fluent in the language during her residence in Moscow. 'Now, ankles first.'

The two women began untying the cords. Anna had expected this, and made herself lie still. Once her legs were free, they each grasped one and pressed down while two of the men moved to the head of the bed. The other man pointed his tommy gun at her.

'You see, Countess,' Kronsky explained, 'it is on file, and your record confirms, that you can be absolutely deadly. So you will forgive us for being careful. Otherwise we might have to shoot you. And Premier Stalin does want you back in Moscow, unharmed. His orders about this were

165

quite specific. With the proviso, of course, that having you dead would be preferable to not having you at all.'

Her wrists were free, but the two men were still holding her arms, and the women her feet, and the gun was still pointing at her head. The odds were simply too great, even for her. And now she was rolled on to her face, her arms brought down behind her back, and her wrists again handcuffed, this time together.

'There we are,' Kronsky said. 'Now we can all go to the toilet together.'

Anna looked past him, at the tommy gun. How odd, she thought, that I have been in this business for three years, and I have never actually fired one of those.

'Clive!' Joe shook hands. 'You old son of a gun. I won't ask what brings you to Washington. But you're welcome. How long is it now?'

'Five years since I was last here,' Clive acknowledged. 'And if I remember rightly, you were quite keen on me leaving again.'

'Well, some of your methods were a bit extreme, even for us. Sit down.' He indicated the chair before his desk, sat himself, and waved a curious Margaret from the room; she had not been his secretary five years before. 'But I would imagine that this time you are not looking for someone, at least not with the intention of taking him out.'

'But I *am* looking for someone, as I am sure you know,' Clive said. 'And as this is in the nature of a flying visit, I need to contact her as soon as possible. As we're officially on different sides of the fence, I need your help.'

'Relax, old buddy. It's done.'

'Eh?'

'Well, I knew Anna was here, of course. So the moment I was informed that you had landed in New York, I took her out to lunch and put her in the picture. That was two days ago.'

'Have you seen a lot of her?'

'No. Lunch was the first time. I reckoned it was best that she should contact me, if she wanted something.'

'And she never did?'

'Nope.'

'But she was glad to hear from you. I mean, you saved her life.'

'Yeah. I think she was glad to see me. She was even gladder when she heard what I had to say.'

'And she's all right?'

'She is more beautiful, more Anna, than I even remembered.'

Relief came as a great sigh through Clive's nostrils. 'Did she tell you what she's doing here?'

'Gathering information for the Reich. It seems they're confused by our behaviour, the way we are pouring aid into both Britain and Russia, but apparently aren't interested in going to war in their support.'

'I have to say, old friend, that that confuses us as well.'

'Yeah,' Joe said sombrely. 'I know your PM

167

has been virtually begging the President at least to issue a declaration of intent that he will not stand by and allow the Japanese to take over Indonesia or Malaya. Lord Lothian has been on Cordell Hull's doorstep every day with the same objective.'

'All without the slightest result,' Clive said bitterly. 'You won't even agree to staff talks.'

'I know how you feel. I can only repeat to you what I told Anna. The President was re-elected last November on a pledge to keep America out of the war. He is not going to break that pledge. He cannot. There are enough people in this country who feel that he shouldn't be in the White House anyway, as the rules had to be bent to give him a third term.'

'And does he, do you, understand the situation that would arise were Japan to decide to take advantage of the European war and take over South-East Asia? Frankly, I don't think we could cope. It could mean the end of the Empire.' He regarded Joe. 'I suppose your people would be quite happy with that.'

'Some of them. I don't happen to be one of them, although I would argue that there are areas where things could be improved. But there it is, old buddy. As I told Anna, the only way this country is going to go to war is if it is actually physically attacked. And I don't think anyone is going to be nuts enough to do that.'

'She came here to find that out?'

'I think that was top of her list. But she sure wants to see you.'

'Snap. You said you could help with that.'

'I said it is all arranged. I'm to invite her out to lunch, and after lunch, take her back to my apartment. We ... ah ... had a trial run of this when we met a couple of days ago, and there were no repercussions. Her bosses know she's here to gauge public opinion, and getting close to someone like me is an obvious way to do that.'

'I see. How close?'

'Well, we had to make it look good. So this time, you'll be waiting at my apartment, and I'll just push off again. For as long as you require.'

Again Clive regarded him, this time for several seconds. Then he said, 'You're all heart, Joe. But I agree, I don't think we can improve on that plan. When?'

'I'll call her now. She has to name the date.' He picked up his phone, trying to avoid looking at his friend. 'Margaret, would you put a call through to the German Embassy. I'd like to speak with the Countess von Widerstand.' He then replaced the phone. 'She's a good girl – Margaret I mean. But sometimes I get the feeling she thinks she's my mother.'

Clive nodded. 'I have one of those. Now, tell me about this new set-up of yours. Rumour has it you've created your own MI6.'

'Loosely. There's so much going on in the world right now that's beyond the reach of agencies like the FBI.'

'So, will we be seeing you in England again some time soon?'

169

'Could be.' The phone rang, and he switched on the speaker before picking it up.

'The Countess von Widerstand isn't available right now, Mr Andrews.'

'Oh. Damn. Well, leave a message for her to call me when she is free.'

'Yes, sir. However, there is a gentleman who would like a word.'

'What gentleman?'

'A Herr Riedeler.'

'Ah ... you'd better put him on.' He gazed at Clive.

'Trouble?'

Joe put his hand over the mouthpiece. 'I hope not. But he's Gestapo. Head of Embassy Security.'

Clive felt his muscles tightening as he remembered the head of Embassy Security in Moscow, who had almost brought Anna down.

'Herr Riedeler,' Joe was saying pleasantly. 'What can we do for you?'

'I hope you can help us with a small matter, Mr Andrews.'

'Shoot. In a manner of speaking.'

'Well, sir, I believe you had lunch with the Countess on Wednesday. This is according to one of our staff, Herr Stoltz.'

'That is absolutely correct. Is there anything wrong with that?'

'Of course not, sir. The Countess is free to go where she wishes, and eat with whom she wishes. But I wonder if you could tell me where she went after the meal.'

'This goes with her absolute freedom of movement you were talking about, does it?'

'I am not prying, sir. But that was two days ago, and the Countess has not yet returned to the Embassy.'

'What?' Joe shouted.

Clive had difficulty in keeping quiet.

'Now, sir, I repeat that it is not our business to inquire into the Countess's movements, but the fact that we have not seen her or heard from her for two days is disquieting. The Ambassador is becoming worried. So if perhaps you could tell us where she intended to go when she left your lunch, it may be of great help in locating her, and reassuring us that she is all right.'

'She said she was returning to the Embassy,' Joe muttered, trying to think, but his brain was overwhelmed at the possibility that something might have happened to Anna.

'Thank you, sir. Would you have the exact time she left the restaurant?'

'It would have been just after four o'clock.'

'Sir?'

'Shit,' Joe muttered, and took a deep breath as he looked at Clive, who in any event appeared to be on the verge of an explosion. But much as he disliked the Gestapo, he reckoned they were at least as efficient at tracing people as the FBI. And if Anna was in any danger ... As far as they were concerned she was one of their own. 'It was not the restaurant,' he said. 'We finished the meal at about one thirty, and she accompanied me to my apartment.'

171

'Ah ... until four o'clock?'

'We had an important matter to discuss. I am sure you realize, Herr Riedeler, that the Countess and I had a previous acquaintance, in Moscow earlier this year. Your people in Berlin know of it.'

'Of course, sir. So she left your apartment at four o'clock. That would be where, sir?'

Joe gave the address.

'Thank you, sir. But you do not know where she intended to go then.'

'I have told you, she intended to return to the Embassy. I did not go down to the street with her, but I believe she was going to catch a cab.'

'It is no more than half a mile from your address to the Embassy, sir.'

'Perhaps she did not feel like walking.'

'Of course, sir. I was only thinking that if she did catch a cab, she would have been here in ten minutes. Say, four-fifteen. So she left your apartment and went downstairs to catch a cab. But you were not with her, so you cannot say for certain that she did so.'

'No, I cannot. But I imagine the concierge would have seen her. He might even have seen the cab.'

'That would indeed be very helpful. Would you object if I sent one of my people round to interview your concierge?'

'I would welcome it. I would like to know if anything has happened to the Countess as much as you would.'

'Thank you, sir. You have been most cooperative. I will keep you informed of any developments.'

Joe replaced the phone. 'Slimy bastard. But I guess he really wants to find our girl, so good luck to him.'

'Do you really have no idea where she might have gone, what she might have been doing for two days?'

'I wish I did,' Joe said, as convincingly as he could. He had no doubt that she had been picked up. By the FBI, or the Soviets? He wouldn't put it past either of those to take unilateral action and risk the consequences. And boy, he thought, are there going to be consequences.

'I do feel,' Clive said mildly, 'that we need to be absolutely straight with each other in this business. I am sure that Anna means as much to you as she does to me.'

'Of course she does.'

'So what exactly was the topic of conversation that kept you occupied for two hours? In your apartment.'

'I told you. She wanted to know under what circumstances we would enter the war.'

'And it took you ten minutes to convince me that there are no circumstances short of a direct attack on the USA that would bring you into the war. That leaves one hour and fifty minutes unaccounted for.'

Joe sighed. 'OK, OK. But it was neither a rape nor a seduction. She felt she owed me for saving her life in Moscow. You must know what Anna is like more than anyone else. She always pays

173

her debts. And when the debt is one of gratitude, well...'

'She is willing to disburse a few of her assets.'

'I guess so. You may now punch me on the nose, if you wish. Although I would like to say that the moment I told her you were in New York her interest in me totally disappeared.'

'And you told her this before, or after, ah...'

'After. So I'm a louse. But I could die happy on that one memory.'

'I'd prefer you to stay alive, at least for a while. Where do we start looking?'

'There are two possibilities.' Joe outlined the events that had surrounded Anna's arrival.

'But,' Clive said when he had finished, 'you say she knew of the danger from both those sources. I mean, Anna is not the easiest woman in the world to snatch, if she doesn't want to be snatched.'

'But even Anna can become over-relaxed.' Joe looked thoroughly embarrassed.

'You mean she had just had a thoroughly satisfying fuck.'

'Well ... I actually meant that she had just found out that in a couple of days she was going to be with you. And I guess she felt pretty secure, here in Washington.'

'All right. I promise I won't punch you in the nose until we find her. So let's start looking.'

'We'll have to do it my way. I know the ropes around here. So you go back to your hotel and sit tight. I'll call you.'

'Oh, yes?'

'Listen, I swear I will take no action, in any direction, without first filling you in.' He picked up the phone. 'Margaret! I need to see the boss. It's urgent.'

Donovan stroked his chin. 'When I gave you carte blanche to handle this woman, I didn't mean you to take it quite so literally.'

'Well, we're old friends...'

'And she owed you a favour. I got that. And I say again, I'd sure like to meet this dame. When you get her back. If you get her back.'

'Sir?'

'Has it occurred to you that she might merely have had her feet encased in cement and be now waving her arms in time to the flow at the bottom of the Potomac?'

'Oh, Jesus Christ!'

'Not a pretty picture,' Donovan agreed. 'On the other hand it's not an FBI picture, either. The Soviets, now, that's another matter. But start with the FBI. You say one of their people was at the restaurant. If his job was keeping tabs on the Countess, he'd surely have followed you to your apartment, and be waiting there when she came out.'

'Holy shit! I never thought of that.'

'You mean you didn't spot him.'

'Well...'

'I get the picture. You were so wrapped up in what you reckoned was about to come your way that you stopped being a forty-four-year-old veteran and became a sixteen-year-old kid on his first date. I have just *got* to meet this dame. However, you can bet your last dollar that he was there. So, maybe he called up support and nabbed her when she left. But you tell me she's not an easy woman to nab, at least when she's on her feet rather than her back. Anyway, it doesn't make sense for the FBI to decide to pick her up after she's been here more than a month, doing nothing subversive. I don't suppose there's any chance she's been setting you up on this?'

'None at all.'

'I'll accept that. But this agent was there, and if he was doing his job, he'll have seen exactly who did pick her up, and he'll have noted the make of the car and the number plate. Go see Fisher and get that info. Pull rank if you have to. I'm at your shoulder.'

'You have my eternal thanks, Wild Bill.'

Donovan grinned. 'Just remember, when she turns up, I'm the guy taking her out to lunch.'

'So you've lost your girl,' Lawrence Fisher remarked. 'Haw, haw, haw.'

Joe kept his temper. 'So here's where you give. Contrary to orders, you had a man on her.'

'I take my orders from J. Edgar, not your lot.'

'One of these days you may be in for a nasty surprise. I want to see his report.'

'Confidential.'

'You are treading on very thin ice,' Joe told him.

'So what's the big deal? Loomis has nothing

that'll help you.'

'He saw her leave the building.'

'Sure. She walked right by him and didn't even notice him.'

'She had a lot on her mind. So he saw where she went.'

'She got into a yellow cab.'

'And he didn't follow her?'

'He heard her tell the driver to take her to the German Embassy. So he figured that was it for the day and went home.'

'I want the number of that cab.'

'I reckon we can let you have that. What, you saying she's gone off with a taxi driver? After spending two hours shacked up with you? She sure must be randy.'

'Look, just get me that number. And tell me something: you had any contact with Kronsky recently?'

'I guess I'm not his favourite person right now.' Fisher frowned. 'You're not serious?'

'Someone has her. Kidnapping is still a Federal offence, ain't it?'

'He wouldn't dare.'

'Well, just let's suppose he did dare. Having received orders from Beria.'

'Shit!'

'Good point.'

'If the Reds have her, she's either dead or out of the country.'

'We'll work on the principle that she's alive until we turn up a body. As for getting her out of the country, the first thing you do is put an embargo on any ship leaving the east coast for Europe, at least until she's been searched.'

'I can't do that. J. Edgar would never go for it.'

'Tell J. Edgar to give Wild Bill a call.' Joe stood up. 'Meanwhile, just in case they're holding her some place, I want a list of every house within a fifty-mile radius of this office which belongs to or is rented by the Russian Embassy.'

'You reckon she's that close?'

'I'm playing a hunch.'

'You realize that we're not supposed to rough up the Soviets right now? They're flavour of the month with FDR.' Fisher held up his hands. 'OK, OK. Your Wild Bill can even square it with the boss. But let me ask you something: your entire bunch got the hots for this chick? Or is she that important?'

'She is to us,' Joe said, and left the office.

'That is one hell of a long shot,' Clive remarked.

'You got any better ideas?' Joe asked. 'And it's not just guess-work. Figure this: Anna hails what she assumes is a cab outside my apartment building, tells the driver to take her to the Embassy. Now, she hasn't been here very long, and she may have been on Cloud Seven, but she has been shown around this old town, and she knows that the German Embassy is only a few blocks from my place. Like I say, she may have been in one big day dream, but she was going to wake up, sooner than later, when she was driven for ... well, you tell me. Fifteen minutes, half an

178

hour? And when she wakes up and realizes that she ain't being carried to the Embassy, boom-boom. Now, the Soviets may not know all about her, but they know enough, after that explosion in the Lubianka, to be sure she's not just going to scream for help if she's being kidnapped. They'll have allowed a certain time, then that cab must have pulled in some place, preferably some place nice and quiet, but pretty close, where they had their goons waiting for her, presumably with sufficient force to subdue even Anna. I happen to know that she wasn't armed.'

'What you are saying is that they probably put a bullet in her right there and then,' Clive said miserably.

Joe shook his head. 'That doesn't fit. Kronsky asked Fisher to have her arrested and deported, so that they could take her back to Russia for a show trial. Fisher refused, so they decided to do their own thing.'

'After a month?'

'If I'm right, and I'm sure I am, they would first of all contact Moscow to get the OK for unilateral action, and having got that, it was a case of taking the first opportunity that presented itself. I reckon they've had her under surveillance from day one, despite being warned off, but she's never been alone, always had someone from the Embassy with her. And the fact that she was being shadowed wasn't being noticed by anyone, me included. I spotted the FBI tail easily enough, but didn't reckon on the Reds. You have to give them credit. They watch

179

and they wait. And suddenly, she drops her German minder and has lunch with me. No chance there: they know who I am. But then she accompanies me back to my apartment. They must have hurried, arranged the cab and the drop-off point. They probably could hardly believe their luck.'

'But if you had come out with her...'

'The plan would have been aborted, and we, and she, would have been none the wiser. Oh, I'm a dummy to let her leave on her own. But that doesn't alter my thesis, that as it was a matter of seizing the moment, they can't have had any immediate arrangement for getting her out of the country. That had to be set up once they had her. Ergo, ten will get you a hundred that she's still here.'

'Joe, she was snatched two days ago. That's a lot of time to set things up. And when you think what she might have been suffering throughout those two days ... Christ almighty!'

'Don't you think it's burning holes in me as well? Oh, fuck it!' His outside telephone was buzzing. He flicked the switch. 'Andrews.'

'Joe?'

Both men sat bolt upright. 'Anna!'

'Oh, Joe, it's so good to hear your voice. Listen, I have a problem.'

Joe looked at Clive; her voice sounded as softly calm as ever. 'Where are you?' he asked.

'That's part of the problem; I don't know.'

'What? Listen, are you all right?'

180

'You could say I have a few ruffled feathers. They'll smooth out.'

'But where have you been these last two days? We've been worried sick.'

'Well, I should think so too,' Anna said severely. 'I was picked up by these people and brought to this house. They took me completely by surprise. I suppose I was thinking of other things.'

'I get you. These were Russians?'

'NKVD.'

'And they took you to some house. But you don't know where it is.'

'They shot drugs into me and laid me out. But I'm pretty sure it's in Washington. It was still daylight when I woke up, so I couldn't have been out for more than half an hour. Then I was here.'

'Right. And they've held you there for two days. How many of them?'

'Six. Four men and two women.'

'Shit! But now they're letting you use the phone.'

'Well, not exactly.'

'You mean you've got loose. Good girl. But if they're not with you at the moment, why don't you jump out of the window and run like hell? At least as far as the next house. There are other houses?'

'Oh, yes. But I don't really want to do that.'

'Why in the name of God not?'

'I have no clothes.'

'What?'

'They took away my clothes,' Anna said patiently. 'I mean, the clothes are here but they're all torn.'

'OK, OK. I take your point. But there are enough of them left to cover your vital statistics, right? If you don't want to appear in public like that, well ... these people have an automobile, I presume?'

'Yes. It's in the garage.'

'Well, maybe the keys are in the ignition. Grab it and drive like hell. Anywhere, away from there. Until you get your bearings.'

'I couldn't do that,' Anna protested.

'Why not?'

'I don't know how to drive.'

'What?'

'I don't know how to drive,' Anna repeated, still with great patience. 'No one ever taught me. The SS taught me just about everything I know, but not how to drive. They didn't consider it necessary. And if I try it now, I'll be arrested by your traffic police, as well as for indecent exposure. I'd hate that. Anyway, these people...'

Joe was taking deep breaths, apparently in an endeavour to prevent himself from having a stroke. Clive took the speaker. 'Anna!'

'Clive?' Her voice went up an octave. 'It's so good to hear you voice. Listen, I need your help.'

'Of course we're going to help you, Anna. But we need information. These people seem to be allowing you an awful amount of time to yourself.'

182

'Well, yes they are—'

'Right. Well, if you don't feel that you can leave the house, why don't you call the police, from where you are? I know you can't give them an address, but surely you can give them the telephone number.'

'There isn't a number, not that I can see.'

'Ah. Right. Well then keep them talking for five minutes, and they'll be able to trace the call.'

'I don't think that would be a good idea, either.'

'Anna...'

'Can't you trace the call from where you are?'

Clive looked at Joe, who shook his head.

'We don't have that facility in this office. Now listen, we are going to find you. But it may take a few hours. We are going to have to ask you to suffer these people for that time. Can you do that?'

'Of course. They aren't troubling me any more.'

'Well, that's something. Don't tell me you've managed to charm the pants off a bunch of NKVD people?'

'No, I didn't think that would be practical. So I had to kill them.'

Six

Paradise

There was a moment's silence while the two men looked at each other. Then Clive said, 'There were six Russian agents, and you killed them, one after the other? Didn't they try to do something about it? I mean, about what was happening?'

'It wasn't quite like that,' Anna explained. 'They had this tommy gun, and I managed to get hold of it. I'd never fired a tommy gun before. I mean, it was just out of this world. It took about ten seconds. But there's a most awful mess.'

'Ah...'

There was a tap on the door, and Margaret came in. 'I'm sorry to interrupt, Mr Andrews, but the list of houses the Russians own or rent here in Washington has just come in from the FBI. Mr Fisher wants to know if you would like him to investigate any of them.'

Joe seemed to awaken from a deep sleep. 'No,' he said. 'Definitely not. Tell him we'll handle it.'

'Yes, sir.' Margaret looked from one to the

other of the two obviously shell-shocked faces, and left the room.

Joe took the speaker. 'Anna, we're on our way. Just sit tight.'

'And you'll bring some clothes. You can get them from the Embassy.'

'I don't think that would be a good idea, right now. We'll find something.'

'When you come, will Clive be with you?'

'Yes,' Joe said, not altogether regretfully.

William J. Donovan gazed at the young woman seated on the other side of his desk. He could not remember ever having seen a more attractive sight, even if she was wearing a somewhat shapeless dress and low-heeled shoes, and her hair was untidy, while there was a complete absence of make-up. But there was a good deal of very expensive jewellery. That she also looked distinctly out of sorts enhanced rather than detracted from her beauty. 'I have been hearing a lot about you, Countess,' he remarked.

Anna tossed her head. 'You have me at a disadvantage, sir. Your people,' she gave Joe a disparaging glance, 'refused to allow me to return to my Embassy and obtain some proper clothing. So I am reduced to wearing these cast-offs.'

'Mr Andrews was following my instructions,' Donovan pointed out. 'Surely you realize that you have placed us in a rather difficult position. I mean, six dead bodies—'

'It was the tommy gun,' Anna explained. 'I

had never fired one before. Once I started I could not stop. Not that they did not deserve to die...'

'All six of them?'

'They raped me.'

'All of them? I understand two of them were women.'

'All of them. I do not like being raped.'

'Actually, I have never met a woman who did. Like being raped, I mean.'

'Especially by women,' Anna added.

'Absolutely. Perhaps fortunately, not all women react quite so ... comprehensively to the situation.'

'They were Russians.'

'And you do not like Russians either?'

'At this moment, no.'

'Let us hope for better times.'

'In Germany, when something like this happens, I telephone the SD and they come and take the bodies away and clean the place up, and nothing more is heard of the matter.'

'And, ah, "something like this" happens quite often, does it? In Germany.'

'It has happened before,' Anna said modestly.

Donovan scratched the back of his neck.

'Sadly,' Joe commented, 'we don't have quite the same facility over here. Dead bodies have to be accounted for.'

'When I had that trouble in England, last year,' Anna said, 'MI6, Clive, sorted it out.'

'The trouble being...?' Donovan was interested.

'Well, three Gestapo agents tried to arrest me.'

'Don't tell me. You shot them all.'

'Well, what else was I to do? If they had succeeded in taking me back to Germany I would have been executed.'

'Absolutely. And this man Clive...' He looked at Joe.

'Clive Bartley, MI6.'

'My British Controller,' Anna explained. 'He's here now.' It was her turn to look at Joe. 'He is still here, isn't he?'

'Oh, indeed. He's waiting for you.'

'Just wait one moment,' Donovan said. 'You mean an MI6 agent is involved in this?'

'I am an MI6 agent,' Anna reminded him.

'Yeah. But this other guy ... Holy shit! I beg your pardon, Countess.'

'Bartley is not involved,' Joe said. 'At least, he wasn't. He came across in order to contact Anna, and, ah, discuss her work.'

'But he's involved now.'

'Only in the sense that he's upset at having one of his people kidnapped.'

'And you say, Countess, that he is your Controller. I think I need to meet this guy. Unofficially, Joe.'

'I'll arrange it. But the point, Anna, is that the six bodies in that house were not Gestapo. They were accredited foreign nationals.'

'Were they all accredited Russian nationals?' Donovan asked.

'Actually, it doesn't appear as if they were. It's obviously too soon for us to be certain, but from

187

such documentation and other evidence as we have found so far it would seem that five of them were US citizens, although certainly Communist sympathizers. Unfortunately, as you know, sir, Kronsky is definitely accredited to the Russian Embassy. Or was, I should say. On the other hand, they were all engaged in the plot to kidnap the Countess.'

'Equally unfortunately,' Donovan pointed out, 'we only have the Countess's word that that is what happened.'

'Are you calling me a liar?' Anna asked, her voice quietly dulcet.

'I wouldn't dream of it. But we need to face facts. If this story breaks and the media gets hold of it, and starts investigating, as they certainly will ... I mean to say, what a story! Beautiful woman kidnapped and raped by six Communist sympathizers, including a Russian official, who then manages to get free and kills them all. How did you manage that, anyway?'

'It was difficult. They kept me tied to the bed—'

'Naked?'

'Yes.'

'But they didn't take away your jewellery.'

'They did take away my jewellery. I took it back when I ... well...'

'When you had finished killing them. You still haven't told us how you managed to do that.'

'You keep interrupting me,' Anna said coldly. 'I said they kept me tied to the bed while they took turns at raping me. They let me out of bed from time to time to go to the toilet. But as I never resisted them, they gradually got careless, and with their weapons. Especially the tommy gun. So this morning they left the gun on a chair while they took me to the bathroom. There were only four of them present. So I wriggled free and reached the gun. When they heard the shooting, the other two, including Kronsky, came running into the room.'

'I guess we all make mistakes,' Donovan conceded. 'What a mess. However...' He gazed at Anna. 'You do understand that you are in deep trouble without our help.'

'But you are going to help me,' Anna said. 'I mean, you are on our side, aren't you?' She glanced at Joe.

'Not visibly,' Donovan said. 'At least, not right this minute. We are going to help you, Countess. But, well, quid pro quo, right?'

Anna stared at him. 'You will have to explain that, sir.'

'My office is engaged in setting up a series of information-gathering points in Europe. Just so we can keep an eye on what's going on. I think it would be very useful to have you on our payroll.'

'Payroll?'

'How much do the Brits pay you, right now?'

'Why should they pay me anything?'

'Countess – Anna – you are working for them.'

'I am working for the destruction of Nazi Germany.'

'But you are working. People usually get paid for working.' He did some more neck-scratching as he realized she had no idea about what he was speaking. 'OK, how much do the SD pay you?'

Anna gazed at him.

'How do you live, for Christ's sake? *Where* do you live?'

'I have an apartment in Berlin.'

'How do you pay the rent?'

'There is no rent. The apartment belongs to the SD.'

'I see. And that jewellery you're wearing...'

'Is their property, yes.'

'But you have to live, buy groceries.'

'I have a bank account.'

'Right. Now, how much money goes in there? Say, monthly.'

'I have no idea.'

'Say again?'

'There is always money there. They monitor it, and pay money into it whenever they feel it needs topping up.'

'You sure you want these guys to lose this war? OK, OK. We'll sort something out. Will you work for us?'

'As long as it does not clash with my work for MI6.'

'Right. Joe, I need that meeting with this guy Bartley.'

'Yes, sir.'

'Meanwhile, this lady has to disappear, entirely, while I try to sort this out.'

'Ah...' Joe and Anna looked at each other.

'You want me to take care of that?'

'She's your baby. If you'll excuse me, Countess.'

'Virginia,' Anna said. 'You promised to show me your home in Virginia.'

'Who lives there?' Donovan asked.

'My mother. She's a widow.'

'And?'

'She would be absolutely trustworthy. And I know she'd enjoy meeting Anna.'

'And I assume she carries adequate life insurance. Just joking, Countess. OK, Virginia. I don't want to know more than that. But you stay there until you hear from me. And Countess, if I hear from you – that is, via any newspaper report or radio broadcast, for whatever reason – I drop the whole thing and turn you over to the FBI.'

'There are some details to be worked out.'

'Tell me about it. I thought you weren't interested in money.'

'I must have my clothes, and my maid.'

'Maid? Holy shit! Don't tell me she's SD as well?'

'Of course she is not. She works for me. She is a good German, but if I tell her I am working for the Reich in visiting Virginia for a while, she will not question it.'

'Well, I guess, if you really want to have her around. But if you go back to the Embassy, there will be questions.'

'The Embassy will also believe anything I tell them. You do not seem to understand,' Anna

191

said, with her invariable modesty, 'that I am a senior officer in the SD, with carte blanche to do as I please, as long as I deliver what is required, and I have always done that. If I do not return there and reassure them that I am all right, they will make a fuss.'

'Point taken. OK, but get in and out of there as rapidly as you can.' He stood up, held out his hand. 'Meeting you has been one of the great experiences of my life. I look forward to our next meeting, when maybe we'll have time to have lunch together.'

'I think that would be very nice. But before we go any further, I wish to see Mr Bartley.'

'You will. But I think that will also have to be in Virginia. You handle that, Joe, as you know this guy.'

'Thank you.' Anna smiled at them both.

'That dame is an experience,' Donovan said. 'How the hell did you get hold of her?'

'I thought Joe filled you in,' Clive said.

'Yes, he did. But I didn't altogether believe him. Now...'

'Can you sort it out?'

'By bending one hell of a lot of rules, and a few arms as well. I have to go to the very top. But he'll support me. If I can convince him that we have a recruit of such potential.'

'It's tricky,' Clive said. 'Our countries are not officially allied.'

'We share quite a lot of confidential information, at various technical levels.'

'I wouldn't altogether describe this as a technical matter, Mr Donovan. I'll have to square it with my boss, when I get back to England.'

'Which will be when?'

'I leave at the end of next week.'

'Soon enough. Anna isn't going anywhere for the next few weeks. But you need to bear in mind, Mr Bartley, that her survival could well rest on her willingness, and yours, to share.'

'I will remember that.'

'Well, then, good luck. I take it you'll be visiting Joe's home for a day or two?'

'Yes, sir. We have a great deal to discuss.'

'I bet you do. I guess you must know the Countess pretty well.'

'I think I can say that I know her as well as it is possible to know her.'

'There's a canny answer. So what makes her tick? I mean, she looks like the debutante of the year, sweet twenty-one and never been kissed, and all the time she's the ultimate femme fatale. And when pushed she seems to act like one too, with the accent on the word *fatale*. But for the rest ... she doesn't seem to be interested in money; she doesn't really have a home; I know she doesn't have a family, at least available ... But she can't be a spy all the time. I mean, what sports does she do? What music does she like? Does she have a guy? Or maybe a gal. She seemed pretty fond of that maid of hers.'

'I can't answer any of those questions, Mr Donovan. I only know, although she would

193

probably deny it, that she was horrendously traumatized as a girl. Can you imagine a seventeen-year-old, brought up in a refined, intellectual home, convent-educated, being handed a gun and directed to kill a living target?'

'Shit! And she did it?'

'She reckoned she had no choice, if she, and her family, were going to survive. That has been her driving force ever since. I know she dreams of an afterwards, a better life, but she knows she has to get there herself. You asked me what makes her tick. I would have to say hatred – hatred of the men who made her what she is.'

'What about the men who are taking advantage of what she is?'

'Right now, Mr Donovan, we are the representatives of that hope for the future. If we let her down, I think we would have to break every mirror in existence, so we would never have to look at ourselves again.'

Donovan considered him for several minutes, then he nodded. 'Give her my love, and make sure she understands that I'm on her side.'

'Isn't this heavenly?' Anna waved her arm as she walked beside the river; the gesture encompassed the trees, the grass, the bird calls, the gentle whisper of the water, as well as the still warm autumnal sun. Ahead of her the two spaniels frisked.

'Yes, Countess.' Birgit panted. Anna took long strides, and the maid, nearly a foot shorter, had to scurry to keep up with her. 'Are we staying here long?'

'I don't think so, more's the pity. But let's enjoy it while we can.'

The house was in sight now, the very picture of a southern mansion with its overhanging roof supported on the high pillars. It had apparently been in the Andrews family for two hundred years, and had thus seen both the War of the Revolution and the Civil War pass by. It was still surrounded by cotton fields, although the vast acreage it had once overseen had greatly dwindled as the years had gone by. It made Anna feel entirely humbled that while she had been forced to play the aristocrat over the past three years – so much so that she had almost come to believe her own pseudo-persona – Joe Andrews really was an aristocrat, who never attempted to impose his background upon anyone.

To be able to live the rest of her life in such surroundings, without a care in the world ... She waved her hat at the labourers in the fields, who had stopped work to watch her. Anna Fehrbach out walking in a summer frock and with her hair loose was always worth watching. They waved back enthusiastically, while she reflected that to men like Himmler and Heydrich, and even more Hitler, these amiable black people were sub-human.

The dogs were barking, and Anna saw, parked on the drive before the house, one of those huge American cars that people of all classes seemed to drive. Her heartbeat quickened. She and Birgit had been driven down here, two days

195

previously, in a similar huge car, by one of Joe's assistants, a very serious young man who had definitely taken to heart his boss's stricture, that the Countess von Widerstand was a person of great importance and not to be subjected to questions or even conversation. Well, she had not been in the mood for conversation herself. The events of the previous few days had been far more upsetting than she would admit even to herself; for all the sexual experiences of her life, that had been a new and most unpleasant one.

She had become used to the fact that her beauty, her allure, seemed to attract men, and some women, to an extraordinary degree, just as she had come to accept that her survival depended upon sleeping with whom she was commanded. This had invariably been distasteful, but once the event had commenced, as it were, she had been in command. Except possibly with Heydrich. But he was merely a recurring nightmare. She had never been strapped to a bed and raped before. The sex itself had been meaningless; the humiliation had been equalled, in her life thus far, only by her session in the SD torture chamber. The desire to destroy those people had taken over her mind. For all her protestation to Donovan and Joe that she had not realized just how lethal a weapon a tommy gun could be – a protestation she had felt necessary – she knew that her fascination had been less with the weapon than the effect it was having on the hateful creatures in front of her. At that moment she had indeed been a monster. But it was not a moment she regretted.

Since then she had been caught up in a situation she could not control. Explaining that she was engaged in something very big and very secret to the Ambassador had not been difficult. Realizing that her existence depended on two men she did not really know, and whose motives she could not entirely fathom, was disconcerting. Most disconcerting of all was knowing that she was virtually within touching distance of Clive, and she had not even been allowed to see him since he and Joe had come to her rescue.

But now the presence of another large car meant that something was at last happening. Eleanor Andrews had a large car of her own, of course, and a chauffer to drive it, but both of these were to be found in the garages behind the house when not in use. So, the dogs had charged ahead, still yapping loudly, and there was Eleanor standing on the downstairs veranda, waiting for her.

She was a tall, stately woman, thin like her son, and – also like him – somewhat lugubrious of face, although she too could produce a flashing smile. What she thought of the situation Anna had not yet deduced; she apparently trusted her son absolutely and was prepared to fall in with his wishes, however unconventional. Thus she had accepted Anna, and her maid, without demur, asked no questions, and indeed had been absolutely charming. Now she was smiling.

'We have a guest,' she announced. 'Who I

believe you were expecting.'

'Oh!' Suddenly Anna was breathless. It was actually only just over three months since she had last been in Clive's arms, and on that never-to-be-forgotten day in the American Embassy in Moscow she had been as disoriented as she was now. Two days at the mercy of Ludmilla Tserchenka had done that to her. There again she had known only the desire to kill, to be avenged, and miraculously she had been given the opportunity. To find herself suddenly alone with Clive so soon after that event had been overwhelming; she could remember little of what they had said, or even what they had done. And now he was here again, and again courtesy of Joe Andrews. She wondered if her gratitude to Joe was not more for arranging these meetings than for saving her life.

Eleanor had been studying her face. 'You do want to see him?' she asked, suddenly anxious.

'Oh, yes.'

'Oh, I am glad. He had a letter from Joe, and, well, after reading it, I put him in your apartment, and told him to wait there for you.'

'I owe you so much.' Anna kissed her cheek. 'You must think I am an awful liability.'

'I would describe you as an unequalled asset, in any society, my dear. So, off you go. Lunch is in an hour. I'll have yours sent up, shall I?'

Anna opened the door of the suite she had been given, Birgit having tactfully remained downstairs; the maid spoke only a word or two of

English and was therefore a rather isolated figure, although Eleanor's housekeeper was enthusiastically trying to teach her the language.

Clive had been standing by the window, looking out. He turned at her entry and she was soon in his arms, kissing him with a desperate intensity. 'I didn't think you were missing me that much,' he said when he got his mouth free. 'Especially as you were having such a busy time.'

She blew a raspberry and sat on the bed to unlace her walking shoes. 'Do you believe everything you hear?'

He sat beside her. 'In your case, yes. Because it's usually true.' Gently he forced her back to lie down, rested on his elbow beside her. 'Oh, my darling girl. When I think of those thugs...'

'I had to do it, Clive. Once they got me on a boat to Europe...'

'Absolutely. I was thinking of the fact that they raped you.'

'Well, that made it easier.'

'And you're not harmed?'

'I don't think so. But you'd better make sure.' She got up, took off her dress, then her underclothes.

'We have a lot to talk about,' he remarked.

'How long have you got?'

'I'm afraid only a couple of days. You know what Billy's like.'

'How is the old buzzard?'

'More buzzard-like every day.'

'And I assume I am still not his dish of

the day.'

'I have an idea that he is secretly as much in love with you as any other man.'

'Brrr.' Naked, she lay down beside him. 'Hold me, Clive. Hold me very tight.'

'You don't mean you want sex? After what you've been through.'

'No, I do not want sex, not right this minute. Although I'm hoping it will happen, eventually. I just want to be held in your arms.'

He obliged, nuzzled her hair as he hugged her. 'What was the worst?'

'The knowledge that out there, all the time, there are people waiting, watching, planning my destruction.'

'There are going to be a hell of a lot more, when this breaks. You do realize that?'

'Must it break?'

'Here in the States, perhaps not. I have tremendous confidence in Donovan. And Joe. But what happened must filter back to Moscow in due course. You have to pray that no Russian army ever marches into Berlin, at least while you are there.'

Anna frowned. 'Can that possibly happen?'

'It doesn't look too likely, at this moment. But ... You know your people have come to a complete halt, still short of Moscow?'

'That's because of the weather. As soon as it improves they'll be on the march again.'

'Darling, the weather is not going to improve, until next April at the earliest. You know that.'

'They are still totally confident in Berlin.'

'Yes, but none of your big boys has ever spent a winter in Russia. You have.' She hugged him tighter yet, and he kissed the top of her head. 'You know we'll bring you out, whenever the going gets really rough.'

'And you know I can't come out, at least for the foreseeable future.'

He tilted her head back to kiss her mouth. 'I just wish I had your guts.'

They were interrupted by the arrival of lunch. Anna put on a dressing gown and left Clive in the bedroom while she admitted the house-keeper into the sitting room. 'Is Birgit being looked after?' she asked.

'Oh, indeed, Countess. She is such a sweet child.'

'Thank you.' She closed the door and was joined by Clive. 'A bottle of cold hock.' She held it up. 'Quite a good one, too. Isn't Eleanor a dear?'

He sat opposite her. 'Almost too good to be true. How long have you known her?'

Anna poured. 'Two days.'

Clive put down his fork.

'Don't panic,' Anna said. 'She's Joe's mother, and absolutely trustworthy. Joe says so.'

'And you trust him.'

'Don't you?'

'I'm not quite sure.'

'Ah.' She drank some wine. 'I should explain that.'

'You don't have to.'

'I want to. You remember Chalyapov, my target in Moscow?'

'I never actually met him.'

'But you knew all about him. Well, of course, Heydrich knew all about how I got out of the Lubianka. He is quite sure Joe wouldn't have risked so much if he hadn't been my lover. So Joe was my target here. A job of work. It took some time. My brief was the same: don't push, let him come to me. They were quite sure this would happen very rapidly. Well, so was I. But it didn't. We even saw each other at a couple of parties, and he took no notice. I won't pretend I wasn't a bit miffed. But he was apparently sizing me up, and watching what I was doing, very carefully. He's a cautious man in some ways. Then all of a sudden he picked me up, took me back to his flat, and, well ... I was working, and he gave me a lot of valuable information. But I also felt I owed him a lot more than one. It was only afterwards that he confessed that he had moved, then, because he had learned you were in New York, and reckoned that once you got to Washington, there'd be no more room for him.' She gazed at him. 'And he was right.'

It was his turn to drink some wine. 'As Joe himself confessed. But you didn't have to confess anything.'

'I told you, I wanted to.'

He leaned across the table to squeeze her hand. 'This information...'

'Berlin wanted to know under what circumstances the States would enter the war. Joe convinced me there were no circumstances, barring an attack on America, that would bring them in.'

'What about the Final Solution?'

'I didn't tell him about that. I asked him, hypothetically, what would be US reaction if the Nazis started murdering the Jews on a big scale, and he said they would not even regard that as a *casus belli*. So, what about the Final Solution?'

Clive grimaced. 'They won't buy it.'

'Do they suppose I made it up?'

Her tone had not changed, but he could tell she was bristling. 'No, no. But they suppose you must have overheard some hypothetical conversation and taken it seriously. It's just too outrageous a concept for the average civilized Englishman to be able to accept.'

'Suppose I told you that I was present in the Chancellery, seated in a chair before Hitler's desk, when Heydrich made the proposal.'

'You mean you're that close to the Fuehrer?'

'I was on that occasion. And the odds are I will be again. He seemed to take a shine to me.'

'Well, that at least proves he's human. But that could be very interesting. It could be vital.'

Anna put down her knife and fork. 'I hope you're not thinking what I think you're thinking. Berlin is not Moscow, and Hitler is not Stalin. And I didn't even make that one. Anyway, I thought you British didn't go in for skulduggery like political assassination.'

'As Billy said to me just before I left London, if we are going to win this war we are going to have to start thinking as thuggishly as the enemy. But there is no way we are going to sacrifice you. So you reckon your job here is finished?'

'Yes. But no one knows that except us. I can stay here as long as you're here.'

'And then it's back to Heydrich. You'll be going to Prague?'

It was Anna's turn to pull a face. 'No. I have been seconded to Reichsfuehrer Himmler. Anyway, I don't have very happy memories of Prague, as you know.'

He nodded. 'And you're probably well out of it now. Your ex-boyfriend has been cutting quite a swathe.'

'Doing what?'

'Well, just for starters, the day after he arrived, he arrested the Bohemian prime minister, Elias, and had him deported to Germany and sentenced to death.'

'Shit!'

'The sentence has, we believe, been commuted to imprisonment, but we're not sure that's much of an improvement. Anyway, Heydrich is arresting people all over the place, and hanging quite a few of them.'

'He said he'd clean the situation up in a year, and be back in Berlin.'

'When he will want you back again.'

'I suppose he will.'

'Anna...'

'Please, Clive. You know there is nothing either you or I can do about the situation, until you win the war. I wish to God you'd hurry up and do that. Meanwhile...' She wiped her lips with her napkin. 'Let's make love. These two or three days may have to last me a long time.'

'I won't say welcome back,' Baxter commented. 'You're two weeks overdue.'

Clive seated himself before the desk. 'A few things came up.'

'Including your dick, I suppose.'

'I will overlook that piece of gratuitous vulgarity,' Clive said. 'And I won't bore you with the difficulties, not to mention the hazards, of getting across the Atlantic, especially coming this way. However, have you heard of the OSS?'

Baxter considered. 'Doesn't ring a bell. Does it stand for something?'

'It stands for the Office of Strategic Studies.'

'Is that supposed to interest me?'

'It should, because it certainly will in the days ahead. It is a brand new and top-secret US State Department. Something like us, with knobs on.'

'Which is so secret they told you all about it?'

'Things came up.' He held up his finger. 'Just don't say it. This department is headed by William Donovan. Maybe you've heard of him?'

'The fellow they call Wild Bill? And they've put him in charge of a secret government department? They need their heads examined.'

'Or they are moving in our direction, for all their denials. He's still recruiting, finding his feet. But one of his first recruits was Joe Andrews.'

'Your old buddy-buddy. So?'

'Well, there was a problem, with Anna.'

'Oh, Jesus Christ! There is always a problem with Anna. What now?'

'It involves the Russians.'

Baxter reached for his pipe.

'Obviously, they regard her as a German assassin who tried to bump off Stalin.'

'She *is* a German assassin who tried to bump off Stalin.'

Clive ignored the interruption. 'And who managed, mysteriously, to escape the Lubianka. Obviously, they would like her back, to stand trial. And unfortunately they discovered that she was in Washington.'

'Don't tell me they nabbed her?'

'Yes, they did.'

'Shit!'

'Why, Billy, I never knew you cared.'

'I have never denied that she is useful to us. And I had something important for her to do. Ah well, if she's gone, she's gone. I don't imagine they are going to let her get out of the Lubianka again.'

'Anna is alive and well and is at this moment sunning herself in Virginia.'

'You mean this OSS lot got involved and got her out? Good for them. But won't there be repercussions?'

'The repercussions are likely to be endless. She wasn't actually rescued by the OSS. Well, not until after the event. Anna very seldom needs rescuing by anybody.'

Baxter paused, fingers deep in his tobacco pouch. 'Oh, Jesus! Don't tell me. How many?'

'There were apparently six Russians, or Communist sympathizers, involved in kidnapping her and taking her to a remote location.'

'From which she escaped. How many did she have to shoot to get out?'

'Ah ... all of them.'

Baxter dropped the pouch; tobacco scattered across the blotting pad.

'Fortunately,' Clive hurried on, 'she had already contacted Joe, and his people were able to help. As I said, there are bound to be repercussions, but I know they are hoping to get Anna out of the country before the story breaks.'

Baxter used his hand to sweep tobacco back into the pouch, clearly concentrating hard. 'You do understand, Clive, that the Russians are our allies?'

'I prefer to think of them as bed-mates of convenience.'

'That may be so, but we simply cannot have one of our people going about bumping off their operatives in droves.'

'The Russians do not know that she is one of ours.'

Baxter began to fill his pipe. 'I suppose that's something.'

'But the Americans do now. At least, the OSS does.'

Baxter struck a match. 'You mean your buddy-buddy Andrews did not prove as trustworthy as you thought?'

'I mean that in order to dig Anna out of her hole, he had to employ the resources of his entire department, including Donovan.'

'Well, then, that's rather blown her, hasn't it? Not that it matters.'

'Not necessarily. They are willing to make our secret their secret. But they want a share.' Again he hurried on, as Baxter stared at him. 'I told them, of course, that I could not agree to anything without the consent of my superiors.'

'I think that was very wise of you.'

'But I think we should agree.'

'Because if we don't agree, they will throw Anna to the wolves, or the Soviets, or whatever.'

'There is that point, certainly. But there is an even more important point: if we agree to share our top agent in Germany, at their request, well, that's virtually co-belligerency. The OSS was set up by Roosevelt himself, and is subject only to him. Therefore, whatever they do has his approval.'

'I thought you knew the Yanks well enough to understand that they don't share, they take over.'

'Anna is our girl. And she will remain our girl.'

'Because she's your girl.'

Clive met his gaze. 'Yes.'

Baxter returned the stare appraisingly; he had known Clive long enough to tell when his subordinate was unsure of himself. 'I'll go along with what you propose. It so happens that we need Anna to carry out a most important task for us. She is at last going to earn her keep.'

Clive raised his eyebrows. Billy had always been sceptical about using Anna at all.

'Let's talk about her German boyfriend, Reinhard Heydrich.'

'Come in, Countess.' The Ambassador came round his desk to take Anna's hands. 'You have read the report?'

'Yes, your Excellency.'

He escorted her to a comfortable chair, sat beside her. 'I have, of course, lodged a formal protest, but they are adamant. "Behaviour inappropriate for a foreign diplomat and harmful to the interests of the United States." What really annoys me is that they have supplied no information as to what this "inappropriate behaviour" is. Or was.' He paused to regard her, hopefully.

Anna shrugged. 'I suppose it has something to do with the fact that I found it necessary to seduce a senior official in the Administration.'

'Good heavens!' The ambassador was suitably shocked.

'I'm afraid it goes with the job,' Anna pointed out.

'Ah! Yes. And have you succeeded in, ah, obtaining the information Berlin requires?'

'Yes, sir. I think I have done that.'

'Then you are to be congratulated. Now, I imagine you will be pleased to be getting home.'

What he meant, she knew, was 'we will be pleased to see the back of you'.

'You will be travelling by a Portuguese

vessel,' he went on, 'called the *Pakoma*, en route to Lisbon. We have informed Berlin of this so there should be no trouble with U-boats. I will wish you good fortune in carrying out your, ah, future duties for the Reich.'

'Thank you, sir.' Anna stood up. 'Heil Hitler!'

As the Embassy had clearly washed their hands of her, she had no worries about leaving the building for her lunch date. Birgit stayed behind to complete their packing; they were boarding that evening. She had hoped Joe would be there, but Donovan was alone, at least at the reserved table; she did not doubt that he had a number of his people strategically placed as bodyguards.

'Countess!' He squeezed her glove. 'Or may I call you Anna?'

'Please do. What do I call you?'

'I think, on this occasion, Bill.' He gestured her to a chair.

'And on other occasions?'

'In public, I suppose it should be Mr Donovan, as I am now your employer.'

'One of them,' Anna reminded him.

'Oh, quite. Shall we order?' The maître d' was hovering.

They chose, and an aperitif arrived.

'I promised myself this treat, from the moment Joe first told me about you,' Donovan said.

'What treat?'

'Lunching with you.'

'Oh. I didn't reckon I could have made much of an impression when we first met. I must have looked like a bag lady.'

'Then I would have to say you would have been the most glamorous bag lady ever. But very human.'

'And now?'

'Oh, now, you're incredible.'

'But inhuman.'

'I hope not.'

'Ah.'

'Do you always consider everything in the ultimate?'

'In my life it usually comes to that, Mr Donovan. Bill.'

'And you survive by anticipating.'

'You could be right. I've never really thought about it like that.'

'But you have survived, which is good. I gather there have been situations before. Like in the Lubianka.'

'Yes.'

'And others?'

Anna drank some wine. 'Yes.'

'Dare I ask how many? Please believe me, I'm not prying, per se. I like to know as much about my employees as I can.'

'You understand that you are not my principal employer, Bill.'

'I understand that. I'd give a whole lot to know which is number one.'

'MI6 is number one. As long as they do not compromise my position. You know about that?'

'About your family? Joe filled me in. So we're

number two. As long as we don't compromise your position in the Reich.'

'As long as you don't do anything that might compromise my family. And let's face it, Mr Donovan – Bill, right now you are a fringe player as regards the future of either me or my family.'

'You are a singularly forthright young woman. But you're damned right. I can only say that it's the profound hope of myself, and my people, that that may change, one day. One day soon. But you understand that you have to keep in contact with our people in Berlin.'

'I understand that I am placing myself in very great danger, unless these people are absolutely reliable.'

'There will be only one, until Joe can get there. And I am sure you'll agree that he will be absolutely reliable. You have the contact information?'

'Yes. But did you say that Joe is coming to Berlin?'

'Just as soon as it can be arranged. I would have thought that would please you.'

'It pleases me very much. It's just that he never mentioned it.'

'I told him that I would put you in the picture. He's pretty pleased too. But right now, you haven't answered my question. Which was how many times have you had to extricate yourself from a situation like that Russian one? Joe has told me about the Lubianka.'

'I agreed that there have been others.'

'Yes, you did. How many?'

'I'd have to think about that.'

'And you can still smile about it. Well, let's rephrase the question. You have obviously had to shoot your way out of a few situations in your time. Have you any idea how many people you have had to hit to do that?'

'You are asking how many people I have had to kill.'

'The two aren't necessarily synonymous.'

'In my case, they are.'

He studied her for several seconds while their main course was served. Then he said, 'Yes. I imagine they were. Have you any idea?'

'Oh, yes. It is now twenty-one.'

Donovan had raised his wine glass to his lips. Now he almost choked. 'Holy sh— I beg your pardon. How old are you?'

'I am twenty-one years old.'

'One for every year of your life. Tell me, have you ever heard of our most famous outlaw?'

'I suppose you mean Jesse James.'

'Well, I guess that's right. But I wasn't thinking of him. The guy I had in mind wasn't technically an outlaw at all, in the sense of robbing banks or trains. He was a hired gun. His name was William Bonney. They called him Billy the Kid.'

'I have heard of Billy the Kid.'

'Well, they reckon he was the deadliest killer in the West. But by the time he was twenty-one he had only managed nineteen kills.'

'Am I supposed to be flattered?'

'You sure have to be respected.'

'I am glad you said that. The way I look at it, sir, is that I am fighting a war. If I were a fighter pilot who had shot down twenty-one enemy aircraft, would they not call me an ace, and give me a medal?'

'That is a very good point. Maybe, when this business is over, we'll be able to arrange that.'

'Would you?' Her face lit up in a way he had not seen before, and which redoubled her beauty, if that were possible. 'I shall look forward to that.'

'So shall I. The trouble with Billy the Kid was that he never got past twenty-one. He was killed at that age.'

Anna gazed at him. 'I know,' she said.

Seven

The Mission

'I have received a coded telegram from London,' Joe announced. 'MI6.'

'Well, now. Don't tell me they've changed their minds about sharing Anna,' Donovan said.

'It reads: "Imperative contact A on arrival. Please advise ship and destination. Regards C."'

'Hmm.'

'Do you think they're trying to pull a fast one?'

'I'd say it's more likely that something has come up.'

'Then shouldn't they be sharing it with us?'

'Simmer down,' Donovan recommended. 'The deal was that we share *Anna*, not every scheme or problem the Brits may have. You'll be seeing Anna in a month, and I'm sure you'll be able to persuade her to tell you what's going on. When does she dock in Lisbon?'

'I think the second.'

'Five days. Give Bartley the info he wants.'

'Just like that?'

'Joe, we have persuaded these people to work

215

with us, at least in this direction. We need to play it straight until we see how things turn out. I can't see that any crisis involving Anna or what she does has arisen over here, apart from the big one, which both we and MI6 know about. I imagine that Bartley is as uptight as you are, and is uptight because she's been hanging about over here for the last few weeks instead of hot-footing it back to Berlin. You say she's got everything she came for?'

'As far as I know, yes.'

'And Bartley knows that?'

'Yes.'

'And I assume he also knows that you and the Countess are not exactly restricted to surnames only?'

'Well...'

'It's an axiom of our business that any controller who gets too fond of one of his people is a risk, both to the agent and himself. And when he gets to the stage of being jealous of her he becomes a walking disaster. I would hate you to go down that road, Joe, although I admit it wouldn't be difficult. As for Bartley, he's not our concern.'

'Anna is. She's certain to be met by Nazi agents in Lisbon.'

'Joe, I have an idea that she's handled this sort of situation before. And we damned well know she can handle situations. Reply to that telegram, absolutely straight, and we'll keep our fingers crossed.'

'Yes, sir. And if Anna winds up in Ravensbrueck? Or against a wall?'

'Joe, I just told you: we are taking on a fully fledged agent who has proved her worth, and her ability, time and again. We can't play nursemaid. If she goes down the drain, you have my permission to shed a tear. And you know what, I may just join you. Go send that telegram.'

Rodrigues the purser was a dapper little man who wore his cap at a rakish angle and was clearly in love with his moustache. But he was equally clearly in love with his most glamorous passenger, as was the entire crew and most of the male passengers. And now he had a reason for approaching her, confidentially. Even if he had no idea how he was going to be received. 'You'll excuse me, Countess.'

Anna was sitting in a deckchair on the boat deck, where she was somewhat removed from the rest of the passengers. It was an extremely cold December day, and she was as well wrapped up as she had ever been in Moscow, wearing her sable with a matching hat, a scarf wrapped round the lower half of her face. However uncomfortable, she was waiting for a first sight of land. This was only her second trans-Atlantic voyage, and although to her relief she had not suffered from *mal de mer* on either occasion, she had been acutely aware that she was challenging the most dangerous stretch of water in the world, right at that moment. Of course, Himmler had guaranteed her safety, but that did not mean that every U-boat captain had received the necessary orders.

But now it was nearly over. And then? She had no idea to what she was returning. But she had just enjoyed, once the Russian business was behind her, the most relaxing period of her life. And despite all that had happened, and might yet happen, she had a greater sense of ultimate security than at any time since March 1938. Both the Brits and the Yanks were now on her side, and surely between them they could accomplish the salvation not only of her but of her parents and Caterina as well.

And land was just over the horizon, after more than a week at sea. They had peeled off from the Liverpool-bound convoy and been able to increase speed two days ago. So she smiled. 'Certainly, Señor Rodrigues. What can I do for you?'

Rodrigues licked his lips. 'I have a message for you.'

Anna raised her eyebrows.

'I'm afraid ... well...' Nervously he held out the form, on which the radio operator had written: 'Belinda unwell. Details in Lisbon.'

Anna's features remained calm, even as her heart pounded. 'Thank you, Señor Rodrigues.'

'Is it serious?'

'I hope not.'

'Ah. Well, we will soon be in harbour.' He pointed. 'Portugal.'

Anna looked to the east, and made out the distant low cloudbank. And what would be awaiting her there? She felt the tension creeping through her body. If she did not know what project Himmler would have dreamed up for her this time, she knew that he, and Hitler, had to be pleased with the news she was bringing back, which meant that they could continue with their plans without fear of American intervention.

But this message ... Belinda was her contact word, chosen by Baxter in a rare moment of humour, because it was the name of Clive's English girlfriend. MI6 had to know that she would be met in Lisbon by members of the Embassy staff, that she would hardly be left to herself, and that she would be on her way to Berlin within twenty-four hours. If they intended to attempt personal contact in those circumstances, Belinda had to be very unwell indeed. And yet the thought of perhaps seeing Clive again so soon had her spirits surging. So, back to patience.

It was a slow journey past Cascais and up the Tagus, with the sandbanks to starboard and the hills of Estoril to port. But Customs and Immigration came alongside in a launch while they were still underway, and the passengers were all processed by the time they docked.

'The Countess von Widerstand,' remarked the Immigration Officer, peering from her passport to her face. 'You are staying in Portugal?'

'Sadly, no. I am just passing through, on my way home.'

'And your home is?'

'Berlin.'

'Of course. I will wish you a pleasant stay in our country and a safe onward journey.'

'Countess von Widerstand!' The slim young man in the well-cut dark suit and the little moustache clicked his heels and bent over her hand. 'This is a great pleasure. My car is waiting.'

'My maid, and my things,' Anna said.

'They will be taken care of and brought to the Embassy.'

Anna turned to find Birgit, who had become temporarily lost in the throng of passengers behind her, but who now forced her way towards her. 'It is so good to feel dry land beneath my feet, Countess.'

'Absolutely. Now, Birgit, I am going with...?'

Another click of the heels. 'Helmuth Essermann, Countess.'

'And you will be coming with...?'

Essermann indicated another very well dressed man, although older and stockily built. 'Johann Udermann, my assistant. He will see to your transport, Fraulein, as soon as all the luggage is ashore.'

'Oh.' Birgit looked disappointed.

'I will see you at the Embassy,' Anna assured her, and got into the back seat of the Mercedes saloon. Essermann sat beside her, and the car moved off. 'May I ask in whose custody I am?'

He gave a quick smile. 'My dear Countess, I am your escort. My card.'

220

Anna glanced at it. *Shit,* she thought. *SD!* 'I am flattered, Herr Essermann. Am I in danger, or under arrest?'

Another deprecatory smile. 'Reichsfuehrer Himmler merely wishes to ensure your safe return, Countess. I am entirely at your disposal.'

Which means, she thought, *that you are going to be at my elbow throughout the journey.* Well, that was a conundrum Clive would have to solve, as she had no idea where he was.

The Ambassador had obviously been given a file on her, and was positively obsequious. As a result, so was his staff.

'Do you think we could go to a bullfight?' Birgit asked as she dressed her mistress for dinner. 'I have always wanted to see a bullfight.'

'What a bloodthirsty little creature you are,' Anna commented. 'I hate to spoil your anticipation, but I think in Portugal they do not actually kill the bull. At least not in the arena.'

'Oh. Are we going to Spain from here?'

'We will be driving through Spain, certainly, to catch a train in Madrid. But I understand that is all due to happen tomorrow. Aren't you in a hurry to get home?'

'Oh, yes, Countess, but it has been a lovely holiday. Not at all like Moscow. That place, Virginia, oh, it was heavenly. And the people were so nice.'

'Well, maybe we'll be able to go back there, one day.'

'But I don't understand about that man who

came to spend a few days with you.'

'You mean Mr Andrews? It was his house, goose.'

'No, the other one. The one who came before Mr Andrews. Wasn't he English?'

Anna frowned. Birgit had never dared question, or even mention, any of the other men who had drifted through her life. So much so that she had never considered the possibility that the maid might be doing some private thinking. Birgit had accepted that the death of Hannah Gehrig's daughter Marlene in Moscow had been suicide: she had had no idea that Marlene had been another who had come too close to the truth. Nor had she pursued the matter of Pieter Schlutz. Of course, by the time she had come home that day all trace of what had happened had been removed, but she did know that she had left the man handcuffed and at the mercy of her mistress.

Now suddenly she had become a menace. But Anna was reluctant to consider getting rid of her. She refused to believe that she was either cold-blooded or vicious. As she had told Donovan, she believed that she was fighting a war; that it was a very private war was her business. And in wars, people got killed. Those were enemies. It was difficult to regard Birgit as an enemy.

But if she was not to be disposed of, she had to be taken on board, in so far as it was possible, and it would involve lying. But Anna had long discovered that just about any lie will be accepted if it is big enough and plausible enough: she had been living nothing but a lie for the past three years. So, watching the woman in the mirror as Birgit piled her hair on the top of her head, she said, 'Yes, Mr Bartley is English. Do you know what I do, Birgit?'

'You work for the SD, Countess.'

'And do you know what the SD does?'

'No, Countess.'

'But you know it is a government depart-ment?'

'Yes, Countess.'

'Well, I can tell you, in the strictest confi-dence, that the business of the SD is the gather-ing of information, about other governments, and what they are doing, or planning to do. To accomplish this, we have to have agents placed in important positions all over the world, gather-ing information, and it is my business to visit these agents and receive the information, and take it back to Reichsfuehrer Himmler.'

Birgit's eyes were as big as saucers. 'You have met the Reichsfuehrer?'

'My dear Birgit, I have met the Fuehrer him-self. But the Reichsfuehrer is my boss.'

'And Herr Bartley is one of your agents? And Herr Andrews?'

'Yes.' Anna's mind, always inclined to be mis-chievous when given the opportunity, could not help but have a mental giggle at Clive's reaction were he to know how she was labelling him.

'You must like them both very much,' Birgit said slyly.

'That goes with the job. We must keep them happy.'

'Do you think I could become an agent for the SD?'

'Who knows? If you are good, I will mention the matter to the Reichsfuehrer.'

'Ooh, Countess.'

Anna stood up and studied her jewellery; tonight she was wearing a pearl choker instead of her crucifix. And the looming crisis seemed to have been averted, hopefully forever. 'That looks very nice.' She tuned her head at a knock on the door. 'See who that is, will you? If it's from the Ambassador, tell him I'm coming right down.'

She checked her evening bag, and then Birgit returned bearing an enormous bouquet of flowers, mainly roses. 'From the Ambassador.'

'Oh, good lord! He's a married man!'

'And there's a note.' She was obviously dying to open it.

Anna took the envelope and sat down to read it. *I will find you in Madrid. I am an old school friend named Judith. Belinda.*

Anna suddenly felt very cold, and then equally very hot.

'Are you all right, Countess?' Birgit asked anxiously.

'Yes,' Anna said. 'It is a rather extravagant personal compliment, that is all.' She opened her handbag, took out her gold lighter, and set fire to the note, dropping it into an ashtray.

'Countess?' Birgit was aghast.

'I do not think it is a sentiment the gentleman would wish to be broadcast,' Anna said.

Then it was necessary to go down to dinner, and be the beautiful sophisticate everyone expected, charming men and women alike with her smile and her air of innocence. Her brain was spinning, in the short term wondering which of the Embassy staff was the British agent who had delivered the note.

But the longer term was the more thought-consuming. She was going to be contacted, and not by Clive. But if they were taking such a risk it had to be something of the most vital importance. Essermann was now at her elbow, where he spent the entire evening. He was not actually seated next to her at dinner, but opposite her, watching her every move. Was this physical attraction merely him obeying his orders to protect her, or was it suspicion? But that was paranoia. The point was that he obviously had no intention of letting her out of his sight.

As they were leaving at dawn the next morning she had every excuse to retire early. She did not really expect to sleep, but the bed seemed to sway to and fro as her bunk on the ship had done, and she had had sufficient wine to dull her senses, and awoke perfectly fresh at five, in time to have a bath and breakfast before going down.

Birgit was of course in a state of high excitement, obviously dying to ask if her mistress had made contact with her secret admirer, but not daring to raise the subject.

They again travelled in two cars, both Mercedes saloons. Birgit and Udermann were in the front vehicle, Essermann and Anna in the rear, sitting together in the back seat. 'I'm afraid it is an all-day drive to Madrid,' Essermann explained. 'But it is interesting countryside, and we shall stop for lunch.'

Anna inclined her head. Much as she was telling herself that it would be pointless and perhaps dangerous either to speculate or anticipate, she could not help wondering what the next few hours would bring. America had been a different world to anything she had known. That even included her encounter with the NKVD. That apart, the overwhelming sensation had been one of living in an utterly confident society for the first time in her life. They knew that with a vast ocean to either side of them, and the strength to dominate either of their immediate neighbours, to north and south, they were totally secure from the problems of the rest of the world. Even in non-military matters, as Joe had pointed out, they had all the natural resources, save perhaps for fringe necessities like tin or rubber, and all the food that they required. They feared no one, and thus had no need to hate anyone.

What a contrast to Europe, she thought. Even the Nazis, so apparently powerful, were driven by fear. They had climbed on to the back of a tiger, and whipped the beast into movement. Now they dared not halt that forward momentum, much less attempt to dismount, because if they did the beast was liable to turn and devour them.

'A brown study,' Essermann remarked. 'Did you have a difficult time in the United States?'

'I would not say so,' Anna replied. 'I got what I wanted. What Reichsfuehrer Himmler wanted,' she added for good measure.

'Then perhaps you are unhappy at the thought of returning to Germany.'

She turned her head. 'Why should I be unhappy about that, Herr Essermann? Germany is my home.'

'Of course. Do you not think that as we are to be close companions for the next two days, we could drop the formality? My name is Helmuth. And you are...'

Here we go again, she thought. 'I am the Countess von Widerstand, as I think you know.'

He had been inclining towards her, his hand sliding across the seat. Now he jerked upright, and the hand was withdrawn, while his features froze.

Anna smiled at him. 'I really do not wish to hurt you, or you career, Herr Essermann, but I think that you should know that I am the personal property of Reichsfuehrer Himmler.'

Now he seemed to coagulate. The rest of their journey was a silent affair. But Anna could not control her growing tension as they approached the capital, simply because she had no idea what to expect. It was surprisingly cold when they reached their hotel, just on dusk, and she put on her sable, which she had discarded for the journey. 'Madrid is quite high up,' Essermann explained, and having apparently decided to make the best of a bad job, added, 'Will you join me for dinner?'

'Certainly. If you will give me time to have a bath and change my clothes.'

'That is not a problem. The Spanish eat very late. Shall we say, eight o'clock in the bar, for an aperitif?'

'That sounds delightful.' Anna entered the foyer, where Birgit was waiting for her. 'Do we have to check in?'

'No, no,' Essermann said. 'That is taken care of. Udermann!'

His aide stepped forward with a key.

'And my maid?'

'I have mine already, Countess. I am across the hall.'

'Well, then, eight o'clock, Herr Essermann.' She turned towards the lifts, and was checked by a shout.

'Anna! Anna Fehrbach! What brings you to Madrid?'

The woman hurrying towards her was approximately her own age, not very tall but decidedly elegant, with rounded features and red-gold hair, which, like Anna, she wore long. Her clothes were expensive, and she carried a very small dog in her arms. And she was speaking German.

'Judith?' Anna asked. 'Can it be you?'

'It is so good to see you, after so long.' Judith kissed her on the cheek, while the dog nuzzled her breast. 'You'll never guess who I bumped

228

into the other day. Belinda! You remember Belinda?'

'I do indeed,' Anna said. 'But ... what are you doing here?'

'I asked you the same thing, remember?'

'Ahem,' Essermann remarked.

'Ah,' Anna said. 'This is Herr Essermann. Herr Essermann, allow me to present Fraulein—'

'No, no,' Judith said. 'I am married. Did you not know? It was in all the papers. I am now the Countess de Sotomayer.'

'How lovely for you,' Anna said. 'And your husband?'

'He is somewhere around. He is joining me here for dinner. Anna! You must dine with us. Carlos would love to meet you.' She lowered her voice into an arch whisper. 'But I must warn you, he's in real estate and can be a bit of a bore. He's certain to try to sell you something.'

'Sounds exciting,' Anna said. 'I'd so like to meet him. I'm sorry, Helmuth, you will have to excuse me for this evening. But we can have lunch and dinner together tomorrow on the train. I will see you in an hour, Judith.' She patted the dog on the head, smiled at the flabbergasted Essermann and hurried to the lift.

She was still panting when she gained her room. Clive was here after all, and in an hour she would be with him. She did not suppose they would be able to do more than talk, unless they were very fortunate, and of course it was only a few weeks since they had last been together, but

229

as she never knew how long they would be separated each time, each time they could see each other was a bonus.

I am in love, she thought, kicking off her shoes, and then wondered if he was also having it off with the rather glamorous young woman who was pretending to be his wife.

A tap on the door and Birgit came in. 'Ah, Birgit, did you have a nice drive?'

'It was very boring, Countess. That man Udermann hardly said a word.'

'His boss was rather uncommunicative too,' Anna agreed, which was somewhat unfair on Essermann, she thought. She then frowned as she remembered that Birgit knew Clive by sight. Birgit appeared to have entirely accepted her explanation as to their relationship, but to see him again so soon, and in such surroundings ... On the other hand, Birgit should not be in either the hotel bar or the main dining room. It was still a risk, though. 'Run me a bath, would you?'

'Yes, Countess.'

She hurried into the bathroom. Anna undressed and followed, to stand in the doorway. 'I hope you are being well looked after.'

'Oh, yes, Countess. It seems a very comfortable hotel.'

'And what about your dinner?'

'Udermann wishes to take me out. He claims to have been in Madrid before, often, and to know a very nice restaurant.'

'I hope you accepted.'

230

'Well ... I don't really like him.'

'It pays to get on with SD agents.'

'Have I your permission, Countess?'

'Of course you do. Ah.'

There was a rap on the door. Anna had anticipated this. She wrapped herself in the towelling bathrobe supplied, which came to just below her thighs, and herself opened the door. 'Is there a problem?'

'I wish to speak with you,' Essermann announced, his gaze drifting down to her exposed legs.

'Well, that is obvious,' Anna pointed out, and stepped back. 'I hope you are not going to let my bath water get cold.'

Essermann entered the room and closed the door. 'You are welcome to take your bath, Countess. We can talk while you do so.'

'I must say,' Anna remarked, 'you deserve ten out of ten for perseverance. But I do not think that would be a good idea. I am sure the Reichsfuehrer would not approve.' She sat on the settee and crossed her knees, the bathrobe riding up. Essermann sat opposite; she reckoned he could just about see her pubic hair. 'So what is it you wish to say?'

'I cannot permit you to fulfil this dinner engagement with that woman.'

Anna raised her eyebrows. 'You cannot permit? Are you my superior officer?'

'You are my responsibility.'

'My safety is your responsibility. I am hardly going to be at risk in the middle of a crowded restaurant when dining with an old friend.'

'The woman is an impostor.'

'What makes you say that?'

'Well, Countess de Sotomayer. What sort of a name is that?'

'I have no idea. She may well be an impostor, at this moment. But I know she was at school with me. We were the best of friends. To snub her now would be both rude and suspicious. Anyway, the best way to find out if she is an impostor is to have dinner with her.'

'But don't you realize, Countess, that if she was at school with you, she will know that your family, and yourself, were arrested in 1938, and will want to know what happened and why you are now apparently a wealthy socialite?'

'Of course she will not. Judith is a year older than me, and she left school, and indeed Austria, in 1937. She may wish to know what it was like, what happened, after you people moved in, but I can easily handle that.'

'I do not like it.'

'Then I suggest you stop thinking about it. Birgit?'

The maid had appeared in the bathroom doorway. 'Your bath is ready, Countess.'

'Thank you.' Anna uncrossed her legs and stood up.

Essermann stood also. 'I shall have to put this in my report.'

'Of course. You must put in your report everything that you think necessary. I will see you in the morning, Herr Essermann.'

232

He was, of course, in the bar when she entered, but at a table by himself on the far side of the room. In any event, she had eyes only for Clive, who was seated with his 'wife', and rose as she came towards them.

'Fraulein Fehrbach.' He bent over her hand. 'How nice to meet you.' He spoke German. 'Judith has told me so much about you. You'll take a glass of champagne?'

'Thank you.'

There was a bottle in the ice bucket on the table; beside it was a folder, lying on top of a briefcase. Anna sat down; Clive poured, and sat beside her. Judith smiled at them both.

'Judith tells me you may be interested in buying real estate,' Clive said, continuing to speak German; there were people seated quite close by and waiters drifting to and fro. 'I have some very good properties here. Would you like to look at them now, or after dinner?'

Anna could tell that he was very tense, which was unusual for Clive. 'I think I would like to look at them now, Count.'

'Well, then...' He opened the folder, spread it in front of her.

Anna sipped her drink and scanned the page. There were two properties advertised, with exterior photographs. But the text, commencing with the first one, had nothing to do with property.

Adolf Hitler will be fifty-three next April, and we are informed that he is not in the best of health. You may be able to confirm this. Anna recalled the pill-taking ceremony at the Wilhelmstrasse and the banter that had gone with it. *Whether this is true or not, our source informs us that he is being pressured by his advisers to name, and install, a successor. Since the defection of Hess, this successor has been assumed to be Goering, but Goering is in even worse health and is also a drug addict. Goebbels would seem ideal, but the fact that he is a cripple rules him out as the leader of a nation of Aryan supermen. Thus it must be Himmler. But we are informed that Hitler recognizes Himmler as an essentially uncertain man, capable of carrying out orders, but not of giving them. We are reliably informed that Hitler is inclining towards Heydrich.*

Anna raised her head. Clive was gazing at her. 'You may have an opinion on that too,' he said. Anna resumed reading.

This cannot be permitted to happen. We identify Heydrich, thanks in part to your reports, as the strongest, most clear-headed, ruthless and therefore dangerous man in the Nazi regime. Were he to be given supreme power the consequences could be catastrophic. We are thinking in particular of his role in devising this so-called Final Solution.

We are informed that this appointment may well be made when Heydrich returns from his Prague mission, probably this coming summer, and of course, when he is back in Germany, surrounded by his people, he is virtually untouchable. Save perhaps by you. But we are reluctant to sacrifice you, at this time. How nice to be needed, she thought. *Therefore his elimination must take place before he leaves Prague. We wish you to engineer things so that you join him there. We do not wish you to endanger yourself. A picked team is being sent from England, who will contact you via the Belinda code. Your task will be to provide them with whatever information they need as to Heydrich's movements and timings. That is all you need to do. You may grieve most whole-heartedly when he is dead. Until then, good fortune. Belinda.*

Anna closed the folder. 'These houses appear very warm, but they are made of essentially cold materials, aren't they?'

'All houses are basically cold, Countess. Anna. May I call you Anna?'

'Please do.'

'How warm they can become depends on who lives in them. However, I wish you to know that if none of those properties interest you, you have the right to say so. In fact, I do not care for any of them myself, and have told my associates this. But they insist I should show them to you.'

'They do interest me, Count. To own a property like this has long been my dream. It's just that I have not seen a proposal like this before.'

'I know. I suppose, when you come down to it, all property companies are basically alike. I can only promise you that no one is going to let you down this time.'

'And I must believe you. But you do realize

235

that if I purchase this property, the neighbours may not be very happy. It may involve them in a great deal of inconvenience, to say the least.'

'We have taken soundings in the neighbourhood, and they are for it. Regardless of the possible consequences.'

'Then I would certainly like to look at it. But there may be a problem. My business affairs keep me extremely busy. I may not be able to arrange a visit to the prime site.'

'If you cannot, we will understand. But my associates would be very disappointed. It really is necessary that we start selling. Right away.'

Anna nodded. 'If I can possibly get away, I will do so.'

'I am sure you will. There is one more thing for you to read.'

Anna turned the page. *The codeword is Operation Daybreak.*

'Operation daybreak,' she muttered, committing the words to memory.

'Well, then,' Judith said brightly. 'Shall we eat?'

Anna tapped the folder. 'I would hate to think of this falling into the wrong hands. Someone might whip the property out from beneath my nose.'

Clive picked up the folder and placed it in his briefcase. 'Wherever this folder goes, I go with it.'

'Will I see you again?' Anna asked over dinner.

'Of course. But not on this trip,' Clive said. He

continued to speak German, but there was such a babble of conversation and noise in the crowded restaurant that the risk of anyone being able to overhear what he was saying was minimal. 'I'm on my way back to London tomorrow, and I think it would be too risky for us to attempt to get together tonight.'

'Oh.' Disappointed, she looked at Judith.

'You will see me,' Judith said. 'As I am established as a Spanish national, I can travel throughout Europe as I please.'

'Judith will act as our go-between.'

'I see. And Bartoli?'

'What are your feelings about Bartoli?'

'I'm afraid I don't find him very reliable. He's too uptight.'

'Our own opinion. We haven't heard from him for a month.'

Shit, Anna thought. Had something gone wrong with the disposal of Edda Hedermann? But she decided not to involve Clive in that problem; there was nothing he could do about it, anyway.

'But as he knows all about you,' Clive said, 'we can't just fire him. So you will continue to use the Boutique, and so will we. But we do not wish him to know anything about this property, or about Judith, who will contact you personally.'

Anna smiled at the titian-haired woman. 'I shall look forward to that. Well...' She finished her wine.

'Anna...' Clive's hand drifted across the table

to touch her fingers. 'You are *not* to become personally involved. Information as to times and routes is all that we require of you. If anything were to happen to you...'

She moved her finger against his palm. 'But you want our man out of the equation.'

He hesitated a moment, then nodded. 'It could play a vital part in winning the war.'

'What was that man showing you last night before dinner?' Essermann asked, sitting opposite Anna as the train rumbled north, out of Spain and into France.

'A real estate brochure. That is his business, do you not remember? Real estate.'

'And he seriously supposed you would be able to buy one of his properties?'

'I have no idea. Perhaps he looked at my jewellery and made the assumption that I am a wealthy woman.'

'What did you tell him about yourself?'

'I told him nothing about myself, Herr Essermann, because he did not ask. He accepted me as a friend of his wife's, and she comes from wealthy parents.'

'Which is no doubt why he married her. But she must have asked after you?'

'I told her I am working for an Austrian clothing firm. Now, really, Herr Essermann, you have asked too many questions. I would like to be left alone.'

He snorted, but looked out of the window. Anna closed her eyes. She had refused to think about the situation overnight. But now it was very necessary, both on a personal and a professional level. Almost from the moment she had entered the SS training camp, three and a half years ago, she had recognized that she was being trained for a specific purpose. To learn about men in all their aspects had been because she was required to deal with men, in all their aspects. To learn how to kill, whether with a weapon or her bare hands, and to do so ruthlessly and remorselessly, had surely not been so that she could amuse herself on her day off.

But her marriage to Bordman, as commanded by her employers, had dulled the edge of her perception of the future. She had been fulfilling a useful, even a vital, task for the Reich. Thus the command that she should assassinate Churchill, the task for which she now knew she had been trained from the beginning, had come as a shattering bolt from the blue. MI6 had extricated her from that looming catastrophe, even if she had had to help herself by committing mass murder.

When, the previous year, she had been sent to Moscow for the express purpose of seducing the womanizing commissar Ewfim Chalyapov, Stalin's right-hand man, she had waited for the order she knew had to come, as indeed it had. She owed her survival on that occasion to Joe Andrews, and so she had gone to the States with considerable apprehension, and it had actually turned out worse than she had feared. Once again she had survived thanks to the assistance of gallant – or were they merely lecherous? – men. But she had no idea how Himmler was going to regard her deportation, as it had happened before he had been able to tell her what her real mission was. At least she had been able to obtain the vital information that he had sought.

It had never occurred to her that the British Government would in turn seek to employ her as an assassin rather than merely a spy. But as Clive had said, all governments, however ostensibly upright and honest, were the same colour when it came to fighting a war. So, were they writing her off? She was sure that Clive was deeply concerned about the risk they were asking her to take. But Clive had made it very clear from the moment of their first acquaintance that for him the job, the eventual victory of his country, was far more important than the life of any individual. As it had to be for her – even if the life involved was her own. That victory remained the only hope for her parents, and while she dreamed of being there to greet them when they emerged from their prison, the important thing was that they should eventually emerge. She had to believe that Clive would honour his word.

So, time to replace doubts with professionalism. That meant getting to Prague, and resuming life as Heydrich's bed-mate. And *that* meant persuading Himmler to humour her ... and Heydrich to want her back.

She realized that her gloved hands were tightly clenched, and hastily spread her fingers and rested her hands on her knees.

Eight

Plots

'Anna!' Heinrich Himmler held her hands, but did not, as she had feared, draw her forward for an embrace. 'Welcome home. I hope you have a great deal to tell me. You are home far sooner than I expected.'

'Indeed, Herr Reichsfuehrer.'

He gestured her to a chair. 'You had no difficulties?'

Perhaps he had not, after all, intended her to murder. Or was he laying one of his traps?

She shook her head. 'None I could not surmount. But the Americans knew who I was, as I knew would happen. And when they discovered that I was seeing a lot of their important people, they deported me.'

Himmler nodded. 'Ribbentrop was informed by the Ambassador. And they did not even have the courtesy to give a reason. These people are barbaric. But are you saying that you learned nothing of value?'

'I learned everything you wished to find out, Herr Reichsfuehrer.'

He raised his eyebrows.

'I can give you a categorical assurance that America has no intention of entering this war. Oh, they do not like us, and they would like to see us defeated, which is why they are supplying the British and the Russians with material, but Roosevelt was only re-elected for an illegal third term on the guarantee that he would never send American troops to fight in Europe unless something quite exceptional happened.'

'Ah! What is this something quite exceptional? Our plans for the Jews?'

'No. I specifically raised that point, without of course going into any details. And they assured me that while all their sympathies were with the Jews, they had no intention of fighting for them. The only thing that would bring the United States into the war would be for us to attack them. I assume we have no plans to do that.'

'Of course we do not. Anna, you are a treasure. The Fuehrer will be delighted. He may well wish to see you again.'

'Thank you, Herr Reichsfuehrer. May I ask if it is possible for me to take a brief holiday?'

'I wish it were.' He took off his glasses and polished them. 'I would like to ask you a very personal question.'

Oh, Lord, Anna thought. But she smiled. 'Of course, sir.'

She watched him get up, walk round his desk and her, and go to the doors. These had been closed after her entry. Now he carefully turned the key to lock them. Then he returned to his desk, while Anna's brain whirred. Did he intend to rape her here in his office?

He sat down and stared at her. 'Tell me about your relationship with General Heydrich.'

'Sir?' She was taken entirely by surprise.

'You were his mistress, were you not?'

'Ah ... yes, sir.'

'Were you happy with that? Or did he force you?'

Not for the first time in her life, Anna felt that she was picking her way through a minefield. 'He was my commander, sir.'

'And you always do what your commander wishes?'

Here we go, Anna thought. 'It is my duty to do so, sir.'

'He confided to me, once, that he thought you hated him. In fact, that having you submit to him, knowing that you hated him, gave him greater pleasure than actually, ah, having you.'

Anna licked her lips.

'Does that anger you?'

She stared at him.

'I made him what he is, you know,' Himmler continued. 'Ten years ago he was a washed-up naval officer. He had just been cashiered. Do you know what for?'

'General Heydrich has never discussed his background with me, sir.'

'He was cashiered for womanizing in a most blatant and disgusting manner. He even used to smuggle women into his cabin on board ship.'

'Good heavens!' Anna said, suitably shocked.

244

'I saw his potential, and took him into the SS. I promoted him, introduced him to the Fuehrer. And now he wishes to betray me. Me!'

'Sir?' Now Anna was genuinely shocked, while all manner of possible scenarios raced through her mind.

'This is in confidence, of course, between you and me.' He peered at her.

'Of course, sir.'

'I have discovered that he means to displace me as Reichsfuehrer. What is more, I have learned that he plans to have himself named by the Fuehrer as heir. Can you believe that?'

'Ah ... no, sir. May I ask, does the Fuehrer know this?'

'Who knows what the Fuehrer knows, and does not know? I do know that he was very impressed by Heydrich's proposal for dealing with the Jewish question. Well, you know that. You were there.'

'Yes, sir. May I ask, is that progressing?'

'It is. Slowly. We have chosen a site for our first camp, a place called Auschwitz, securely hidden away in the Polish countryside. Work has started, but God knows when it will be ready. It is Heydrich we have to worry about. The Fuehrer is also very impressed with his handling of the Bohemian question. He is talking about bringing him back here before the summer. That will be to take my place.'

'Excuse me, Herr Reichsfuehrer, but do you know this for a fact?'

'What are facts? I watch, and I listen, and I

draw conclusions. It is my job. You have to help me, Anna. I want you to go to Prague.'

Just like that, she thought. *All my problems, solved by a simple over-anxious idiot.* But the implications... 'To do what, exactly, sir?'

'Oh, I am not seeking his assassination, not at this time. That might raise difficulties. I want you to resume your close relations with him, find out just what he is thinking, just what are his plans. If I am right, and he seeks to replace the Fuehrer, it may well be that his plan is to do this sooner rather than later. The Fuehrer may be fond of this upstart, but he will not entertain any discussion of the succession. He becomes quite demonic whenever the subject is raised. If you can obtain proof, or even a strong indication, that Heydrich is laying plans for after ... well, after the Fuehrer's possible retirement, and I can inform the Fuehrer, I think that will be the end of Herr Heydrich. Do you not agree?'

'I am sure you are right, Herr Reichsfuehrer.' Anna was having trouble controlling her thoughts, to stop them from running away from her. There were suddenly so many possibilities. But in the immediate future, she had to decide whether to go along with this frightened but still so powerful little man, and if she did, to obtain whatever she could from such a perilous relationship.

'But do you think that the Reich-Protector wishes to have me back?'

'Oh, my dear Anna, of course he does. He wanted to take you with him, last August. He

246

was very upset when I persuaded the Fuehrer that you were the ideal choice for the American assignment.'

You could have fooled me, Anna thought. 'You do realize, Herr Reichsfuehrer, that you are asking me to undertake a very dangerous mission. If General Heydrich were to discover, or even suspect, what I am about...'

'I do realize that, Anna. I have turned to you because I believe that you are a devoted servant of the Reich. Of me.'

'I try to be,' Anna said modestly.

'And do not think I will forget what you have done. You will serve at my side, forever.'

'That is very gratifying, sir. But I must ask, suppose something did happen to me, my family...?'

'They will be my concern. I give you my word that no harm will ever befall your family.'

Oddly, Anna believed him. He might be the nastiest, most devious man she had ever met, but he had an ineradicably old-fashioned view of such things as personal honour: he would never willingly break his word. Could there be anything else to be gained? She dared not press her luck too far, and if the British plans were successful ... He had said he did not wish to risk ordering Heydrich's assassination, but if he *were* assassinated, by an apparent Czech patriot, he would surely have to be pleased. 'That is a great relief to me, Herr Reichsfuehrer. What if General Heydrich discovers what I am about and has me arrested, and interrogated?'

'I am still his superior officer, Anna. No matter what may happen, I will protect you. You have my word. Now, go to your apartment and await further instructions. It will take me a day or two to set up your new posting.

So, Anna wondered as she left Gestapo Head-quarters, *have I fallen entirely on my feet, or have I got myself into something too deep for even me to handle?* But obviously a successful assassination would cut the Gordian knot, as it were. And she had definitely, even if by accident, accomplished her first duty as required by London. They had to be informed of that.

She took a taxi to Antoinette's Boutique, strolled into the showroom, and paused in consternation as Edda Hedermann hurried forward. 'Countess! How good to see you. Did you have a good trip?'

'Yes, thank you.' What the shit was going on? But Clive, even if he had his own doubts, had told her to continue using Bartoli as long as the Italian knew nothing of Operation Daybreak. So she smiled at the woman in turn. 'Is Signor Bartoli free?'

'He is in the fitting room. With a customer,' she hastily added as Anna turned towards the inner door. 'I will tell him you are here. Would you like to wait in the office?'

'Thank you.' She went in and sat down. This was another occasion when she wished she smoked. She could not imagine how Hedermann was still around. And, since she was still around,

248

how the Boutique was still functioning.

The door opened. 'Anna! It is good to see you back. How was America? It is a country I have always wanted to visit. I have relatives there, you know.'

'How very nice for you. Close the door.'

'Still giving orders, I see.' But he obeyed and went behind his desk. 'I assume your communication is urgent, as always.'

'Why is Hedermann still here?'

'Should I not employ my wife?'

'Your *wife*? Are you mad?'

'I think I am perfectly sane. Which is more than I can say for most other people around here.'

'I left instructions...'

'Anna, you do not give me instructions. You bring me information for transmission to Basle and thence London. I understand that your solution to every problem is death, but that is not civilized, nor is it a Christian point of view.'

Anna stared at him. He had definitely lost his senses. 'Well, unless you wish me to transmit a very long message to London, concerning you, you had better explain just what is going on.'

'It is very simple. You told me that Edda was suspicious of our activities, and had confided her suspicions to her Abwehr boyfriend. I do not know the truth of that. Edda swears that she never knew anyone named Schlutz, and he has never been around here.'

'That is hardly surprising, is it? Unless you believe in ghosts. The fact remains—'

'That she was suspicious. But it was less of what we might be doing outside of the office, as it were, than what we were doing inside it. I was able to reassure her about that.'

Anna regarded him for several seconds. His inability to understand what was necessary for their survival was incredible. And there was nothing she could do about him, without orders from London. But still, he was her line of communication with London. 'And you seriously suppose that because she is your wife she will not betray you? Us?'

'She loves me,' Bartoli declared proudly. 'Anyway, I have outlined the situation to her.'

'You have done *what*?'

'There is no need to be agitated. I have told her that you, we, are in the pay of Mussolini, who requires us to keep him informed, if we can, of Nazi plans. They are inclined to do things, as you know, without informing the Duce.'

'And she accepts this? Is she not a Nazi herself?'

'Lip service. She is a Nazi because all her friends are Nazis. She does not truly believe in their principles.'

Anna sighed. Her sense of well-being was entirely gone, and her irritation was increased by the thought that she was virtually at the mercy of that creature outside. But then, she had always been at the mercy of this creature in front of her. It was a situation that had to be put right, as rapidly as possible. 'Very well,' she said. 'I will trust in your confidence. Now I have a very urgent message for London.'

'All your messages are very urgent,' he grumbled, and pulled a sheet of paper towards him. 'Yes?'

'Position achieved. Leaving in a week. Essential I see Judith before then.'

Bartoli studied what he had written. 'Leaving for where? And who is Judith?'

'Just send that message.'

'You are not supposed to have any secrets from me.'

Anna stood up. 'Every woman has her secrets, Luigi. It is vital that London receives that message tomorrow. Ciao.'

'It is so good to be home,' Birgit confided. 'I mean, America was very nice, but there is no place like home, is there, Countess?'

'Well, don't start to feel too comfortable,' Anna advised. 'We are moving on in a few days.'

'So soon? Where are we going?'

'Prague. You will like Prague. It is a beautiful city.'

'But ... will we be gone long?'

'I have no idea. It may be a few weeks.'

'Then we will miss Christmas.'

'I am sure they celebrate Christmas in Prague,' Anna pointed out. 'Was it not the home of Good King Wenceslas? Now, serve lunch, and then I must go to the gym.' She had not had a chance to work out during her visit to the States.

251

Clive put the transcript on Baxter's desk. 'She seems to have overcome the first hurdle without difficulty. She must have done it the day she got back to Berlin.'

'Like all women,' Baxter commented, 'she sees difficulties where none exist. And why is she so anxious to see Judith? I knew giving her another contact was a mistake.'

'In my opinion,' Clive said, 'giving her this assignment at all is a mistake.'

'Because you promised her that we would never let anything happen to her? May I remind you that you had no authority to make such a promise. If she is working for us, she is working for us, and therefore she has to accept the same risks as any other field agent. Anyway, where is the risk, for her? She is not to be involved in the assassination. All she has to do is say where, and when.'

'If something goes wrong, and it usually does, and any of our people are picked up and inter-rogated, they are very likely to give her name as part of the group.'

'None of our people are supposed to allow themselves to be taken and interrogated. They all have their suicide capsules. I presume Anna has one?'

'Can you ever really look at yourself in the mirror and say to yourself, "I like that man"?'

'I hope one day to be able to look in the mirror and say to myself, "it was all worth it, because we won the war".' Baxter pointed with his pipe.

'As I have told you before, you have made the cardinal and inexcusable error of falling in love with one of your agents. That comes close to making you unemployable. Remember that.'

Clive stood up. 'Yes, sir. Have I your permission to contact Kruger? If, as you say, this is the most important assignment you have allotted to Fehrbach, it is surely at least equally important to keep her happy until the assignment is completed.'

Baxter considered, briefly. Then he nodded. 'You have permission. But I do not want Kruger to be personally involved in Operation Daybreak.'

Anna was awakened from a deep sleep by Birgit hovering anxiously by the bed. The light was on, but it was still dark outside. 'What in the name of God ... What time is it?'

'It is just gone six, Countess.'

'And you have woken me up? It had better be important.'

'There is a gentleman here to see you, Countess.' She lowered her voice. 'An officer.'

'At this hour?' Anna threw back the covers and got out of bed. Birgit hastily wrapped her in a dressing gown. Anna peered into the mirror, and dragged hair from her eyes. But anyone calling on her at six o'clock in the morning had to take the rough with the smooth. She thrust her toes into slippers and stalked into the drawing room, paused to regard the anxious young man in the black uniform who was standing by the

253

window. 'We have met before.'

'Of course, Countess.' He clicked his heels. 'Captain Dorff.'

'I cannot remember where.'

'In the gymnasium, in August, Countess. I remember it as if it were yesterday.'

Well, you would, Anna thought. *I was naked when you came in.* 'Don't tell me,' she said. 'The Fuehrer wants to see me. At six o'clock in the morning?'

'Conventional time means nothing to the Fuehrer, Countess. He habitually works all night and then sleeps until noon. He is about to retire now. But he wishes to see you first.'

Oh, my God, Anna thought. Just like that. 'You can't expect me to come like this.'

Dorff studied the dressing gown. 'I think you should put something on, yes.'

'If I am going to see the Fuehrer, I need to have a bath.'

'I do not think a bath is required, Countess. When the Fuehrer says now, he generally means *now*. There is an important matter he wishes to discuss with you.'

In bed, Anna thought grimly. She hated having to have sex with anyone unless she was properly physically prepared. And in any event, the thought of having sex with Hitler was too much for her brain at this time of the morning. But this was not a force she could combat, at least at this moment. 'Very well,' she said. 'Give me five minutes.'

* * *

She dressed as she had that August morning when they had first met, remembering that he had clearly liked her appearance, washed her face, cleaned her teeth, put on her sable as she had no doubt it was freezing outside, and joined Dorff. It was actually snowing, and the Mercedes saloon slithered to and fro.

'I don't suppose you have any idea what this is all about?' she ventured.

'I do, actually, but I think the Fuehrer would rather tell you himself. I can tell you that there has been a very dramatic development. But I would beg you not to ask me anything more.'

Anna decided to leave it: they were only a few minutes away from the Chancellery. But she could not imagine what very dramatic development could possibly have occurred that could involve her. Or indeed, that Hitler would be so excited about. Had the Wehrmacht finally captured Moscow? But that could hardly be considered a very dramatic development, since it had been repeatedly claimed that the fall of the Russian capital was imminent.

The Chancellery was a blaze of light, and filled with excited people. Didn't they ever sleep? But there was no Frau Engert. Dorff himself escorted her up the stairs and into the Fuehrer's office. There were several people present, but not Himmler, Anna saw to her surprise. In any event, at her entry Hitler waved them all away, and a moment later they were alone.

'Countess!' As on the occasion of their first

255

meeting he held her hands and gave them a gentle squeeze. 'I am sorry I have not seen you since your return from America. I have been somewhat busy.'

'Of course, my Fuehrer.'

'But I have read your report. Sit down. Sit down.' Anna took the chair before his desk while he returned behind it. 'It is very interesting. You are to be congratulated. And you are certain that the Americans have no wish to go to war?'

'I have that information on the highest authority, sir.'

'Unless they were to be attacked.'

'That is what they told me.'

'Well, tell me this: if they were to be attacked, are they *capable* of going to war? Have they the will? And the means? They are a pleasure-loving people, are they not?'

'They enjoy their prosperity, sir, yes. But I think they would fight if they felt that prosperity was under threat.'

'And the means? Could they, for example, put a hundred divisions into the field, in the immediate future?'

'No, sir. I think it would take them some time to mobilize an army on a European scale. If they were to be forced to go to war now, they would have to rely on their fleet to protect them for the time necessary to raise an army. That could be several months or even a year.'

'And if they did not have a fleet?'

'Ah...' He had this habit of firing unanswer-

256

able hypothetical questions at people. 'They do have a fleet, sir. I think it is about the largest fleet in the world.'

Hitler actually laughed; it was the first time she had heard him do so. 'That is no longer true, Anna. At dawn this morning, that is, just after midnight last night our time, the Japanese navy destroyed the American Pacific fleet.'

Anna stared at him in consternation. 'Sir?'

'They are claiming that nine battleships have been sunk. Nine battleships, for the loss of a handful of aircraft! It is the greatest, the most decisive naval victory in history.'

Anna continued to stare at him in disbelief.

'So, tell me,' Hitler went on, 'what will the Americans do on finding themselves virtually defenceless?'

Anna drew a deep breath. *Joe*, she thought. *What will Joe do? And Wild Bill Donovan?* 'They will fight, sir.'

'But you have agreed that they cannot be in a position to do so effectively for several months. Perhaps even a year. Thank you, Anna. You have confirmed my own opinion.'

'You think Japan can defeat them, sir?'

'It is very difficult to determine what the Japanese are thinking, or hoping to achieve. This attack, I mean ... well, it is completely out of the blue.'

'You mean you did not know of it, sir?'

'No one knew of it. It is a master stroke, of both secrecy and execution. But it presents us

257

with an unexpected opportunity. No, I do not believe that Japan can defeat the United States, militarily, by itself. I mean, in terms of occupying mainland America, or even a part of it. But they can certainly gobble up what they are after, the Philippines and the Dutch East Indies and Malaya for the raw materials, the tin and the rubber – and above all, the oil that they need. More importantly, from our point of view, they are going to consume all the Americans' attention and strength for the foreseeable future as Washington attempts to redress the situation. That is what we want, don't you see? I have always known that one day I would have to confront America. Frankly, I had supposed it would be after I had completed the conquest of Europe. What you have told me seemed to confirm that proposition. But now ... Did not an English playwright say something about a tide in the affairs of men, which, taken at the flood, leads to everlasting success, but if missed, dooms a man to perpetual failure?'

'William Shakespeare, sir.'

'Of course. Can you not see, Anna, that this is the flood tide? At this moment Japan has the strongest fleet in the world. We have the strongest army. Between us there is nothing we cannot achieve. So now is the moment to shatter the Americans. Don't you understand that if they are involved in a war against both us and the Japanese they will have to cease supplying the Russians, and the British, with the arms, the ammunition, the vehicles and equipment, that

258

they must have to continue fighting us?'

Anna swallowed. 'You mean to join Japan in a war against the United States?'

'That is what I have been saying.'

'But, my Fuehrer, is it necessary?' *It sounds like suicide*, she thought.

'It is my will to do so, Anna. Besides,' he added, a trifle ingenuously, 'I gave that fellow Matsuoka my word, when he was here last year, that if Japan became engaged in hostilities with America, we would back them to the hilt.'

'You mean we have a treaty with them?'

'No, no. There was no formal treaty. Just my word.'

'Which may have inspired them to carry out this attack. One would have supposed they should at least have told you what they were planning.'

'They are a secretive people. All Asiatics believe in secrecy. And they have brought off a great coup. Thank you, Anna, your assessment of America has been of enormous help to me. I shall not forget it. Now leave me. There is work to be done.'

'Yes, my Fuehrer.' Anna stood up. 'Heil Hitler!'

Not for the first time Anna left the Chancellery in a swirling mental fog. That Germany, Italy and Japan, with almost no natural resources between them, could dream of taking on Great Britain, Russia and now the United States, who between them possessed, controlled or had access to just about every natural resource in the world, was a concept of utter madness, a gambler's throw based entirely on the belief that Germany and Japan, at least, possessed the greater martial tradition and determination. As if every day of Russian resistance, not to mention more than two years of British defiance, had not already proved that wrong. As for the Americans ... she recalled what Joe had told her. She wondered what Hitler would have said if she had related that conversation, in full, to him.

Should she tell London what was about to happen? They were going to find out soon enough, and telling them perhaps a day or two in advance could not possibly be of any value. They could warn Washington, but if America was already at war with Japan, as she was sure it would be by now, and thus mobilizing like mad, it would hardly make a great deal of difference. Besides, she was reluctant to return to the Boutique, at least until after she had seen Judith; she was increasingly convinced that Bartoli was now a serious liability.

Anyway, in a few days she would be off to Prague. She wondered if what had happened would make any difference to London's plans for Heydrich. But she was committed to carrying out Himmler's instructions.

She returned to the apartment, and then went to the gym for a vigorous work-out, watched as always with glowing eyes by Stefan. 'Was America as exciting as they say, Countess?' he asked as she showered.

'Why, yes.'

'And did you have to shoot anybody to get out?'

'Of course. I had to shoot six people.'

He blew a raspberry of disbelief. 'But now you are back for a while.'

'About three days.'

'What?'

Anna towelled herself dry. 'Does this concern you?'

'Well...' He flushed. 'It is difficult to keep an eye on your fitness when you are away more often than you are here.'

'I am a trial,' Anna agreed. She laid down the towel and picked up her cami-knickers.

'Countess,' he said. 'Anna. May I ask a favour of you?'

'I thought we had been through that,' Anna reminded him.

'I know. I apologize. It will not happen again. But would you give me permission to take your photograph?'

'My photograph?' Anna was surprised. When she had lived in England, she had been photographed extensively for *Tatler* and many of the other glossy magazines and newspapers that had found her good for circulation figures, but those had always been without her permission and therefore hardly more than hurried snapshots. She had never actually posed for a picture. She found the idea quite amusing. But... 'I am not very presentable at the moment. I will stop by some time when I am properly dressed and made-up.'

He licked his lips. 'I would like to take it now, just as you are. I have a camera here.'

Anna gazed at him, then looked down at herself; she was still holding the cami-knickers against her naked body. 'I see. You wish to become very popular with your friends.'

'No, no. I swear it. I will never show it to a soul. It will be my personal memory of you.'

He was such a desperate little man, so desperate to have sex with her that he would settle for masturbating to a photograph. She supposed that was the ultimate compliment that could be paid to any woman. 'And who will print your photograph?'

'I print my own. Photography is my hobby.'

'Well, then,' Anna said. 'I wish to have a copy.' It would be something to give to Clive. Just in case.

Birgit was wildly excited. 'Have you heard the news, Countess?'

'I am sure everyone has heard the news by now,' Anna pointed out.

'Did you know it was going to happen when we were in America?'

'No. I don't think anyone knew it was going to happen. Except the Japanese, of course.'

'But will we still be going to Prague?'

'Of course. What happens in the Pacific is hardly likely to affect us here.' *At least, not immediately*, she thought.

She sat on the settee with a glass of schnapps.

She was in one of her periods of limbo, and she never enjoyed those. She was awaiting final instructions, both from Himmler and from London, without having any idea what those instructions were going to involve. She wondered which would arrive first, and nearly spilled her drink when the doorbell rang.

Birgit hurried to open it, and entered the drawing room to say, in a stage whisper, 'It is the lady we met in Madrid.'

'Ah.' Anna got up and hurried into the lobby. 'Judith! How good to see you.'

Judith embraced her. 'It is good to see you too.' She indicated a valise by her feet. 'Is it possible to stay the night? It is so difficult to find a hotel room in Berlin nowadays.' She gave a little giggle. 'Half of them seem to have been knocked down.'

'Well, they are targets for the RAF. Of course you must stay the night. Come in. Birgit, put this case in my bedroom.'

'Yes, Countess,' Birgit said disapprovingly. 'Ah...'

'I am not throwing you out, silly,' Anna said. 'The Countess de Sotomayer will sleep in my room.'

Birgit looked more disapproving yet, but she carried the valise down the corridor. Anna showed Judith into the drawing room. 'There are only the two bedrooms, you see. And she has one.'

'Ah. But...'

'Oh, she is assuming we are lovers. She would like to be one herself. Schnapps?'

263

'Thank you. You mean you and she...'

Anna poured. 'Oh, good God, no. She knows her place. But I suspect that she feels that if any woman is ever going to get into my bed, it should be her.'

Judith gave one of her giggles. 'But you have just invited me to your bed.'

'Yes,' Anna said thoughtfully. 'I have.'

'I can hardly wait.' Judith sat beside her on the settee, sipped her drink, and lowered her voice. 'Can we talk? They told me it was urgent.'

'Not now,' Anna said, and smiled at her. 'When we are in bed.'

'You must forgive me,' Anna said as they undressed after dinner. 'I do not wear clothes in bed.'

'I am glad of that,' Judith said. 'Neither do I.'

Anna got between the sheets. 'What a pity we never did know each other as schoolgirls.'

'Yes.' Judith lay beside her. 'Were you as exquisite then as now?'

'I think I was somewhat thinner.'

Judith giggled. 'So was I.'

She was actually the more voluptuous of the pair, although her legs could not match Anna's for length. Anna took her in her arms, and Judith kissed her mouth. 'You do not mind?'

'I think you could grow on me.' Anna hugged her. She had the strangest feeling of well-being, a total lack of tension that she had seldom felt before, certainly not since that heavenly interlude in Virginia. 'How long can you stay?'

Judith's breath rushed against hers. 'I must return to Spain tomorrow. Is this room bugged?' she whispered.

'Yes.'

'But can you not turn it off?'

'Yes, I can. But as I never do, it would look suspicious. Just stay close.' Anna massaged her breasts and shoulders. 'The tape is regularly checked. I think we should gasp from time to time. Did London get my message?'

'Of course.' Judith did some massaging of her own. 'Did you doubt that?'

'I am not happy with the situation.' Anna told her about Bartoli and Edda and Schlutz.

'You think she is a plant?' Judith's mouth was against her ear.

'No. I think she is a very ordinary woman. Therefore she is at the mercy of her emotions, of which jealousy is the most common. Bartoli cannot keep his hands off anything in a skirt.'

Judith's hand slipped lower. 'You mean he has had you?'

'No, he has not. But he would like to. The point is that if he falls out with his wife, as he is bound to, she may well do something stupid.'

'I will report that to London. But it will take time to set up a new Control.'

Anna kissed her some more. 'Can you not be my Control?'

'I would like that very much.' Judith found what she was looking for. 'I will see if it is practical.'

'Tell me about Prague.'

265

'Oh, yes.' Judith's fingers became less urgent as she concentrated. 'Your contact is a man called Telfer. He is a doctor.'

'The Hradcany has its own medical staff.'

Judith's chin moved up and down against her shoulder as she nodded. 'He is not an ordinary doctor. He is a chiropractor, a bone-setter. You must strain your back, as soon as you get there. Can you do this?'

Anna smiled into her hair. 'As I will be required to sleep with Heydrich, that will not be difficult.'

Judith's movements became lively again. 'He is vigorous?'

'Very.'

'Well, you are in pain, a problem you have suffered before, and you have been given the name of this man. He is actually quite well known, and outside of Bohemia too, so there should be no problem. Now, the people coming in from England will arrive in a few days' time.'

'How?'

'They will be parachuted.'

'Can they hope to be undetected?'

'They will be dropped in a remote area, and they know where to go to find a safe house. They will make their way to Prague, and they will await your instructions. Our people there will conceal them. As soon as possible, you must make up a plan of campaign and convey it to the doctor. Now, Anna, you must not, under any circumstances, become involved. London is very insistent about this. Date, place and time

266

are all that is required of you. Some notice is necessary, of course.'

'I understand. London is aware of what is going on in the Pacific?'

'Everyone is aware of that. They are cock-a-hoop. They know that with America on their side, they cannot lose.'

'That's not the opinion held here.'

'Well, they can hardly dare think anything else, can they?'

'But London wishes Operation Daybreak to go ahead.'

'London regards it as top priority. But you must understand that as regards us, you are out of touch until it is finished.'

'I understand,' Anna said. The temptation to tell this utterly delightful bed-mate about Himmler's plan for bringing down Heydrich was enormous. But if Operation Daybreak was already under way, that might be to over-complicate matters. And however delightful Judith was, this was still only the second occasion they had ever met; her desire to get close to her might not be entirely innocent.

'So you will make it as quick as possible,' Judith whispered. 'I should like to see you again, soon.'

'I think I would like that too,' Anna said. 'Now, I think, for the sake of our listeners, that we should both indulge in some heavy breathing.'

'Are you afraid?' Judith asked later as they lay

267

quietly together.

'I cannot afford to be afraid.'

'I am afraid.'

Anna turned her head, sharply; their noses touched. 'You?'

'We have to be taken, one day. And then ... God, when I think of it.'

'There is no reason for us to be taken,' Anna insisted. 'As long as we are careful. And if we are, well, you have your capsule. Don't you?'

'I am never without it.'

'You don't have it now?' Anna asked in alarm; she had spent the past couple of hours kissing this woman.

'It's in my handbag.'

'Ah.'

'I carry it in my mouth, of course, whenever I am in public.'

'Well, then, you have nothing to worry about. One bite, and oblivion.'

'How brave you are. But suppose it didn't work, or you couldn't make yourself bite? Can you imagine what it must be like to be stripped naked by a bunch of strange men, to be tied up to be flogged, to have them finger your sex while they put electrodes into you ... I would go mad.'

'I have been though all that,' Anna said.

Judith rose on her elbow. 'You ... what?'

'It was a few years ago. I wasn't working for MI6 then, so I didn't have a capsule. But you know, I'm rather glad I didn't, because I'm still here. You can survive anything if you are

268

determined to do so. Now go to sleep. Nothing is going to happen to you.'

But Anna herself lay awake, staring into the darkness. *Shit,* she thought. She had been counting on this woman's strength. Now...

'Have you known the Countess de Sotomayer long?' Himmler asked.

The question came out of the blue. Anna was packed and ready to leave on the noon train, and she had in any event been surprised when he had come personally to see her off, as it were, as his final instructions had not differed greatly from those he had given her in his office. She was to watch, listen, and report. She was to supply the names of everyone Heydrich met in private, and, of course, where possible, convey the gist of their conversations. 'But you must not endanger yourself in any way,' he had repeated.

'I shall endeavour not to, Herr Reichsfuehrer.' *How sweet all these people are,* she thought, *sending me into the utmost peril and solicitously warning me not to endanger myself.* 'I assume General Heydrich knows I am coming?'

'No.'

'Sir?'

Himmler had given her an envelope. 'This is a personal letter from me to him, in which I explain that circumstances have made it necessary for you to be removed from Berlin for a few weeks, and that I am therefore sending you to him as a personal assistant. I am sure he will welcome you.'

'Surely I should know what these circumstances are?'

'That is what I have come to tell you. You have fallen foul of the Reichsmarshal, who has formed the opinion that you have been poisoning the Fuehrer's mind against him.'

Anna realized that her mouth was open, and hastily closed it; she had never met Goering in her life.

'This will place you firmly in General Heydrich's camp, as he still regards Goering as the principal obstacle in the way of his being named as heir. In these circumstances, he is almost certain to confide his fears and hopes, and perhaps even his plans, to you. Pillow talk, eh?'

'But if he raises the matter here in Berlin, will not the Reichsmarshal deny any knowledge of me?'

'Of course. But he would do that anyway, would he not?'

Anna felt like scratching her head: this was becoming more and more complicated, and dangerous, with every moment. 'Is not the Reichsmarshal still the second most powerful man in Germany?'

'He thinks so, certainly.'

'Thus if word of this gets back to him...'

'By that time you, and I, will have brought Heydrich down.'

'And I will be regarded as his creature, to be brought down with him.'

'Have I not sworn to protect you, Anna? I am a man of my word. And with Heydrich gone, for all Goering's posturing, I will be the second most powerful man in the Reich.'

And I will be utterly at your mercy, Anna thought. But was she not anyway? There were so many factors to be taken into consideration, and now came this question out of the blue. But of course her SD monitors would have felt the visit of an unknown woman, who had spent the night, was worth reporting. And Essermann had no doubt also reported their Madrid meeting, as he had said he was going to do.

'We were at school together,' she explained now. 'And then we met by chance in Madrid.' She allowed herself one of Judith's giggles. 'Her husband tried to sell me real estate.'

'She is Spanish?'

'No, she is Austrian. Her husband is Spanish.'

'And she followed you here.'

'Well, you know how it is, sir. One meets an old friend, and one is polite, and says the conventional things, like "do look me up if you are ever in Berlin". One never expects that sort of invitation to be taken up. I was amazed when she appeared.'

'Did she not tell you why she was in Berlin? If not to see you?'

'Well...' Anna attempted to look embarrassed. 'She did not tell me, although I think she was here on business.'

'But she spent the night here.'

How much had Birgit overheard of their conversation? 'She told me that she had been unable to find accommodation in any hotel. So I agreed

271

that she could sleep here.'

'In your bed.'

'Well, I did not wish to put my maid out.'

'The tape indicates that you and this woman were ... close.'

'We were close friends as girls.'

'And she wished to resume the relationship. I see. The things that go on in convents, eh, when the nuns are asleep.'

Fortunately, Anna thought, he did not seem to be aware that the convent she had attended in Vienna did not take boarders. 'I am sorry, Herr Reichsfuehrer,' she murmured. 'I live a very lonely life.' She fluttered her eyelashes, the clearest signal she could possibly send.

But it was to no avail. 'You will soon be re-united with General Heydrich. But, according to your file, which I looked at this afternoon, when you were at SS training school you once broke the arm of a girl who, ah, made advances to you.'

'Yes, sir. But that girl was not Judith.'

'You are discriminating. That is good. Does General Heydrich know of your, ah, inclinations?'

Chance would be a fine thing, she thought. 'I have never told him, sir. I do not think he would be interested. General Heydrich is very single-minded.'

'Still, I think it would be a good idea not to tell him. Let us share this little secret, just the two of us, eh? You do realize that homosexuality, whether indulged by men or women, is a

272

criminal offence punishable by imprisonment?'

Anna stared at him with her eyes at their widest, and he patted her hand. 'However, as I have said, it shall be our little secret.'

Something else to bind me to him, Anna thought. 'I shall be eternally grateful, Herr Reichsfuehrer.'

'Of course. However, these, ah, feelings of yours are a weakness, a chink in your armour. I think it would be very unwise for you to see this woman again.'

Shit! Anna thought. There was a problem, certainly if Bartoli was going to be taken out. 'If that is what you wish, sir.'

'Yes, that is what I wish.' He stood up, straightened his belts. 'Now, I will also wish you a good journey, and look forward to hearing from you, very soon.'

Anna waited, for as always he was regarding her like a large cat – although he was some inches shorter than her – crouching over a particularly succulent mouse. But, as always, he merely squeezed her hands and left. She simply could not make up her mind whether he was himself a homosexual, or was simply afraid to place himself at the mercy of a woman who he knew could kill. Or now, of course, whether he did not wish to take a lesbian to his bed.

What a fuck-up. And yet, that night with Judith had been rather fun ... until the disquieting end.

'Is the Reichsfuehrer angry with us, Countess?' Birgit's tone could be every bit as innocently dulcet as Anna's.

'Is that any concern of yours?' Anna inquired. 'And what do you mean, us?'

'Is my future not irreversibly tied to yours?'

Anna considered this and recalled that many people had assumed that Marlene Gehrig's 'suicide' in Moscow had been caused by an unrequited love affair with Birgit. A love affair she knew had been far from unrequited. The maid had never aspired to her bed, but had that simply been because Anna had never hidden her aversion to any sex unless commanded to it ... Until Virginia, and the presence of Clive for those unforgettable few days. That unavoidable insight into her true character should have more than ever convinced the maid that her mistress was not a lesbian, but the mental intimacy created by the situation had definitely embold-ened her to ask questions. And the night with Judith had clearly led her to some provocative thoughts.

Once again, the question arose: was she too dangerous to be allowed to continue? But Anna remained reluctant to harm the woman to whom she had become so close over the past couple of years. Besides, it would be highly dangerous, with Himmler also in a question-asking mood, for Birgit suddenly to have a fatal accident. And anyway, she was unlikely to prove a problem until after this assignment was over, by which time, if everything went according to plan, all things might be possible.

So she smiled. 'Why, yes. That is probably

absolutely true. I think that is something we should both remember, at all times.'

'Anna?' Reinhard Heydrich stared at his protégée in amazement. 'What are you doing here?'

The office was in the Hradcany Castle, looking out from its hillside over the many spires of Prague. Anna had indeed found the return to the Czech capital more evocative than she had expected, or wanted. Stepping out of the train at the Central Station, as she had done only eighteen months ago, had brought back the most vivid memories; her leaving the train with that apparently civilized man who had shared her compartment from Dresden, who had suddenly seized her arm, pushed a pistol into her ribs, and told her to take him up to Meissenbach, waiting for her on the platform. She had reacted with instinctive and unhesitating violence, as she always did in such situations. She destroyed Reiffel with a blow to the neck, seized his pistol, and opened fire on the two men standing on the far side of the platform, who had also drawn their guns. English agents, of whom London had not informed her because they had had no idea she would be visiting Prague!

It was an incident that, however personally tragic, had left Heydrich, and by projection Himmler and then Hitler, in no doubt that she was the best they had.

'Reichsfuehrer Himmler sent me,' she said now.

Heydrich frowned. 'To do what?'

275

'To be with you.'

'You have quarrelled with the Reichsfuehrer?'

'No, sir. He has explained the situation in this letter.'

Heydrich took the envelope, gestured Anna to a chair, and then opened the letter. His expression never changed as he read it, but then his expression never changed, whatever might be happening around him.

He laid down the sheet of paper. 'It appears that you have been interesting yourself in things that are outside of your duties.'

'Not intentionally, sir.'

'I did not know that you had ever met Reichsmarshal Goering.'

'I have not met him, sir.'

'Then you need to explain this situation.'

Anna took a deep breath, but if this man was soon to die, he was hardly going to have the time to discover whether or not what she told him was a lie. 'My mission to the United States was a success, sir. I was able to bring back the information the Fuehrer required.'

'You mean you convinced him that now was the moment to go to war with the Americans?'

'I did not know what he intended, Herr General. I only know that he was pleased with my report. He saw me privately.'

Heydrich raised his eyebrows.

'In his office, sir. He wished to discuss many things. He told me that he was not as fit as he would have liked, and that he was considering appointing an heir, someone to share his duties and responsibilities, and in time take over entirely.'

Heydrich's face remained expressionless. 'He asked your opinion on this?' His tone suggested that he was wondering if the Fuehrer was not more ill than was supposed.

'No, sir, he did not. Not in so many words. He told me that his obvious successor was the Reichsmarshal. And then he sort of paused. I realized that I had to say something. So I said, "is not the Reichsmarshal the same age as yourself, my Fuehrer?"'

'He is four years younger,' Heydrich said.

'That is what the Fuehrer said. But then he added, as if to himself, "and his health is not good". And then he looked at me, and said, "Tell me, Countess, who you would choose as the next Fuehrer, if you were I?" I was so surprised I could not speak, so he said, "Do not be afraid to speak your mind. Your mind is the equal of half a dozen so-called savants. And what you say will never be known to anyone save me."'

'So you said...?'

'I said that it should be someone young, and virile, with a proven record of leadership.'

'And he said...'

Anna looked suitably embarrassed. 'He said, "You are thinking of Heydrich." And then he pointed at me. "Because he is your lover."' She bit her lip.

Heydrich continued to study her for several seconds. Then he said, 'I have not shared your bed for four months.'

'That was your decision, Herr General, not mine.'

Heydrich preferred not to comment on that. 'And you think that your conversation, despite the Fuehrer's promise of confidentiality, got back to the Reichsmarshal.'

The ice was suddenly growing thin. 'I only know that I realized I was being followed.'

'And you told the Reichsfuehrer. And you also told him of your conversation with the Fuehrer? I was under the impression that he had ambitions himself.'

'His ambition is to serve the Reich, sir.'

'Even if that means serving under me?'

'He admires you greatly, sir. He is proud of having been able to give you the opportunity to prove your worth, and of the manner in which you have done that.'

'Has he slept with you? What is he like in bed?'

'I have never had sex with the Reichsfuehrer, sir.'

'You are telling me that you have been chaste for the past four months? You?'

Anna's gaze never flickered. 'I have never had sex with any man unless commanded to do so by you, Herr General.'

'Do you know, Anna, I cannot make up my mind whether you are God's gift to mankind, or the Devil's handmaiden.' He picked up his house phone. 'Haussmann? I wish an apartment prepared for the Countess von Widerstand, who is rejoining my staff. She will be down in a

moment.' He replaced the phone. 'You understand that my wife and daughter are with me, so
a certain amount of discretion is necessary.'
Anna gulped; she had not anticipated having to
work at destroying this man virtually before his
family. 'However, my wife does not like living
in a castle, so we have taken a house outside the
city. I will be able to see you from time to time
when I am here, and we will ... discuss your
duties.'

Anna stood up. 'I will look forward to that,
Herr General. Heil Hitler!'

She desperately needed a bath: she was dripping
sweat. But once again everything was falling
into place; she could have asked for no better
reception.

Major Haussmann was one of those handsome
young SS officers who was clearly nervous of
his famous charge as he escorted her along a
corridor. 'Where is my maid?' Anna asked.

'I will send her to you, Countess, together with
your luggage.' He opened a door. 'I hope this
will be satisfactory?'

Anna went into the apartment, which had big
windows overlooking the inner lawns of the
castle, and was light and airy. However ... She
crossed the lounge and opened the door to the
bedroom, which had an en-suite bathroom. She
turned to face Haussmann. 'It is very small.
There is only one bedroom, and no kitchen.'

'It is the best I could do at such short notice,
Countess. If we had known you were coming...'

'How do I eat?'

'There is the canteen...' He paused on seeing her expression.

'And where does my maid sleep?'

'Quarters will be provided...'

'I like my maid to be available at all times.'

'I understand, Countess. I promise that I will obtain better accommodation for you within twenty-four hours. Now I will send your maid to you...'

He was definitely overawed. So why not take advantage of that? It could do no harm and would lay the groundwork for when she was with Heydrich. She gave a little grunt. 'Oh!' Then she sat down.

Haussmann had gone to the door. Now he turned sharply. 'Countess? Is something the matter?'

Anna breathed deeply for several seconds. 'I have this pain.'

'Oh, Countess!' He hurried back to stand beside her. 'Is there anything I can do?'

'It is my back. I hurt it in the gymnasium a few weeks ago and it does not seem to get better.'

'Ah. Perhaps if I were to rub it...' He paused optimistically.

'It is not muscular. I think I have pinched a nerve. But thank you.' She smiled bravely. 'It will wear off.'

'Well, you must tell me if I can help in any way.' He returned to the door, reluctantly.

'Perhaps there is a way,' Anna said.

He turned again, this time eagerly. 'Countess?'

'I was told there is a very good chiropractor in Prague. A man called Telfer. Have you heard of him?'

'Everyone has heard of Dr Telfer, Countess.'

'Have they? That is excellent. Do you think you could obtain an appointment for me to see him? I am sure he would be able to relieve me.'

'I am sure he would have been able to do so. Unfortunately ...'

Lumps of lead suddenly appeared in Anna's stomach. 'Yes?'

'It will not be possible for him to see you, Countess.'

'Why not? What has happened to him?'

'The day before yesterday, Dr Telfer was knocked down by a motor car.'

'Oh, my God!' Anna cried. 'Is he all right?'

'No, Countess. He was killed instantly.'

Nine

Counter-plots

'Oh, my God!' Anna said without thinking.

'Countess? He was not a German, you know. He was a Bohemian.'

He was clearly finding it difficult to reconcile her very obvious concern at the death of an itinerant foreigner with her reputation as a professional assassin; she needed to be careful. 'It seems such an irrelevant way to go,' she improvised. 'And he might have been able to help me. But the pain is wearing off. Send up my maid, will you, please, Captain.'

Haussmann hesitated a last time, then clicked his heels and left. Anna went into the bathroom and switched on the water, then stripped off her clothes, which were even sweatier now. *Of all the fucking awful luck*, she thought. A misfortune which had left her completely out on a limb. Telfer was to have been her only contact in Prague. Without him she had no means of contacting the assassination squad. And here in Prague she had no means of contacting London to inform them of the situation. What a fuck-up!

'Haussmann tells me you have some back trouble,' Heydrich remarked. 'At your age? That is remarkable.'

Anna lay with her head in the crook of his shoulder, her hair scattered around her, her legs splayed. His love-making had been as violent and one-sided as always, leaving her feeling almost punch-drunk. Yet he expected her to have an orgasm every time he entered her, and such was her ability to concentrate on what she was doing that more often than not she did. Actually, it was not at all difficult, because she could fantasize while it was happening, as she had done in that charnel house in Washington. Now she moved against him, scraping her nipples against his ribs. 'It is just a twinge. I think I pinched a nerve while training. It is gone now.'

'So I observed just now. But he said you told him it was a recurring pain. Why have you not had it seen to?'

'I did mean to have it seen to.'

'Here in Prague? By that fellow Telfer? Why did you not go to a specialist in Berlin?'

'It only happened a week ago, and I knew I was coming here, and someone I mentioned it to said I should go to Dr Telfer as he is the best chiropractor in Europe.'

Heydrich began to slide his hands over her body, his way of conveying a return of passion. 'You're sure it has nothing to do with that bullet wound of yours?'

283

'Quite sure. It is on the other side. Anyway, I shall have to grin and bear it, as the doctor appears to have got himself killed.'

'Yes. I am glad you did not have the time to go to him. He was under investigation.'

Anna raised her head. 'You mean...?'

'No, no. We did not kill him. It was a legitimate accident. Feutlanger – you remember Feutlanger?'

'Yes,' Anna said grimly. She remember the little rat-like Gestapo officer who had handled the investigation into the three men she had killed, here in Prague, the previous year.

'Well, he was investigating some rather guarded but somewhat suggestive phone calls the good doctor made from time to time.'

'You mean his phone was tapped?'

'Of course. I have placed taps on the phones of every intellectual in Prague.'

My God, she thought. Perhaps Telfer's death, however tragic for him and disastrous for Operation Daybreak, had after all been a blessing in disguise for her. Had she visited him, and had he referred to her in one of those mysterious phone calls...

'But as I said,' Heydrich went on, 'that particular investigation must now be considered at an end. I believe Feutlanger brought in his nurse for interrogation, but he learned nothing.'

Which means, Anna thought, knowing Feutlanger's interrogation methods, that the woman was either very tough or she did indeed know nothing of her employer's secrets. In either event, the nurse was clearly too dangerous to be approached. So she remained in limbo.

Heydrich gave her a last squeeze and swung his legs out of bed. 'I must go. I have a dinner engagement. Now, Anna, you know that over Christmas and the New Year I must spend as much time as possible with my family.'

Thank God for that, Anna thought. Apart from sparing her from his sexual attentions, it would give her time to think, and hopefully come up with a solution to her problem. There had to be a solution. Apart from the obvious one that, as Heydrich was turned away from her as he dressed, she could almost certainly get out of bed and kill him before he knew what was happening. But she had been ordered not to get personally involved and she really had no wish to commit suicide, a suicide which would involve her family as well. So she remained lying still, looking at him.

He turned round. 'However, I do not wish you to have a lonely holiday. I have instructed Haussmann to take care of you. You like Haussmann?'

'I have not really thought about it,' Anna said, with perfect honesty.

'Well, he is a very nice chap. He will squire you wherever you wish to go, dance attendance on you, eh?'

Anna had not seen a lot of the adjutant since her first day, but she remembered him coming on strong that afternoon. 'And suppose he wishes to do more than dance, Herr General?'

285

Heydrich knotted his tie. 'I imagine he dreams of getting into that bed. Well, you could humour him, I suppose. Life here is rather dull for an ambitious officer.'

And in your opinion, I am nothing more than a whore, Anna thought. *Your whore, to be pedalled around to your favourites.*

Heydrich put on his tunic. 'You will also need him to look after you while I'm away.'

Anna sat up. 'You are going away?'

'I have been summoned to Berlin for a conference with the Fuehrer. I am to go in the New Year.' He smiled. 'Who knows, the scenario you outlined to me last week may be about to become reality.'

Shit, Anna thought. *Shit, shit, shit.* 'Can't I come with you?'

'No. My wife is coming with me.'

'Oh! But ... you will be coming back?'

'Of course. If only to tie things up and hand over to my successor. Do not look so alarmed, Anna. If things turn out as we anticipate, I will be able to offer you the full protection of the Fuehrer-in-waiting, and place you in the most advantageous position I can think of. I will see you tomorrow.'

He left the room, and Anna stared at the closed door. What a total mess. She could have no doubt that he was being summoned by Hitler to make the appointment, and that would mean ... It must never be allowed to happen, Clive had said. But do not get personally involved. It must

286

never be allowed to happen, Himmler had said, but do not get personally involved. And yet she was the only person in the world who *could* be personally involved, who knew that it *was* going to happen.

And there was the temptation to do nothing. If Heydrich became the next Fuehrer, with her as his favourite, she could be the most powerful woman in Germany. In Europe. Perhaps in the world. She might even be able to get her family out of their prison camp. But she doubted that Heydrich, who loved control more than anything else, would ever be prepared to relinquish his complete control over her. And to go down that road, which would mean turning her back forever on Clive and Joe and Judith, would be finally to sell her soul to the Devil, for the rest of eternity.

So think, God damn it, she told herself. You are supposed to be a genius. There is no problem that does not have a solution. But the only solution took her back to suicide. She had spent the last four years in this ghastly business, simply to keep her family alive. To condemn them to death now, even if she went with them, would make a nonsense of those four years, of the twenty-one people she had killed, just to keep her family alive.

Thought was increasingly difficult over Christmas. The Wehrmacht might have failed to take Moscow and be suffering frightening casualties as they endeavoured to hold their ground against both sub-zero temperatures and

Russian counter-attacks, but no one seemed to have any doubt that the offensive would be resumed once the weather improved, and that victory would be achieved this coming summer. Certainly the German colony in Prague found no reason not to enjoy themselves. Haussmann was in constant attendance, but Anna did not find it difficult to keep him at arms' length, partly because she quickly discerned that he was basically terrified of her, and clearly was sufficiently content to be seen everywhere with her at his side, with all of the suggestions that might raise in the minds of his jealous fellow officers. But it was necessary to do a great deal of dancing, and even more drinking, which most nights had her collapsing into bed exhausted. And the date of Heydrich's departure for Berlin, January 15th, was rushing towards them. Once he got on that train...

It was a few days after Christmas, when she had managed to get out on her own for a walk through the city, that she stopped to look in a shop window, and a quiet voice said, 'Well, hi there. Remember me?'

Anna resisted the urge to turn violently, and now she made out the woman's face in the window. 'Judith?! Oh, Judith...'

'I think we should have a cup of coffee,' Judith said. 'There is a shop just over there.'

They ordered, and sat opposite each other at the small table, smiling at each other. Like Anna, Judith wore a fur coat and a matching hat, and appeared her usual confident and ebullient self; if she did indeed live in a state of terrified apprehension, she was apparently able to keep it well concealed. 'Isn't this very dangerous?' Anna asked.

Judith made a moue. 'Yes. But I am doing what I have been told to do. Anyway, London does not feel that the danger is extreme. We are old school friends, are we not, meeting once again by happy chance, and my papers are impeccable. You could at least say that you are pleased to see me.'

'I am delighted to see you,' Anna said. 'You have no idea what has happened.'

'We know what has happened. Why do you think I am here?'

'You? But...'

'This is an emergency. I have been sent in to replace Telfer. I hope you have something for me.'

'You are in contact with Operation Daybreak?'

'I am now in command of it.'

God, if London knew the risk they are taking, Anna thought. But she said, 'That's a relief. Listen...' And she outlined what had happened over the past fortnight.

'And you think he will be confirmed as the Fuehrer's heir on this visit?' Judith asked.

'There is no other reason for him to have been summoned.'

'Then he must never get to Berlin. You say he is leaving on fifteenth January? At what time?'

'He will be catching the eight o'clock out of

Prague Central.'

'Excellent.'

'You think so?'

'That train travels very slowly for the first half-mile, because of all the lines and other trains using the station at that time in the morning. That stretch of track is also overlooked by a derelict warehouse. We could not ask for a better opportunity. Leaving at eight o'clock, he will almost certainly use the restaurant car for breakfast. That has huge windows. He will be a sitting duck for an expert with a high-powered rifle.'

'Do we have such an expert?'

'Yes. You may leave it with me.' Judith finished her coffee, squeezed Anna's hand. 'I have so enjoyed seeing you again.'

'And...?'

Judith made another moue. 'It should not happen again, at least until you return to Berlin. But I look forward to it.'

At last Anna felt she could relax; whatever her secret fears, Judith seemed to be in control of the situation. She returned to the Hradcany Castle feeling on top of the world. The business had been taken out of her hands, and she felt she could simply wait on events; she had no doubts as to Judith's efficiency, as long as she kept her nerve, or the efficiency of the assassination squad sent from London. Even Himmler would have to be pleased if his arch rival was murdered by a bunch of foreign agents.

Her principal problem was that, at least during

office hours, when Haussmann presumably had other duties, she did not have enough to do. To provide a reason for her being in Prague at all, she had been given an office of her own, with all the paraphernalia required – filing cabinets and a telephone and so on – but the filing cabinets were empty and she had no one to telephone. On the other hand, it was a sanctuary, a place where she was safe from even the constant chattering of Birgit, where she could await events ... Her head jerked as there was a tap on the door. Some idiot unaware that the office was occupied, she supposed. 'Come.'

The door opened. 'Countess! I should have come to see you before.'

Anna studied the little man. Feutlanger had always reminded her of a ferret. Now his nose was positively twitching as he surveyed her in turn; she wore a dress, and although she was seated behind her desk, there was a knee-hole and her legs were visible. 'I can't imagine why,' she remarked.

He came into the room, closing the door behind himself. 'Well, it was discourteous of me, to say the least. When I remember how we worked together two years ago after that attempt to assassinate Herr Meissenbach ... Is it true he has since been condemned for treachery?'

'Herr Meissenbach is at present in a concentration camp,' Anna agreed. 'He attempted to betray me – that is, betray the Reich,' she added for good measure, 'to the Soviets.'

'And you always get your man,' Feutlanger

said, in apparent admiration. 'Or woman, as the case may be. I remember as if it were yesterday your interrogating that woman Hosek just before she committed suicide.'

Just before she used the cyanide tablet I had been able to get to her, Anna thought. *Under your very eyes*. 'That whole incident was a foul-up by your people, who had not properly searched her.'

'Oh, I agree entirely,' Feutlanger acknowledged. 'They were disciplined. And now you are back, and Prague is a brighter place. Tell me about the woman you had coffee with this morning.'

Anna was totally surprised, but she reacted strongly, if only to give herself time to think. 'Have you been having me followed, Herr Feutlanger?'

'It is my duty, and that of my staff, to keep an eye on our people, when they are outside of the castle grounds. It is for your own protection. You must know that these people hate us.'

'And you think that I am incapable of protecting myself?'

'If you can see your antagonist, or better yet, reach him, your record indicates that you can take care of anyone. But not even you, Fraulein, can do a lot about a bullet fired from a distance.'

'And your man, lurking, would be able to prevent that happening?'

'Probably not. But he might well be able to identify the assassin and avenge you.'

'How terribly reassuring.'

'You have not answered my question about the young lady.'

Anna had had time to determine how to handle the situation; she did not see how she could do better than continue the cover arranged in Madrid. 'The young lady and I were at school together in Vienna before the war. She is now married to a Spanish nobleman. Her name is the Countess Judith de Sotomayer. She is in Prague on business, and we happened to encounter each other, so we had coffee together. You may put all of that in your file, and I am going to tell the Reich-Protector that I dislike being followed as if I were a common criminal.'

Feutlanger clicked his heels. 'At the end of the day, Countess, even the SD needs the support and assistance of the Gestapo to carry out its duties. Heil Hitler!'

'The poor fellow is only attempting to do his job,' Heydrich explained. 'And he is of course quite right; we do need them to do the spade-work for us. But I will tell him not to be a nuisance as regards you.'

'Thank you. I really do not enjoy having trench-coated heavies breathing down my neck wherever I go.'

'Of course. It will not happen again. Now tell me, do you know this Countess well?'

Once again Anna knew that she had to be scrupulously accurate in what she told this man. On the other hand, she could not imagine Him-mler confiding the Berlin incident. 'I did once, Herr General,' she said. 'When we were at school together. But she was a year older than me, thus she left the convent in 1937, the year before the Anschluss. As you know, I was rather busy after that, so we did not keep in touch. And then, purely by chance, I encountered her in Madrid, with her husband, when I over-nighted there on my way back to Germany. I am sure Herr Essermann, who was escorting me, will remember it. I had dinner with them. The Count is a dreadful bore who actually tried to sell me real estate. Over dinner!'

Heydrich was a difficult man to distract. 'If she left your convent the year before you, she must have been in a higher form. Is it usual for girls of different ages and in different forms to be close friends?'

'Ah ... we found we had a lot in common.'

'I see. And now she has followed you to Prague.'

Once again, thin ice. 'How can she have done that, Herr General? She did not know I was in Prague. She was as surprised as I when we encountered each other.'

'You did not mention that you were coming here when you met in Madrid?'

'I did not know I was coming here when we met in Madrid.'

'Hmm. Still, I think it is not a bad idea for Feutlanger to keep an eye on her. In our business coincidences are always suspicious.'

Damnation, Anna thought. And there was no way she could contact Judith to warn her. While

Judith would be setting up the assassination scenario with total confidence. She became more and more anxious as the day approached, and nearly jumped out of her skin when Heydrich entered her apartment early on the morning of the 15th.

'I am leaving now, Anna. Be a good girl and when I come back we will celebrate together, eh?'

'I am looking forward to that, Herr General.'

He peered at her. 'Are you all right?'

'Sir?'

'You look breathless. Feutlanger has not been bothering you, has he?'

'No, no. But I shall miss you.'

'You have Haussmann.'

'Not quite the same thing, sir.'

Heydrich smiled, and slipped his hand beneath the sheet to caress her naked thigh. 'You are a treasure. But I am only going for three days.' A squeeze. 'And when I come back...'

The door closed, and she was left staring at it. Within the hour he would be dead! It was a quite overwhelming thought. Staying in bed was impossible. She got up, had a bath, then dressed and sat down to breakfast.

'Countess?' Birgit asked, serving. 'Are you all right?'

'Should I not be all right?'

'You look, well...'

'Oh, really, Birgit. Pour the coffee, do.'

She looked at her watch. Eight thirty. The train normally ran on time, so it would have left at eight sharp. It usually took about forty-five minutes to negotiate the immediate traffic before attaining any speed. So ... it should be done now. She gulped at her coffee, and spilled some. Birgit hurried forward with a clean napkin, but preferred not to comment as her mistress was clearly in a bad mood.

How would the news be broken? Right now, she supposed all would be pandemonium at the station; she was in fact surprised that they couldn't hear the racket, or at least the sirens. But at any moment the castle would explode ... A quarter to nine.

Anna got up and went to the window. As the apartment overlooked one of the inner court-yards of the castle she had no means of knowing what might be happening out front, but below her all was peace, with a solitary gardener prowling about the wintry flower beds. She could contain herself no longer, and went down to her office, which meant descending the main staircase and passing through the great entry hall. Sentries, guards and secretaries hurried to and fro. All greeted her, as all knew she was Heydrich's protégée, but none of them gave any indication of crisis.

She closed the door, sat at her desk. How she wished he had some real work to do. The phone rang. She snatched at it. 'Yes!'

'Coffee! Ten o'clock.'

'Oh, God! What has happened?'

'Ten o'clock,' Judith repeated. The line went dead.

Anna slowly replaced the receiver. There had been no time to warn her. But even if there had, they would still have to meet. Telephoning her was incredibly dangerous, for both of them, so something disastrous must have happened. She had to know what had gone wrong, and decide what needed to be done – if there was anything that could now be done. And Heydrich had promised that she, at least, would not be shadowed. A great deal would depend on whether Feutlanger was still after Judith. That she was still here more than a fortnight after their first meeting was unexpected, and apart from being risky in itself, would certainly acti-vate the Gestapo if they knew about it.

So she had to go to the meeting. She felt as if she were riding a bicycle whose wheels had become stuck in a tramline and were carrying her towards an oncoming tram, and there was nothing she could do about it.

She returned upstairs. 'I am going for a walk,' she told Birgit.

'It is very cold out, Countess.'

Anna put on her sable, added her fur hat, pulled on a pair of thick gloves. 'I need the fresh air. I will be back for lunch.'

She walked as casually as she could, but still arrived at the coffee shop five minutes early, although Judith was already there. 'This is very risky,' Anna said, as she sat down. 'The Gestapo are interested in you.'

'Why?'

Anna waited while the coffee was served.

'Simply because one of their people saw me talking with you the other day. I saw them off with the schoolgirl story, and explained that our meeting was entirely by chance. If they were to see us together again...'

'Um. I think the best thing I can do is get out of here.'

'What has gone wrong?'

'Our people were in place, they had a perfect view of the train, and it even stopped, exactly opposite our window, with Heydrich sitting in his window, large as life and clear as day. But as our man was about to make the shot, another train pulled up alongside, and also stopped, blocking the view. He had to wait for it to move, but the Berlin train moved first, streaking away. There was nothing he could do.'

'Shit!' Anna muttered. 'And our people?'

'Oh, they are all right. No one knew they were there.'

'So what happens now?'

'It will have to be set up again.'

'The next time he takes a train out of Prague, it will be to return to Germany as Hitler's heir.'

'He will still have to tidy things up here. You will have to arrange it.'

'Me?'

'As you say, it will be too dangerous for me to remain here any longer. I will leave on this afternoon's train. Your contact from now on will be Professor Corda.'

'Who is Professor Corda?'

'He teaches music. What instrument do you play?'

'I don't play any instrument.'

'Oh, come now. You must have played something at school.'

'I used to play the piano at the convent. But I haven't touched one since leaving.'

'Then it is time you took it up again. Make an appointment to see Professor Corda, and he will set up a series of lessons. I am sure even Heydrich will approve: all Germans are musical. Now I must go.' She reached across the table to squeeze Anna's hand. 'We must get together again when this is over.'

Anna felt a profound sense of loss as she walked back to the castle. Whatever her mental problems, Judith had been such a breath of confident fresh air. Now she was again on her own. As if she had not been on her own a dozen times before, she reminded herself. But she had always hated the sense of isolation that went with her job, her position. That was where her clandestine meetings with Clive, and with Joe in America, had been so important, reminding her that she was part of a team. Judith was another member of that team, and they had shared as much reassuring intimacy as she ever had with either of the two men.

Now, and for the foreseeable future, she was again bereft. And she was stuck with an even more difficult situation. If Heydrich returned as Hitler's deputy, just to pack up his command before leaving Prague forever, all London's plans would be negated. The best they would be able to hope for would be the extraction of their team before they were betrayed and rounded up. And once she moved into the front row, as it were, if they were betrayed, she would be too.

Therefore it made no sense for her to get involved until she had a better idea of what was happening. Even if London were to panic, she reflected, there was no way they could get in touch with her, unless they risked sending Judith back again.

She regained the castle, went up to her apartment, handed her coat and hat and gloves to Birgit. 'Countess, are you all right? You are trembling.'

'Well, it is very cold out there.' Anna poured herself a schnapps, then sat down to get her thoughts into shape. But the more she considered the matter, the more impossible the situation appeared. She could do nothing now until Heydrich returned. But she could do even less if, as she anticipated, he returned merely to prepare to depart again, for good. Unless she undertook the executive action herself. But not only had she been forbidden to do that, she was not in a hurry to sacrifice herself, and the thought of sacrificing her family was impossible. So ... do nothing, think nothing, until Heydrich returned. Then pray for a miracle.

She did not feel like eating in the canteen, but their new apartment had a kitchenette as well as an extra bedroom, so she had Birgit prepare a light lunch, and was just sitting down when there was a knock on the door.

'Get that, will you, Birgit,' she said. 'But I do not wish to see anyone at this moment.'

Birgit hurried to the door and opened it. 'Oh!' she said. 'Ah! The Countess is lunching—'

'This is important,' Feutlanger said, pushing her aside.

'Really, Herr Feutlanger,' Anna protested. 'You have no right to come barging into my private quarters.'

'I have something to show you.'

'Well, it will have to wait until after my meal.'

'I think you need to come now, Countess. It affects someone who is known to you.'

A lump of lead suddenly formed in Anna's stomach. 'Who?'

'The Countess de Sotomayer.'

'What?' Anna pushed back her chair. 'Where is she?'

'Waiting for you. Will you come with me, please? I will bring you back here after.'

'You mean we are going somewhere?'

'That is correct.'

'To see the Countess de Sotomayer?'

'That is correct.'

Anna stood up. Now the crisis had arrived, she was, as always, utterly calm. 'If you have arrested the Countess de Sotomayer, Herr Feutlanger, you have seriously overstepped the limits of your authority. The Countess is a Spanish national, and is very well connected.'

'I am sure you are right, Countess, and I have

not arrested her. But I think she would like to see you.'

'You mean she is in your custody, but you claim that she is not under arrest.'

'That is correct. Shall we go? It will not take long, and I am sure your maid can keep your meal warm for you. But you will need a coat; we are leaving the building.'

Anna put on her sable and hat. She would not have been able to eat anyway, without knowing what had happened to Judith. The thought of anything happening to Judith, whether from a professional or a personal point of view, was unacceptable. But Feutlanger looked neither triumphant nor apprehensive, merely watchful. Patience.

There was a car waiting, and they sat together in the back. 'It is not far,' he said reassuringly.

The lead was beginning to return to Anna's stomach. Suddenly she knew what had happened. But *how* had it happened, if Feutlanger was so confident he, or his men, had not overstepped the mark?

The car stopped in front of the rather bleak-looking building. 'These places are never very pleasant,' Feutlanger remarked. 'But you must have been in quite a few of them.'

'I have never been in a morgue,' Anna said.

'I thought that killing people was your profession?'

'Looking at their bodies afterwards is not. Why have you brought me here? If you have been responsible for the Countess's death, you may be sure that I will report it to the Reich-Protector.'

'That is why I have brought you here, Countess, so that you can report to the Reich-Protector exactly what you have seen.'

The door had been opened for her. Anna glanced at him, then got out of the car, and followed the attendant up the wide steps, Feutlanger behind her. They entered a lobby, and then an inner door was opened for her. Her nostrils dilated, although the only smell was one of disinfectant. A medical attendant, wearing a white coat, clicked his heels and indicated where she should go. There were a dozen raised concrete slabs, every one containing a long mound beneath a white sheet. The attendant carefully raised the sheet from one of them, then removed it altogether.

Anna caught her breath. Judith's naked body was on its back, its head nestling on the mat of titian hair, its green eyes staring sightlessly at the ceiling. Her face was calm and relaxed; as she could have been dead only a couple of hours, rigor mortis had not yet set in. *I will look like this, one day*, Anna thought. *Perhaps one day soon. Will I look as relaxed, as beautiful?*

'I would like you to look closely,' Feutlanger said. 'And tell me if you see any marks, any discolouration, any punctures in the skin.'

Anna had to swallow an excess of saliva. 'You would not have brought me here if there was anything to find, Herr Feutlanger. How did she die?'

'Korvin!'

The attendant pulled Judith's lips apart. *Don't touch her*, Anna wanted to shout, but she did not, and with an effort Korvin parted the teeth. Instantly she smelt almonds. 'You will have to explain this to the Reich-Protector,' Anna said in a low voice.

'Indeed,' he agreed. 'But I am hoping you will be able to explain it to me first. Let us leave this place.'

Anna was happy to get out into the crisp winter air. 'You keep being mysterious. Now I would like some plain speaking. Are you attempting to tell me that the Countess did not die in your custody?'

'That is correct. As you know, Fraulein, I had my suspicions of the Countess. But they were no more than that and, as you say, she was both a foreign national and a lady of apparent importance. So I merely issued my staff each with a photograph of her, and told them to report if she was found to be indulging in any subversive activity. I will admit that they may from time to time be over-zealous. But that is partly your responsibility, after the slating you gave them, two years ago, over their mishandling of the shooting business, and the report you made to Berlin. So, knowing of my interest in the lady, when two of my people, on duty at the Central Station, saw the countess about to board a train for Switzerland, they approached her.'

'And you are saying they did not arrest her?'

'They did not have the time. They stood

beside her and said, "May we have a word, Countess", and a moment later she was dead.

Because she was obsessed with the certainty that she would one day have to kill herself, Anna thought. She had almost been waiting for the moment to arrive.

'My people immediately removed her before there could be a scene, and they also had her luggage.'

'And?' Anna felt the tension creeping through her body. Not that she could accept that Judith would ever be so stupid as to travel with incriminating documents.

'Oh, there was nothing.'

'In other words, your thugs are responsible for the death of an innocent woman.' The car had arrived in the castle courtyard, and the door was being opened for her. 'That will go in my report.'

'If I could have a word in private, Countess.'

'Are you arresting me, Herr Feutlanger?'

'Of course I am not, Fraulein. There are just one or two matters I would like to discuss with you.' He escorted her up the steps. 'It will not take a moment. My office is right here.'

Anna shrugged and entered the office, took off her coat and hat, laid them on a chair, sat before the desk, and crossed her legs. She knew she was still in a critical situation, but she also knew that the only way to deal with this self-important little man was to be even more aggressive.

Feutlanger sat behind the desk. 'The question we need to ask is, does an innocent woman normally walk around with a cyanide capsule in her mouth?'

'As the Countess is dead, we will never be able to ask her that.'

'Well, let me put it another way. If I were to search you now, including inside your mouth, would I find a cyanide capsule?'

'You would not, Herr Feutlanger. And if you were to attempt it, you would find yourself lying on a slab in that morgue, beside the Countess.'

He regarded her for several seconds, then decided to adopt a different approach. 'You knew this woman. You have confessed to that.'

'My dear Feutlanger, your world is closing in on you. Can you think of nothing but confessions and admissions, and lies? You asked me if I knew the Countess, a rather irrelevant question as we had been having coffee together, and I told you that we had been at school together. That was a fact, not a confession.'

'And you have not seen her since. Except today, of course.'

The trap was blatant. 'As you say, I did not see her again before today. But I saw her today, when she was still alive.'

Feutlanger's eyebrows shot up; he had not expected such a ready admission. 'You saw her today? When? Where?'

'Oh, come now, Feutlanger, we met at the coffee shop, this morning, as you well know. She is, or was, apparently a regular customer, and I happened to stop by this morning, so we met again.'

'Again, purely by chance.'

'Why, yes.'

'And what did you talk about?'

'Nothing of the slightest interest to you. Although she did tell me that she had completed her business here in Prague, and was returning to Madrid this afternoon.'

'And you discerned nothing ... unusual in her attitude, in what she had to say?'

'No, I did not. Now, if you will excuse me, I would like to have some lunch.'

She went upstairs. 'Oh, Countess,' Birgit said. 'You were so long.' She opened the oven in the kichenette. 'I hope this is not spoiled.'

'It does not matter. I do not want it.'

'Countess?'

'I am not feeling very well,' Anna said. 'I am going to bed, and I do not wish to be disturbed.'

Rationally, she supposed she was being absurd. If she had killed twenty-one times, this was one death for which she could not be held responsible. As she had thought, Judith had virtually had a death wish, almost a longing to have the tension of her life ended. She wondered if anyone at MI6 had realized by how slender a thread her sanity had hung.

But the death of a woman with whom she had been associated had always distressed her, more than that of any man. Only once had it been premeditated. Elsa Mayers, Hannah Gehrig, Ludmilla Tserchenka had all been instantaneous reactions to dangerous situations; the two

307

women in Washington – she did not even know their names – had been utterly hateful, but even then, while she had been waiting for the moment to take them on, gaining possession of the tommy gun had been fortuitous, opening fire instinctive. Gabriella Hosek had been an act of mercy, to save the woman from the hours of unbearable torture that were about to be inflicted on her by Feutlanger and his thugs. But she could remember as if it were yesterday holding Marlene Gehrig under the bath water until she drowned. She had felt physically sick; she still did when she thought of it.

But Judith ... Had they loved each other? They had made love, certainly. It had been a charade that had come very close to reality. What might have developed out of that she would never know. The true importance of Judith had been that they had shared the same profession, taken the same risks, sought the same ends. And would they wind up in the same place? Naked on a stone slab to be leered at by people like Feutlanger? Anna fiercely reminded herself that dying was not on her agenda, no matter what it took to keep her alive. Or to complete her mission.

'I gather that you have been having an interesting time,' Heydrich remarked.

Anna had not seen him immediately on his return; she had waited for him to come to her to tell her his news, and he had not done so for several hours. Well, she reflected, he had had his family to meet, and clearly he had had a session with Feutlanger. But now he was here.

'Herr Feutlanger seemed to find it so,' she agreed.

'While the odd dead body no longer interests you,' he remarked. 'Even when it is that of a friend.'

'School friendships seldom endure, sir. Frankly I was embarrassed when she suddenly turned up. I am sure you understand that I cannot greet old friends with the news of what I have been doing these last few years.'

'Good point.' He sipped the glass of schnapps she had poured him. 'And she gave you no hint that she was engaged in subversive activities?'

Anna shrugged. 'I think she may have had ideas of perhaps seeking my help, or even recruiting me. But when I told her I was working as a secretary for the Reich here in Prague, she changed the subject.'

'Did this conversation take place the first or the second time you met?'

Damn this man's powers of perception, Anna thought. 'It was the first time, sir.'

'Yet she wanted to see you again.'

'No, sir. She did not want to see me again. As I told Herr Feutlanger, she was apparently a regular customer at the coffee shop. I did not know this until I encountered her the second time. Then I think we both felt that we had to greet each other.'

'And she told you she was leaving Prague to return to Spain. Did you get the impression that she had completed her task here?'

'She told me she had completed her business, yes.'

'But not what that business was.'

'No.'

'Well, I suppose we shall never know the truth of it now. Feutlanger has been able to find no indication of any subversive activities in the city. Although,' he added thoughtfully, 'in view of the past behaviour of these people, that in itself could be suspicious. However, there can be no question that she was engaged in some illegal activity. You say you met her in Spain? At your hotel?'

'Yes, sir.'

'And her husband tried to sell you real estate?'

'Yes. I think, from my clothes and jewellery, she got the impression that I had become a wealthy woman, like her. I'm afraid I did not correct that misapprehension, as I did not wish her prying into my affairs.'

'Absolutely. But it may interest you to know that Feutlanger has made enquiries in Spain ... Well, he wasn't entirely sure how to handle the affair, what to do with the body, how to get hold of the husband, and so on, and he found out that there is no such person as the Count de Soto-mayer, and therefore, of course, no Countess. You had no suspicions of this when you met them? This Count, what did you make of him?'

Anna's brain was tumbling. 'He was a middle-aged man, not very attractive. I'm afraid I did not pay very much attention to him.'

'Yet they picked you up.'

'Sir?'

'Well, Anna, think. If the title was spurious, they were obviously at least confidence tricksters. I would have supposed the last thing they would have wanted was for her to run into an old school friend. At the sight of you, she should hastily have made herself scarce.'

'Unless they thought I would be a soft touch for whatever scam they were engaged in.'

'Good point. It is still a pity that she could not be interrogated.'

'I entirely agree, sir. I cannot help but feel what happened was the result of the heavy-handedness of Feutlanger's mob. May I ask what has happened to the body?'

'Oh, it has been cremated. We had no use for it, and neither did anybody else. In all the circumstances, I think you had a fortunate escape, or heaven knows what you might have been sucked into. Well...' He got up. 'I will see you later.'

'You have not told me the outcome of your visit, sir.'

'Oh, that went as well as we had hoped. I am now the Fuehrer's heir.'

'Oh, sir! Congratulations! Does that mean we will be leaving Prague?'

'Yes. But not right away. He wishes to prepare the ground before the announcement is made.'

'Was my name mentioned?' She held her breath.

'You are a greedy little wanton. I thought it

best not to mention your name, and he did not.' Anna could not stop her breath from escaping in a sigh of relief, but fortunately he again misinterpreted her reaction. 'Do not be disappointed. I have promised you a place at my side, and you shall have it.'

'Thank you, sir. May I ask if a date for your return, for the announcement to be made, was agreed?'

'Why, yes. The Fuehrer feels that the end of May would be most appropriate. That is only four months off. By that time I should have completed my business here. It is a pity we were not able to establish exactly why your old school friend was here, but I'm sure something will turn up.'

'I am sure of it,' Anna said. 'But as we are going to be here for another four months, do you think I could start taking music lessons?'

He raised his eyebrows. 'Music lessons?'

'I used to play the piano at school. I think I was quite good. But of course, once I went to training school I had no further opportunities. Dr Cleiner was not interested in music.'

'Only in making you parade naked in front of him, eh?'

'Yes, sir.'

'He is a nasty piece of work. But you must admit that he is good at his job. After all, he produced you.'

Anna allowed her lip to curl. 'He merely proved to me what I could do, sir.'

'Good point.'

'And the fact is that I really do not have enough to do here. Except when you are free, of course.'

'Well, I have no objections to your taking lessons. But you'll have to find someone here in Prague as a teacher; I do not wish you going back Berlin until I can accompany you.'

Can he really be growing fond of me? Anna wondered. *Or is he merely afraid to let me out of his sight?* 'I think there are people here in Prague who I could use, sir. I have had a Dr Corda recommended to me. Do you know of him?'

Another case of holding her breath; Feutlanger had said that all intellectuals in Prague were under constant investigation and surveillance.

Heydrich considered for a moment. 'No. The name means nothing to me.'

'Then you have no objection if I apply to join him as a student.'

'By all means do so.'

'And will you request Herr Feutlanger not to breathe down my neck every time I visit the doctor? It would be too embarrassing for words.'

Heydrich nodded. 'I will tell Feutlanger that your music lessons are not to be interfered with.'

That was not quite what she wanted, but she dared not press any harder. 'Thank you, sir. I will call for an appointment today.'

Ten

Death in the Morning

Countess! This is an honour and a pleasure.'

Alfred Corda was not what Anna had anticipated, being a very large man, over six feet tall
and built like an ox. His only concession to
being either an artist or an intellectual was his
beard, which, like his dark hair, was streaked
with grey, and his pince-nez. Now he bustled to
help her out of her coat.

Anna took off her gloves, removed her hat,
and fluffed out her hair, while he watched
appreciatively. 'It is good of you to see me,' she
said. 'You are clearly much in demand.'

On her way up the stairs to the office she had
passed several studios, all in use, and indeed the
house was filled with scales and various
discords, not to mention long-haired young men
and dishevelled young women; she wondered if
London's assassination team had been amongst
them.

'But I repeat, this is an honour. We do not
often entertain students from the castle. And
you...'

'I am somewhat mature for a student?'

'No, no. Of course not. May I ask where you obtained my name?'

'You were recommended to me.' Anna glanced at the open door, but there was no one in sight, and there was such a background racket going on she did not suppose there was any risk of her being overheard. 'By Belinda.'

The doctor's cultivated bonhomie disappeared as if she had turned a switch. He too glanced at the door, then went to it.

'I would leave that open,' Anna suggested. 'As we have just met for the first time. If we both face it, we cannot be surprised, but to close it might encourage curiosity.'

He hesitated, clearly unable to make up his mind, or to comprehend what was happening. 'You are from the castle.' It was almost an accusation.

Anna sat down, crossed her knees. 'Can you think of a better place for me to be from?'

He licked his lips, and looked at the door again.

'If you had been betrayed,' Anna said, 'do you think I would have come alone? You would already have been arrested.'

A last hesitation, then he came back to his desk and sat down. 'You could be a Nazi spy, sent to infiltrate...' He paused.

'Operation Daybreak?'

He gasped, and his hand dropped to the desk drawer. But Anna, anticipating the reaction, had already opened her handbag and drawn her

Luger. 'Think,' she recommended. 'If you open that drawer, I will kill you. I can do that with impunity, because, as you have reminded yourself, I am from the castle, and am therefore inviolate. Equally, as I am from the castle, they know where I am at this moment.'

'You...'

'They know that I have come to you to begin a series of music lessons, and that each lesson is to last an hour. They are expecting me back for lunch. Now listen to me, very carefully. The Belinda you know, the Countess de Sotomayer, is dead.'

'What? You—'

'Please keep your voice down, and listen. She committed suicide when arrested by the Gestapo. I am very sorry about this, but you can rest assured that she did not betray you, or me, or any of us. She was, in any event, my deputy.' She had no doubt that Judith's shade would forgive her. 'So her death, while it means that I have had to take over the direct contact with you, also means that there is no change in the overall plan.'

'How can I believe this? London...'

'Have you any means of contacting London?'

'Of course I do.'

'Thank God for that. Then do so immediately. Ask them to name something only I can know.'

'It will take time. It is very dangerous.'

'We have time. At the moment. I will return next week, for another lesson.'

'But for you to take command of such an

316

operation. You are only a girl.'

'Was not the Countess de Sotomayer a girl?'

'Well, no, she was—'

'Only a year or two older than myself.'

'She looked a good deal older. You ... well...'

'I do not look my age. Actually, that has often been an advantage. London will confirm my command, Herr Doctor. But now, shall we begin with scales?'

Not for the first time Anna had been forced to place her life in the care of someone she did not altogether trust. She had no doubts about Corda's patriotism, his commitment to Czechoslovakia, to the death of Heydrich. But she had to have doubts about his nerve.

Her sense of isolation grew, and increased when, at her next lesson, although Corda swore the message had gone off, there had been no reply.

'I do not like it,' he complained. 'They must have decided to abort.'

'I cannot believe that. Is the team still in Prague?'

'It is in the country,' he said cautiously. 'Awaiting orders. They are becoming very anxious.'

'Aren't we all? But the confirmation will come. Be patient.' It was the name of the game.

'Well?' Clive demanded.

Baxter knocked out his pipe. 'Operation Daybreak will go ahead.'

'Even if—'

'It means sacrificing Anna? I put this to them, and their decision was that the death of Heydrich was more important than the life of one of our agents, no matter how important that life may be to you.'

'That is barbarous.'

'As I keep trying to knock into that thick skull of yours, war is by definition barbarous. People get killed. Only the end result matters. Send Corda a message with a question to ask Anna which only she can answer. That should satisfy him. And, Clive, I am sorry about Judith.'

'As I am sure you will be sorry about Anna,' Clive said bitterly.

'Look, her instructions have not changed, except in so far as she is now dealing directly with the operators. She is still required only to supply place and time, not to get personally involved.'

'Anna always gets personally involved,' Clive reminded him, and left the office.

'I have heard from London,' Corda announced at their next lesson.

'Well, thank heavens for that,' Anna said.

'They have sent me a question to ask you, which they say only the genuine Belinda can answer. I do not understand it myself. Are you prepared to hear it?'

'Of course I am.'

'They say I must ask you to give me a number. If it corresponds with the number they have given me, then you are genuine. It sounds like some kind of magician's game. Does it make any sense to you?'

'I think so. The number you want is twenty-one.'

Corda gazed at her, then looked down at the sheet of paper in front of him. 'How could you possibly have known that?'

'It is the number of people I have been forced to kill in the course of my profession.'

Corda's head came up slowly. 'You have killed twenty-one people? How old are you?'

'I am coming up to my twenty-second birthday,' Anna told him, 'but I started young. Now let's get down to business. What is the size of the team?'

'We have three operatives. They are Czechs who left when the country was taken over by the Nazis. They have been serving with the British Army, and are of course volunteers.'

'Do they regard this as a suicide mission?'

'Only as a last resort. There are plans to get them out of the country when the operation is completed. Do you wish to meet them?'

'No.'

Corda raised his eyebrows.

'My orders are not to become personally involved, and under no circumstances must I risk being identified. Had it not been for Sotomayer's catastrophe you would not know I exist. Now, tell me how many locals are involved.'

'I have a team of ten.'

'Ten?'

'The operatives have to be housed and fed and

concealed. They have now been here for some time, waiting to be informed as to their next opportunity. You know what happened the first time?'

'I set it up.'

'They had bad luck.'

'Well, the next opportunity may be the last, if the task is to be completed before the quarry returns to Berlin for good. What is the armament situation? How much high explosive do they have?'

'There is no high explosive. London asked us to procure some, if necessary by raiding Nazi armouries, but this has proved impossible. Your predecessor knew this.'

And never thought to tell me, Anna thought. On the other hand, Judith had also been told that she was not to be involved in the actual operation. 'So what do they have?'

'Pistols, a tommy gun, a high-velocity hunting rifle, and some grenades.'

Shit, she thought. *Shit, shit, shit.* 'Do they realize that, as the plan to use the rifle misfired, and is not likely to recur, with those weapons it will be a matter of getting very close to the victim?'

'Can't we wait until he takes another train journey?'

'It is unlikely that he will use the train again until he leaves for the last time. If we wait until then, and that again misfires, then the operation is a failure.'

'Then what are we to do? Can they be smuggled into the castle?'

'No.'

'You must have a plan.'

Anna had already realized that in view of the limited weaponry available there was only one possible plan. Do not under any circumstances become involved, Clive had said. But Clive had also said that the operation had to be successful. 'Yes,' she said. it will involve a direct confrontation with the bodyguard.'

'You mean a shoot-out in the street?' Corda was aghast. 'They will have no hope of getting away. Heydrich always travels with bodyguards both in front and behind his car. And then there will be traffic, and people...'

'I am aware of all of these things. But I believe it can be done, and that the operatives will be able to get away afterwards. You have a map of the city?'

Corda spread it on his desk.

'Now,' Anna said. 'This is the route he always takes, from the house he is using to the castle.' She traced it with her finger.

'Do you not think we have been over this a thousand times?' Corda asked. 'It is a very carefully selected route. Heydrich may know nothing about Operation Daybreak...' He paused to give her a sidelong glance, as if wondering if even that was true. 'But he is not a fool. He knows how hated he is, and that one day a patriot may take a pot shot at him. So the route is through the very heart of the city, at rush hour every morning, when the streets are packed. The traffic is mostly bicycles, of course; only the Germans or their supporters are allowed a petrol ration. But in addition to the mere numbers of people, the crowds are always infiltrated with Gestapo watching and listening. There is no possibility of anyone drawing a pistol, much less waving a tommy gun, without instant pandemonium.'

'I know all of that,' Anna said. 'But suppose the quarry were to turn off here, preferably without at least part of his escort...' She indicated the corner. 'That leads away from the business centre – goes round it, in fact – and rejoins it just before the castle. There are never many people there, and certainly no Gestapo.'

'But why should he do that?'

'Leave that with me. I will let you know the day, and all you have to do is place your men. Can you arrange a hand-pushed dray cart?'

'I should think so.'

She picked up a pencil from the desk and made a mark on the street plan. 'It should be positioned here. If all goes well the first escort will overshoot the corner. Heydrich's car will turn sharp right. As it does so, the dray should start to cross the road, in front of the rear escort.'

'If the rear escort is an armoured vehicle, as it usually is, will it not simply push the cart out of he way?'

'Almost certainly.'

'Then what will be gained?'

'A minute. Perhaps two. Even as much as five. Every minute counts. Now, you will have a man here, just round the corner, but in a position where he can be seen by the executive operators. A wave of his arm will indicate that this far everything is going to plan. No wave will mean either that something has gone wrong or that Heydrich is simply not turning off. But I am quite sure that he will do so.

'Now, your two executives will be here, at the next corner, where there is the very sharp right-hand bend. One here, with the tommy gun, and one here with a pistol. The car will slow to make the turn. When it does, the man with the tommy gun should be able to spray it with bullets and make his escape before the escort can arrive. They will, in any event, be more anxious to make sure Heydrich is all right than thinking of taking off after the assassin. I will let you know, at one of these lessons, the day the operation can be carried out.'

'How can you be sure he will take this diversion, at any time?'

'I will be in the car.'

'You? But ... you will be killed. I will have to tell my people...'

'No,' Anna said. 'They must be thinking only about killing Heydrich. That a woman is riding with him is her bad luck.'

He stared at her. 'You wish to die?'

'No. And as I know what is going to happen, I should not die. But this is the only way it can be done.'

Confident words, Anna thought, as she returned

to the Castle. She was exceeding her orders, and putting herself in extreme danger. But there was no other way it could be done, no other way Heydrich could be persuaded to place his head in the noose. And if she made a mistake? She would have to rely on Himmler's promise that he would look after her family. As for Clive, and Joe and Wild Bill and Baxter, they would surely be able to deduce what had happened, what she had done; there would be no reason for the Germans to suppress the name of the woman who had had the misfortune to be sitting beside the Reich-Protector when he was killed, and who had died with him.

The question was, when would she be able to make it happen? That depended on her being able to spend the night at Heydrich's house.

'It has been decided,' Heydrich said. 'I am to hand over my duties at the end of May, and return to Berlin on the first of June, when the official announcement of my new position as Deputy Fuehrer will be announced.'

'Oh!' Anna said.

'You don't look very pleased.'

'It's just that I can't shrug off this feeling that once you are back in Berlin and installed as Deputy Fuehrer, you will have no more use for me.'

She was seated at her desk, and he leaned over to kiss the top of her head. 'I shall always have a place, and a time, for you, Anna. I have become very fond of you, you know.'

'Have you, Reinhard?'

'You are about the only rock in my life. You know the situation. We live in a society filled with envy, with plots, with selfish determination to climb on other men's, and women's, backs to reach the goal we seek.'

She wondered if he realized he was talking about himself as much as anyone else.

'But you,' he went on, 'you are different. You wish only to serve the Reich, and within the Reich, me. You are the most faithful of aides.'

Anna swallowed.

His hand caressed her neck. 'Oh, I know that you were coerced into working for us. But I am growing to feel more and more with every day that you are now truly one of us. One of mine. My treasure.'

He was going to have her weeping in a moment. 'I wish only to be at your side, Reinhard.'

'And you will always be at my side, Anna. You have a birthday coming up, haven't you?'

'May twenty-first.'

'When you will be twenty-two years old. May twenty-first. That is just a little too early for what I have in mind. Oh, we shall celebrate your birthday, but that will have to be here in this office. Do you remember that week we spent together in my villa in Bavaria, just before you went to Russia, two years ago?'

'Yes, I do.'

'I have the fondest memories of that week.'

No doubt he does, she thought. He had been at his most brutally sadistic, and she had had to gurgle with pleasure at everything he had done to her.

'Are the memories pleasant for you also?'

'Of the week, oh, entirely. But it was so closely followed by the Meissenbach affair, and then Russia.'

'I know. I feel so guilty about having exposed you to that. It will not happen again.'

'Sir?'

'You are going on no more missions. You have done more than enough for the Reich. Now, as I have said, I want you at my side, always.' His hand was still caressing her neck. 'Take off your tie.'

Anna pulled the knot loose, laid the tie on the desk.

'And unbutton your shirt.'

Again she obeyed, and his hand slipped inside to caress her breasts. She gave an obliging little shudder of pleasure.

'I wish to repeat that week, and I do not know how soon my new official duties will give me the time to spend with you. Listen, as I said, your birthday is too early, but on the Tuesday, that is the twenty-sixth, my wife and daughter are leaving to return to Berlin, to put our house there in order. That gives us five days. I would like you to move in with me for those five days.'

Fortunately, he was still standing behind her, leaning against the back of her head, both of his hands now inside her shirt. He could not see her face. 'People will talk,' she murmured.

'Let them. I will be gone at the weekend, and

326

then I will be Deputy Fuehrer, beyond the reach of gossip.'

'But if your wife were to find out...'

'She too will have to accept the situation. I will make you the first lady of Germany.'

'Do you think Fraulein Braun would accept that?'

'She will have to. She must understand that when the Fuehrer retires she will be yesterday's woman. In any event, she has never sought the limelight. I do not know whether this is her decision or the Fuehrer's.'

'And you think I seek the limelight?'

'Whether you seek it or not, Anna, you belong in it. You belong in evening dress with naked shoulders and half-naked breasts, dripping with diamonds, with your hair loose down your back.'

What dreams men have, she thought. But she had protested long enough, and besides his massaging was now becoming uncomfortable. 'You are turning my head.'

'Anna ... I would like to have a child by you. Would you not like to be a mother?'

Of a monster? 'More than anything else in the world.'

'Well, then, we shall start, on the five days we shall spend together before we return to Berlin. I will fuck you, morning, noon and night, and we will wear no protection.'

Shit, she thought, and not only because of the sex he was threatening her with. 'You mean you will not be attending the office at all during that time?'

At last his hands moved. 'I must, I am afraid. Duty before everything. There is always someone to be hanged, eh? But I shall come in on mornings only, for a few hours. The rest of the days, and the nights, will be ours.'

'You're giving me goose pimples.' she murmured, turning her face for a kiss.

'It must be Wednesday, the twenty-seventh of May,' Anna said.

Corda frowned. 'That is still a month away.'

'It is the first time the plan will be available. But it may also be the last. There can be no slip-ups. And it will give you time to prepare, not only your people but the escape route for the operatives.'

'And you can guarantee that he will use the route on that day?'

'Yes. But I cannot guarantee the exact time. I know it will be early, but it may be half an hour each way. Your people must be in position from half past seven. You say you have three. Remember, one must be on the corner of the turn-off. His task will be to signal the two executives. They should be waiting at the next corner, where the sharp turn is. You say they are absolutely reliable?'

'They are the very best, and they are dedicated.'

'Very good. Now, you can give them the rough outline of the plan, so that they can reconnoitre the ground, but the details are not to be given until the day before, that is, Tuesday the twenty-sixth. On that day you will give them their final orders. These are that they should kill the driver and the bodyguard, who will be sitting beside him in the front, as well as Heydrich, of course. None of the three must survive to say what happened.'

'You are taking a terrible risk. If they are spraying the car with machine-gun bullets...'

'The moment I see them, I am going to drop to the floor of the car. But they must kill the men and then make off. The escort will be close behind.'

'It is still an immense risk for you to take. You are a very brave woman, Countess.'

'Let us just say that I am committed. But I have every intention of surviving.' *As I have done so often before*, she thought. But at this level she had survived only by failing to carry out the assignment. This time there was no room for failure.

As so often before, the waiting was the most difficult part, especially when she had so little to do with her time. Even her music lessons were now redundant, but she maintained them as part of her plan. Every week Corda looked at her with glowing, longing eyes. He was sure she was going to die. But then, Feutlanger looked at her the same way; he knew she was on the verge of escaping him, perhaps forever.

And needless to say, there was a letter from Himmler. *I need what you have, urgently. It is*

329

going to happen on June 1. To which she replied: *It will never happen, my Reichsfuehrer. I have the means to stop it. You will know of it by the end of May.*

And then, finally, the day itself came. Heydrich rested on his elbow as he looked down at her. 'Last night was the best I have ever had. Was it like that for you?'

'The best,' she assured him.

'Anna, I love you. Do you know what I am going to do? I am going to divorce my wife and marry you.'

Oh, my God! She could only put her arms round him and bring him down for a kiss. Only Ballantine Bordman had ever proposed marriage to her before. And this man had less than three hours to live! She hated him, and everything he stood for, everything he had made her do, everything his Nazi regime stood for. She had dreamed of his destruction for three years. And now she felt weaker than at any moment in her life.

He pushed himself up. 'I must go. I have a meeting at nine o'clock.'

She grasped his hand. 'I would like to come with you.'

'It will be very boring.'

'I have some things to pick up. We left in such a hurry yesterday.'

'Well, then, don't be long.'

Birgit was waiting for her. If she had understood for some time that Anna was the Reich-Protector's mistress, this was the first time she

330

had actually slept under Heydrich's roof. She apparently found it difficult to believe that it had happened, or was still happening. 'Are we leaving now, Countess?'

'No, no,' Anna assured her. 'We are not leaving until Sunday. But I need to go to the csstle with the Reich-Protector today. We will be back for lunch.'

She dressed carefully, wore a broad-brimmed summer hat, but as he liked, left her hair loose, secured by a ribbon on the nape of her neck. It was a warm day, and she wore thin gloves.

Heydrich was waiting by the open Mercedes tourer. 'You look enchanting, as always,' he murmured as he sat beside her in the back.

'I feel excited,' she admitted.

'Is there something exciting happening today?'

'No, no. But next week...'

He squeezed her hand.

The bodyguard got into the front seat beside the driver. The front car, which contained Haussmann and another aide, had been waiting, its engine running, and now at a signal from Haussmann it moved off. Heydrich's driver allowed it to move fifty yards in front, then followed. Another fifty yards behind, the third car also fell into place; this was an armoured vehicle and contained four SS men as well as a mounted machine gun.

For the first mile the road was relatively empty of traffic, and what there was hastily pulled to one side as Haussmann's driver blared his horn.

Then the traffic thickened, dozens of bicycles roaming across the road and the little caravan slowed.

'It is always like this,' Heydrich explained.

'I know a short cut,' Anna said.

'Do you?'

'I have used it often. It will take us round the commercial centre and bring us out within a block of the castle. It will save at least ten minutes.'

'You are a knowledgeable little girl. Where is this short cut?'

'There! That corner.'

'Turn right,' Heydrich commanded.

'Major Haussmann ...'

'Let him wrestle with the traffic. It will be interesting to see who gets to the castle first.'

'Yes, sir.' The driver gave a toot on his horn, and swung right into the narrow road.

Anna dared not turn her head, but out of the corner of her eye she saw the dray start to cross the road. From behind them there came the blaring of a horn and then a crash and several shouts. 'What has happened?' she asked in alarm.

Heydrich looked back. 'Some cretin has attempted to cross the road in front of Bittner. He will have to find a new cart.'

Anna, still looking straight ahead, saw a man strolling along the pavement, suddenly raising his arm as if going to scratch his head, and then thinking better of it. Heydrich did not notice, but the SS agent sitting beside the driver did, and turned his head to look at the man more closely. She reckoned that did not matter as within a couple of minutes he should be dead. 'It is the next corner,' she said. 'It is quite sharp.'

The driver braked, and as he did so, a man appeared from around the corner itself, carrying a tommy gun. Anna screamed, and dropped to the floor of the car, waiting for the rattle.

But there was none. Instead the guard opened fire, as did Heydrich, who leapt from the car, drawing his Luger as he did so. 'Damnation!' he snapped.

'That man was going to kill you, Herr General,' the guard said.

'That was his idea,' Heydrich agreed. 'But his gun jammed. What rubbish these people are. And now he has got away.' He turned back to the car. 'Really, Anna, I am ashamed of you, screaming like a frightened little girl.'

Anna slowly started to uncoil herself from the floor of the car, her brain an angry turmoil. *What rubbish*, Heydrich had said with absolute accuracy. How a presumably highly trained assassin could allow his tommy gun to jam at such a moment...

Behind them a horn was blaring as the rear escort finally forced a passage. Heydrich opened the door to get in. 'Oh, get up,' he said irritably.

'Herr General!' the driver screamed.

Heydrich started to turn back, and there was a clang and a huge explosion. The Reich-Protector uttered a startled sound, threw up his arms, and fell forward, striking his head and clearly losing consciousness. Anna pushed herself up and looked down at him; the back of his tunic was stained with blood.

The wrecked car was surrounded by people, mainly soldiers and SS men. An ambulance arrived. Anna sat in the back of the car, knees pressed together and hands clenched. Haussmann sat beside her. 'What happened?' she asked.

'I am hoping you are going to tell me that, Countess. Did you not see?'

'No.' She allowed herself a little shiver. 'I saw a man with a tommy gun. I shouted to warn the General, and then I dropped to the floor. I knew there was going to be shooting. But nothing happened.'

Haussmann nodded. 'According to Zimmerman, the tommy gun jammed, and the would-be assassin ran off. Zimmerman fired after him, but I suppose he was so excited he missed.'

'Then there was a strange noise,' Anna said. 'A sort of clang, and then an explosion.'

'Yes. There was a second man waiting just around the corner, armed with a grenade. He threw this and struck the front bumper, just beside where the General was standing. That probably saved his life.'

'You mean he's not dead?' Anna cried. And hastily added. 'Oh, thank God for that!'

'He's very badly hurt,' Haussmann said, 'But the medics do not think it is life-threatening.'

What a fuck-up, Anna thought. A complete

fiasco. As for what would happen now... 'The assassins...?'

'They escaped. But we will get them. Do you have any idea why the Reich-Protector decided to take this route, so suddenly?'

'It was my fault. He was becoming so impatient with the traffic delays that I suggested we try another street.'

'Hmm. And these people were waiting for him to do that. Very odd. Well, I suppose Feutlanger will work it out. It's his job. Now, you are sure you are not hurt?'

'I don't think so.'

'Still, I think you should go to the hospital and have a check-up.'

'Will I be able to see the Reich-Protector?'

'Not immediately. His back is apparently full of bomb fragment and the medics said he would have to undergo emergency surgery. When he comes round, I am sure he will wish to see you.'

'Has Frau Heydrich been informed?'

'She will be, certainly.'

'And the Reichsfuehrer?'

'All of Germany will be informed, Countess. This is a most dastardly crime.'

There was so much to be considered, top of the list being her own position. Had everything gone according to plan, both the driver and the guard would have died along with Heydrich, leaving her the only person who could explain why he had chosen so sudden and catastrophic a change of route. But both of them were alive, and had overheard the conversation. And Heydrich was also alive, and would remember what had happened. What a mess. One thing was clear: she needed help, desperately, and that could only come from one source.

'Are you sure you are all right, Countess?' the doctor asked, having examined her. 'Your blood pressure is high, and yet you are cold.'

'Well, it was a terrible experience,' Anna pointed out. 'Is it possible for me to see the Reich-Protector?'

'Not today, Countess. He is undergoing extensive surgery, from which he will have to recover before he can see anyone.'

'But he is going to be all right?'

'Oh, yes. As soon as he is well enough to travel, we will transfer him to Berlin for recuperation. It may take some time, of course...'

Anna hurried to the castle. She was dripping sweat even if her temperature was down, and desperately felt like having a hot bath and a lie down. But first things first. 'Put me through to Berlin,' she told the girl on the exchange. 'Gestapo Headquarters.'

'I am sorry, Countess. No calls are being allowed out of Prague at this time.'

'Look, I am SD. I insist upon being given a line.'

'I am sorry, Countess. I am acting under strict orders from Herr Feutlanger, which have been confirmed by General Zeydorf.' The military commander of the city.

'Well, then, put me through to Herr Feut-langer.'

'Certainly, Countess.'

There were various clicks, and then a quiet voice said, 'Gestapo.'

'This is the Countess von Widerstand. I wish to speak with Herr Feutlanger, immediately.'

'I am sorry, Countess. Herr Feutlanger is not in the office at this time.'

'When do you expect him back?'

'I do not know, Countess. It is the attempt on the life of the Reich-Protector, you see. He is investigating.'

She called Heydrich's office, and spoke with Haussmann. 'I know, Countess, there is the most colossal flap.'

'I feel that I must report to Reichsfuehrer Himmler.'

'That has been done, Countess. Herr Feut-langer handled that personally.'

But how had he presented the situation? She wondered what would happen if she went to the station and boarded a train for Berlin. But to flee while her immediate boss was still recovering from the assassination attempt might well be regarded as an admission of guilt, unless she could be absolutely sure of Himmler's support, and while she trusted in his word in personal matters, she could not be sure of his pragmatism. He would undoubtedly be happy were Heydrich to die. But if Heydrich was not going to die, and instead recovered to start making accusations, might the Reichsfuehrer not conclude that his safest course would be to wash his hands of the one person who could betray him?

In any event, the thought of being arrested at the station and brought back to the castle in ignominy was not something she could face.

Birgit arrived with their things; she had been commanded to leave the Heydrichs' house, and was in a state of high excitement. 'Will we be returning to Berlin, Countess?' she asked.

'I imagine so,' Anna said, putting on an appearance of massive calm for all the churning in her stomach. She was used to being in control of situations, or at least to being sure of the backing of a higher authority. Now she only knew that the plot had been a colossal failure; she did not dare return to the music teacher until she could get some idea of what was going on, how far Feutlanger's investigations had progressed, whether or not he had made any arrests. Apart from the executives, Corda had said there were ten other people involved. And a chain is only as strong as its weakest link.

She spent a restless night, and next morning rang for a car. 'Where do you wish to go, Countess?' asked the transport manager.

'Well, really!' No one had ever questioned her movements before. 'I wish to go to the hospital, to visit the Reich-Protector.'

'Ah. Just give me a few minutes to see if a car is available. I will call you back.'

The bastard, she thought. He obviously felt it necessary to check with Feutlanger, who had apparently taken over control of the castle. Well, she reminded herself, he was in charge of security, and there could be no greater failure of security than to have the country's ruler blown up by a bomb. He was probably sweating more profusely than Anna herself.

There was a tap on the door, and Haussmann came in. 'Countess!' he cried. 'Great news! We have them!'

'What?'

'The terrorists.'

'So quickly? They are under arrest? Or dead?'

She was being optimistic. 'No, no,' the major said. 'They are hiding in a church. But we have the church surrounded. They cannot escape.'

'How do you know they are inside?'

'Well...' He looked embarrassed. 'Feutlanger received a tip-off. One of their own people.'

'You mean they were betrayed.'

'That is one way of putting it. This idiot actually went to Feutlanger and tried to bargain the safety of his family, who apparently live in Prague, against information. Well, once Feutlanger got him into that cellar of his, it didn't take long for him to be screaming everything he knew.'

A total fuck-up, Anna thought. They couldn't pick men who knew enough about weapons to be sure they were in working order, and to pick someone who had vulnerable relatives... 'He is having a busy time,' she remarked. 'Do you think they will surrender?'

'Well, General Zeydorf has taken control, and has virtually every soldier he commands surrounding that church. They must either surrender or die.'

'I do not think they will surrender,' Anna said. Did she hope that they would not? Did she dare hope that, so she could live? But if they had been betrayed by one of their own, then Corda would also have been betrayed, and if Corda was in Feutlanger's hands – while Heydrich still lived! So, after all her mental wriggling, her attempts to control events, her orders from London, her instructions from Himmler, it came down, very simply, to herself. And then a capsule? Himmler had sworn he would protect her family. She had to believe that. As for dying, she had a sudden sense of curiosity. The capsule, and then nothing save a beautiful corpse on a concrete slab ... Or hours of agony, after which she doubted her corpse would still be beautiful. But she would have lived up to the moment of her last breath. And either way, she would have completed her personal mission.

'Countess?' Haussmann asked anxiously. He had been studying her expression.

'It is all so ghastly. That there should be men out there, waiting to kill the Reich-Protector. Is he all right? There was to be an operation...'

'The operation has been carried out. I'm afraid they found more damage than they had suspected.'

'You mean he will not live?'

'Oh, his life isn't in danger. But it will be a few days before he can be moved. He's on life support. You know, an oxygen mask, intravenous feeding, that sort of thing.'

'Major Haussmann, Claus, I must see him.'

'I'm not sure he's conscious.'

'Just to see him.' She clutched the major's hand. 'My God! I feel so guilty. If we hadn't taken that road ... I love him, Claus. He is all I have.'

He gazed at her for several seconds, and she wondered if she had gone too far out of her perceived character. But then he nodded. 'Of course. I will arrange a car for you.'

'Countess?' Sister, imposing in her huge winged white cap, looked up from the note. 'This says you are to be allowed to see the Reich-Protector.'

'I am his closest aide,' Anna explained.

'If you are hoping to obtain some information as to what happened, you will not do so. The Gestapo have already been here. But the Reich-Protector is only conscious for a few seconds at a time. He certainly cannot speak.'

'I just want to be with him for a little while. Before his wife gets here.'

Sister raised her eyebrows.

'I am his *closest* aide,' Anna said again.

'I see.' She regarded the note again. 'Well, Major Haussmann says you are to be allowed to see him. Ten minutes only. Nurse!'

* * *

The nurse led Anna along the corridor. 'What a terrible thing,' she remarked.

'Terrible,' Anna agreed.

There was an armed SS guard seated outside the door.

'Sister has given permission,' the nurse said.

He stood to attention, clicking his heels. The nurse opened the door, and Anna inhaled; how like the morgue it smelled. 'Is he ever conscious?' she asked.

'Oh, yes. It comes and goes. But I do not think he recognizes anyone.'

'I would just like to sit beside him for a while. I am sure if he does come to he will recognize me.'

The nurse hesitated.

'I am his mistress,' Anna said. 'Did you not know that?'

The girl gulped. 'Sister said you could stay for ten minutes. I will return then.'

'Thank you.' Anna sat beside the bed, and the door closed. She gazed at Heydrich's face, clearly visible beneath the transparent oxygen mask. The machine throbbed slowly and quietly, as the drip attached to his arm clicked, and the monitor attached to his pulse ticked. The face was calm, relaxed, but then she recalled, it had always been calm, and relaxed, even when he had been ordering her to kill. Now he had given his last order.

She had only ten minutes. There was no time to brood on the past or to consider the future. She stood up, went round the bed, and disconnected the drip. Then she switched off the oxygen pump. The room was suddenly so quiet, with only the pulse monitor ticking, she wondered if the guard would notice. But there was no sound from outside the room either.

Anna waited, holding her own breath. Heydrich's eyes opened. She bent over his face. 'This is your own Final Solution, Reinhard. I have no doubt we will meet again,' she whispered. 'In Hell. Wait for me.'

His mouth moved as if he would have spoken, then the pulse monitor also fell silent.

Anna waited for another three minutes, then switched on the pumps again. She sat down, staring at Heydrich, waiting for any trace of movement of chest or nostrils or eyes. But there was none. Another minute passed, then she got up and opened the door. 'There is something wrong,' she told the guard. 'One of the machines has stopped.'

He looked inside, but obviously could not immediately make out anything amiss, as the two pumps were working rhythmically. 'Countess?'

The nurse came along the corridor. 'I'm afraid time is up, Countess.' She gazed at them. 'What is the matter?'

'I don't know,' Anna said. 'I am sure one of the machines has stopped.'

The nurse pushed her aside. Her practised eye took in the situation at a glance. 'My God!' she said. 'There is no pulse. You,' she shouted at the guard. 'Fetch Sister!'

He ran down the corridor.

'What has happened?' Anna asked.

'The Reich-Protector is dead.'

'Dead?' Anna cried. 'Dead?' she shrieked. 'He can't be dead. He opened his eyes. He saw me.'

'Then you are the last person he ever saw.'

Anna sank into a chair. 'My God!' she muttered. 'What a catastrophe. For me. For the Reich. For the world!'

'Here is Sister,' the nurse said gratefully.

Was it really over? Anna felt that she was swimming in sweat as she sat in the back of the command car to be driven back to the castle. Behind her the hospital was in a state of complete panic, but the doctors had recognized that she was distraught and had virtually ordered her to go home and lie down; they had even given her a packet of sedatives if she felt she needed them. As for Heydrich, there would be a post-mortem, but that could prove nothing beyond the fact that he had simply stopped breathing.

She was determined to get out of Prague and back to Berlin just as rapidly as possible. There was no more reason for either Zeydorf or Feutlanger to keep the city sealed, if they really did have the would-be assassins trapped in that church. She could, in fact, hear the distant sound of firing; the operatives must still be holding out. Brave men, who had done the best they could until they were betrayed. And she could not help them. Nor, presumably, could she help Corda. He must also be praying that they would die before they could be forced to reveal his part in the conspiracy. As for the traitor...

And what did she feel? At that moment, nothing. But she would feel, soon enough. If she had dreamed of Heydrich's death for three years, she had also, during those three years, been closer to him than to any other man. Or woman. He had asked her to marry him. And she had responded by carrying out the most cold-blooded of all her assassinations. Of course he had deserved to die. Of course she felt she had had the right, the duty, to kill him. But that could not negate the guilt of having done so.

The streets were crowded with agitated people. If they could not yet know that Heydrich was dead, they knew of the attempt on his life, and of the fighting going on at the church. It took her driver over half an hour to regain the castle, while at every pause people stared at her through the windows, often, as she was driving in a German car with a Swastika on the bonnet, shouting curses at her and some even spitting. 'They are swine,' the driver commented.

She hurried up the steps and into the great hall. Above all else she wanted a bath. Progress through the hall was also slow, as it was crowded with people, all shouting at each other. Several shouted at her, as her relationship with Heydrich was well known, but she ignored them and finally reached the grand staircase. As she placed her foot on the first step, a quiet voice said, 'A word, please, Countess.'

Anna hesitated. But she was going to have to confront him at some time, so it might as well be now. 'Why, Herr Feutlanger, I had gained the impression that you were avoiding me.'

'I have been very busy, as I am sure you understand. But now...'

He gestured towards the door to the Gestapo offices, and she stepped in front of him. She knew she had to be aggressive, dominating, but was taken entirely by surprise as she stepped through the opened door and had her arms seized by a man standing on each side of the opening. The door slammed shut behind her, and she was forced across the room to a desk; her groin struck the edge of the wood and she fell forward, her face bumping on the blotter.

Desperately she gasped for breath. 'Have you gone mad?' she shouted.

She felt hands on her buttocks, squeezing the flesh through her dress. 'I have looked forward to this moment for two years,' Feutlanger said.

Anna tried to get up, but the two men were holding her arms wide apart, and pressing them down on the desk to leave her unable to move anything except her head and her legs, and she felt that to kick backwards would be as dangerous as it would be futile.

'You *have* gone mad,' she declared, fighting back the rising tide of panic that was threatening to overwhelm her. 'When the Reichsfuehrer learns of this...'

The fingers continued to massage her flesh,

and now the hands moved lower, to raise her dress. 'By the time he does, Fraulein, you will have confessed to everything. You will confirm what Corda has told us.'

Oh, my God! Her worst nightmare. She gave another convulsive heave, but the men holding her arms were too strong for her.

'But first, let us soften you up a little.' His fingers dug into her flesh as he ripped her cami-knickers. 'As I said, I have waited a long time for ... What the devil?'

The door had swung open. 'What are you doing, Herr Feutlanger?' Haussmann demanded.

'Whatever I am doing, it is no business of yours,' Feutlanger snapped.

'But it is business of mine,' said another voice.

It was a familiar voice, even if Anna could not immediately place it. Then she wanted to scream with joy and relief.

'And who are you?' Feutlanger inquired.

'I am Colonel Hellmuth Essermann, of the Reichsfuehrer's personal staff. I have come to take the Countess von Widerstand back to Berlin.'

Feutlanger's hands slipped away as he stood straight. 'You ...'

'Here is my authority.'

Anna's arms were released, and she pushed herself straight, pulling down her dress. She turned to face Feutlanger, who stepped back-wards as he looked into her eyes.

'We are to leave immediately, Countess,' Essermann said.

Anna drew a long breath, and let it go, slowly. 'I intend to see you again, Herr Feutlanger,' she said in a low voice. 'Very soon.' She went to the door. 'Colonel Essermann,' she said. 'You are growing on me.'

EPILOGUE

'So Himmler came up trumps,' I suggested.

'His peculiar sense of honour demanded it,' Anna said. 'My fear, as I told you, was that he would decide to write me off, or that he would not get to me in time.'

'But how did you explain the evidence Feutlanger had obtained from Corda against you?'

'Heinrich was really a very simple soul. I told him that I had learned of a plot against Heydrich's life while attending Corda's music classes, and as my endeavours to obtain something incriminating against the Reich-Protector had proved unsuccessful, and I knew that time was running out, I decided to encourage it. Oh, he said that I should have reported it to him to make the decision, but he was so pleased that Heydrich was dead he did not press the matter.'

'Yes,' I said. 'But Corda knew that you were a British agent.'

Anna shook her head. 'Corda knew what I had told him. I explained to Heinrich that when they discovered that I knew about the plot, the assassins were going to execute me. The only way I could save my life was to convince them

349

that I was a British agent. I did not, of course, tell him how I had done that.'

'Did you tell him that it was you who actually completed the job?'

'No. I have never told anyone that, not even Clive or Joe. You are the first.'

I felt a glow of mental intimacy. But I had to ask, 'And the repercussions?'

Anna hugged herself. 'Lidice? That was terrible. I still have nightmares about it. I can only say that I warned London what was likely to happen, and they said that they, and the Czech Resistance, believed that it would be worth it, to prevent Heydrich ever becoming Fuehrer. Perhaps they were right. I have to hope they were.'

'And did you ever catch up with Feutlanger again?'

Anna gazed at me, and I felt a distinct chill. 'I always pay my debts, Christopher.'

I swallowed. 'So, was Heydrich your greatest coup?'

'Oh, no. There were bigger fish in the sea.'

'Ah. Yes. Of course. May I ask a question?'

'Is that not what you have been doing since we first met?'

'Well ... did you ever sleep with the Fuehrer?'

Anna Fehrbach merely smiled.